NO LONGER
AND **NOT YET**

NO LONGER
AND **NOT YET**

STORIES

JOANNA CLAPPS HERMAN

excelsior editions

State University of New York Press
Albany, New York

Thanks to the following for permission to reprint:

"Perfect Hatred" first appeared in *Italian Americana*, 2001.
"Seeding Memory" first appeared in *VIA: Voices in Italian Americana*, Fall, 1999.
"No Longer and Not Yet" (fall, 1997) and "Snow Struck" (spring, 1997) appear by permission of the *Massachusetts Review*.
"Asparagus Soup" was first published by *Earth's Daughters*, No. 10–11, 1979.

Published by State University of New York Press, Albany

© 2014 State University of New York

All rights reserved

Printed in the United States of America

No part of this book may be used or reproduced in any manner whatsoever without written permission. No part of this book may be stored in a retrieval system or transmitted in any form or by any means including electronic, electrostatic, magnetic tape, mechanical, photocopying, recording, or otherwise without the prior permission in writing of the publisher.

Excelsior Editions is an imprint of State University of New York Press

For information, contact State University of New York Press, Albany, NY
www.sunypress.edu

Production by Jenn Bennett
Marketing by Fran Keneston

Library of Congress Cataloging-in-Publication Data

Herman, Joanna Clapps.
  [Short stories. Selections]
  No Longer and Not Yet : Stories / Joanna Clapps Herman.
     pages cm. — (Excelsior Editions)
  ISBN 978-1-4384-5034-6 (Paperback : alk. paper)
  I. Title.
  PS3608.E759N65 2013
  813'.6—dc23
                                    2013015889

10 9 8 7 6 5 4 3 2 1

For my son, Dr. James Paul Herman, a postdoctoral research fellow at the National Institutes of Health, who knows how deeply proud of him I am.

And for always for my darling and beautiful Bill.

CONTENTS

What are those currents that run between us, filling our rooms, hallways, streets, connecting us the one to the other? When we are with those we belong to, does the air we breathe vibrate at the same pitch? When we fill it with our furies does it irritate the skin? After we're gone is something of our stride left where we once walked? Sometimes we arrive among strangers or in places we've never been and know we are home.

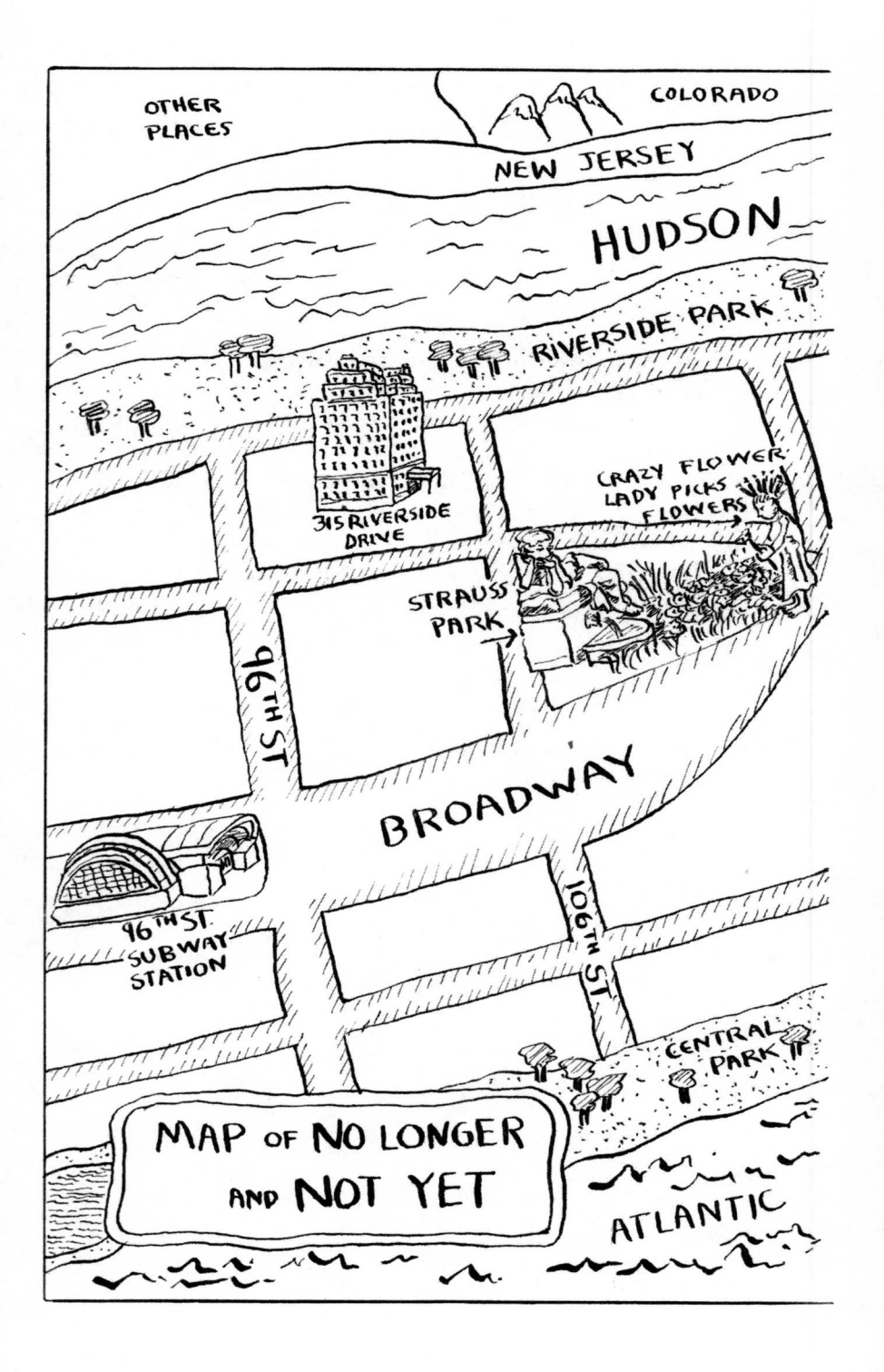

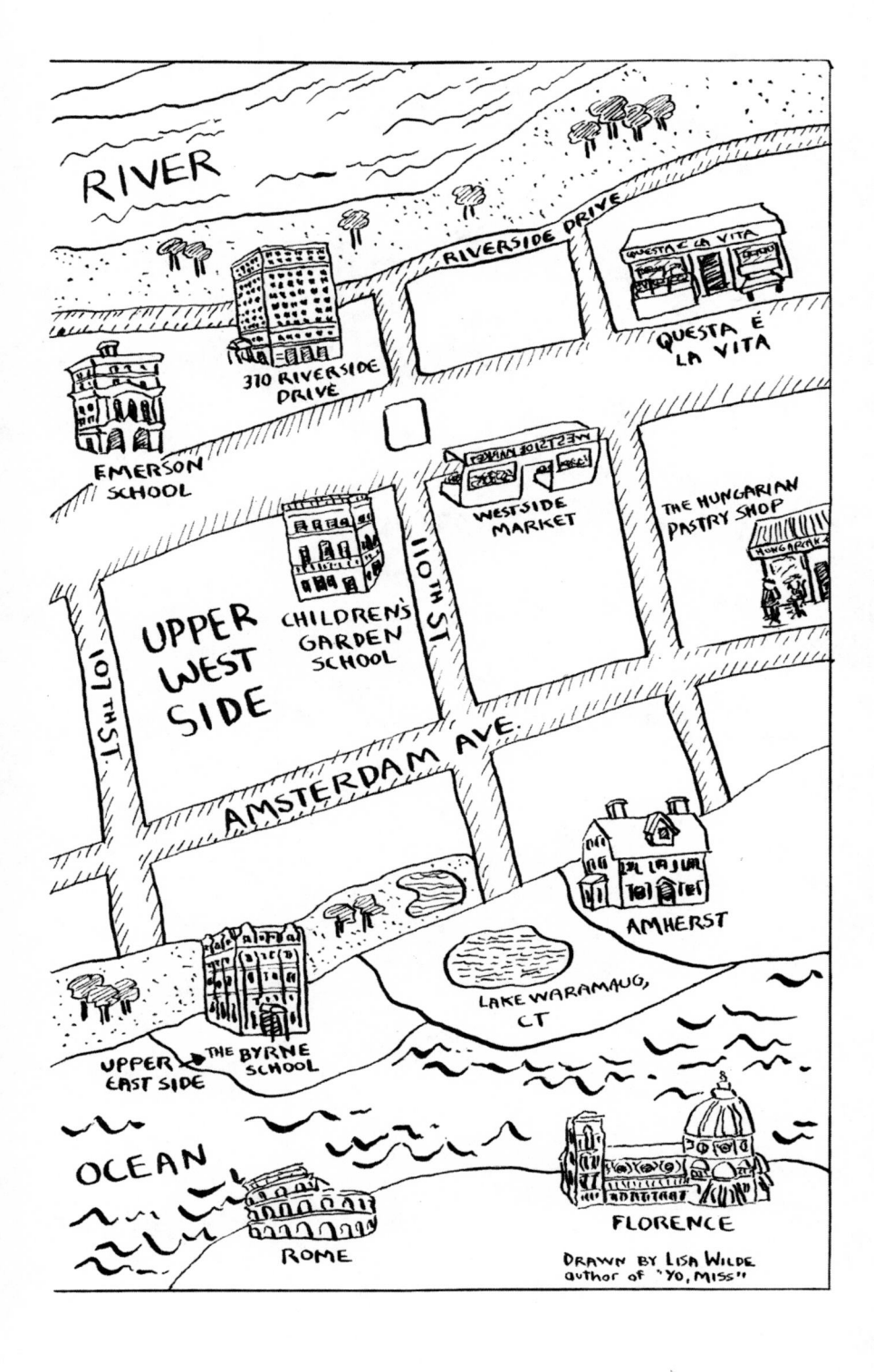

RIVER

RIVERSIDE DRIVE

QUESTA È LA VITA

310 RIVERSIDE DRIVE

QUESTA È LA VITA

EMERSON SCHOOL

WESTSIDE MARKET

THE HUNGARIAN PASTRY SHOP

HUNGARIAN

UPPER WEST SIDE

CHILDREN'S GARDEN SCHOOL

110TH ST

107TH ST

AMSTERDAM AVE

AMHERST

THE BYRNE SCHOOL

LAKE WARAMAUG, CT

UPPER EAST SIDE

OCEAN

ROME

FLORENCE

DRAWN BY LISA WILDE
author of "YO, MISS"

ROMAN BATH

It's an old dinosaur of a hotel, immense, with cramped labyrinthine halls going in surprising directions. Rossolino, narrow-faced, with downy feathers over his lip—the beginning of his moustache—shows Max and Tess to their room. Max and Tess are sweaty and exhausted, the way only road travel can leave you. When the three elbow their way out of the tiny ornate cage the hotel uses for an elevator, Rossolino leads the way, his head perched soberly on a long neck, a flag of red hair flying back from his forehead.

For Rossolino, this is home; he conducts them confidently through each turn, leading them down halls carpeted with rugs of diminishing thickness and design, until the floors creak bare underfoot. They arrive at a small lobby, sparsely furnished with one beast of a chair, carved, clawed, a snarling grimace at its head and a table next to it looking as if it had been mauled by its neighbor. The bowl of vegetation sitting on the table has lost all memory of photosynthesis.

Max and Tess follow Rossolino obediently, juggling awkwardly the assortment of odd plastic bags and overflowing totes that all travelers acquire on long drives, while the young bird of a porter carries their bulky suitcases with ease.

It's six. Max and Tess have been driving since noon, when they'd left Assisi. Max had wept as they came up the stairs from

1

the lower church. "I may never come back. Who knows? These paintings, this civilization, it's . . ." but he hadn't been able to finish.

"But we're going to Rome," Tess reminded him.

Max looked startled, shocked. "You never mentioned *Roooma*." Her recently acquired husband is one for song, soliloquy, schtick.

Though still in the flush of recently assembled devotion, Tess has already stopped trying to attend every performance of Max's constant theater. "You asked for a room with a bath?"

"Would I fail you my Queen?" He bowed, opened the rental car door. "Never."

They had picnicked at the side of the road on newly baked bread, cheeses that surrendered their flavors softly from the heat, tomatoes that burst at the point of the knife, but by the time they were on the outskirts of Rome they had evolved into creatures with sickening membranes of inevitably acquired sweat and dust of the journey. Minuscule Fiats flew by honking, their horns sounding like screaming geese. Tess's dirty hair flapped in her face no matter how tightly she pinned it up—tiny whips of hair lashing small, mean strokes, stinging the skin around her eyes.

"Maaax, get me to the hotel," her words, like a file on metal, grated—even on her. "I'd do anything for a bath."

Max flung back his head and let his laughter trickle down his throat. Tess's irrationality pleases Max. She's requesting magic. He's the man for the job.

"Hey, maybe we could *bagna insieme*, if the tub is one of the big ones?" His eyes rolled wildly, his tongue wagged from side to side in his mouth. He's easily roused, easily launched. He thinks this gesture is seductive.

"Hmmm," Tess turned her head to watch the untreelike cypress slip by.

Inspired, Max leaned out and shouted at the small cars passing them at high speeds, "*Papagallo!*" Mimicking a young Italian guy he had heard fighting with another *vitellone* at one of their road stops.

The fact that now he was calling someone a parrot who hadn't even spoken to him didn't matter to Max. He liked the sound of it. "*Papagallo!*" he shouted again, shaking his fist at the cars passing him.

When they entered Rome, Tess was navigating, something she did well. Tess knew where they were going—*on the map*. But every time she made a decision about which street to take, it was invariably a *senso unico*, a one way, the wrong way.

"It's all right; I'll just keep driving around this piazza until you figure out which street we take." Max had all the confidence in the world in his Tess.

The tiny cars had come from everywhere, their shrill horns screaming, men leaning out of windows to yell, particularly at them. The foul chemistry of exhausted diesel filled their car. When they went around the piazza a second time, the front end of a small blue Fiat cut in front of them, then screeched to a halt. Max slammed his brakes, jerking them forward, one small suitcase swinging into Tess's neck. There had been more yelling, curses Tess couldn't translate, but little movement toward the mark Tess had so carefully made on the map before they left Assisi. As they moved out of that piazza, Tess, peering down at the map, then up at the street sign, realized that they had just driven past a street that held the possibility of leading to their hotel.

"Just tell me which way to go, just tell me." Max's voice pitched up like Tess. He has his own need for sorcery.

"Just tell you? The problem is I *just* don't know!" Tess was furious that she didn't.

"All right." Max pulled over, disgusted. "Let me see the map." They'd pulled up to the hotel in silence.

Now Rossolino places the bags neatly to the side of the door to their room and waits for Tess and Max to reach him. He opens what had once been a solid, if modest, wooden door, but now looks as if it couldn't hold much out. It's not of concern. They want in. A shaft of cool light directs them from the dark hallway into their room. A large, somber chamber waits inside the door. Tess follows the light; Max follows Tess; Rossolino gathers up the bags, guiding them in from behind.

Cool Roman air fills the high, vaulted ceiling, gently coats the walls, and settles quietly on the stone floor. An older world, large, shabby, and calm is laid out before them. The bed's expanse is framed in the mirror that hangs on the opposite wall. Below the mirror is an old porcelain sink, a bidet set in a wooden stand. Under the stand on a shelf sits a white china pitcher. Rossolino deposits the bags near the foot of the bed.

Tess can hear Max searching his pockets for lire. Max is no doubt giving Rossolino something excessive, a habit Tess normally approves of, but now is only cause for further irritation. He is probably raising his wild eyebrows in a vaudeville expression that says, "I know you are an exceptional young duck, and I appreciate your new moustache."

"*Grazie infinita,*" Tess hears Max say. Only infinite thanks will do. Everyone has to love Max, Tess thinks, annoyed that everyone always does, especially since at this moment she doesn't. When Tess opens her eyes, Rossolino's long arm wings the door closed.

Max is standing by the bags. Sweat has glued his shirt to him.

"What do you think?" he asks Tess. "Are you okay about the bath?" as he begins to pull his shirt away from his skin. Max's back is usually a sanctuary in Tess's private country. But as she notices the hair on his back matted to his body she particularly loathes the broad sweaty terrain she sees.

"It's fine," she says breezily. It had been her decision, too, but she's too miserable to be fair.

When they had arrived at the desk downstairs the hotel clerk told them that their original reservation for a room with a bath had been given away. There hadn't been a confirmation. They could either go back to the wilderness of an unknown city or take the room without one.

Max had asked, "What do you want to do?" so ready to be obliging, "Stay or go? Whatever you want." Tess had no choice but to be reasonable. She held that against him.

"We'll stay," Tess had nodded angrily at the desk. As if there had been a choice, she thinks now.

Off to one side of the room is a large armchair with a rounded back and plump arms, fitted with a faded cloth cover. Tess lets herself sink into it, rests her head against the high back and closes her eyes. She feels as if she's being held by a grave parent. Dust particles fill the air between Max and her.

He's taking off all his clothes, all, except for his briefs. He bunches up his pants and shirt carefully over the back of a chair. Small sighs escape from him, bubbles of misery.

"You hungry? There's some bread and cheese left I think."

"Nah," Tess says without opening her eyes. "You?" She asks not to be outdone. "I'll put something together for you."

Nobody wants anything.

Tess walks over to the bed, pulls her dress up over her head, and throws it down. The synthetic fabric lands in a limp heap against the dull luster of the floor. She lays back, her lower legs hanging over the side of the bed. She slips off her sandals, and her dirty feet find the cold, polished stone. In a minute, she thinks, I'll take a birdbath. Each hot muscle relaxes against the rough cotton pattern. She's trying to remember how to bathe in a sink.

"You okay?"

"Yeah. You?" Tess drags her words and breathes out together.

"Yeah."

She just wants to lie there.

Max's bare feet pad the floor. A hollow creak breaks the hush of the room. He is standing in front of the massive wooden wardrobe lodged off to one side. Its chipped veneer matches the bed. Two or three hangers wait crookedly on the pole. The stale smell of old dust, long enclosed, emerges from the wardrobe. Max lines his shoes up at the bottom and covers the hangers with his things. Another creak. Then the water splashing.

"*Tesoro* Tessina," Max sing songs, leaning over Tess when he has finished washing up. He wants this fight over. He didn't care who began, who joined in.

But Tess rolls away, across the bed, then stands up efficiently. She's ready to bathe. She peels away her slip, the rest, tossing them onto the floor. Then she reaches up, pulling the stringy tangles of her hair back and pins them up again.

Max sits on the bed and sinks his head into his chest. He breathes in deeply then lets the air out through his teeth, making his lips flap. His back rounds over even further. This is to let Tess know he's descending into one of his deepest darks. The pact is sealed; they're sworn to this stunned, swollen silence.

Max picks up his paper on the bed and lies back, blocking

her out. Tess goes to the sink and begins by rinsing her face. Just the dust comes off. A film of oil still covers her skin. She soaps it and then rinses it clean. Tess tips her head back, eyes closed, the water dripping down onto her torso. Her face feels made of one piece again. She can almost recognize herself. She bends and puts her elbows into a well of cool water in the sink. Her soapy hands slip up over the round of her shoulder, down to the outside, then reach to soap the tender underside of her arm. She pours water over her shoulder, drawing the cool, white china pitcher along her arm. The water falls into streams over her fingers, the sound of liquid breaking as it hits her skin, the sink and the floor.

A breeze blows in through the windows, billowing the curtains up. The air dries her skin, leaving small maps of moisture evaporating on her body.

When she looks up again at the mirror she sees that Max has closed his eyes. The pages of the *Trib*, anchored by one hand flung across the bed, flutter in the air, waving the words held prisoner in the fields of white. In a dream the small black letters would float off the pages into the air. His body is traveling toward sleep. His lips twitch slightly. "I can't . . ." something, something, "Who are you guys . . .?" he asks tensely falling off the rocks of consciousness.

I should cover him, runs through Tess's mind. Instead she leans over the rounded porcelain edge of the sink.

She hears the squawk of rusted metal behind her as Max turns in the bed. When she looks up into the mirror she sees that the sound isn't from the bedsprings, but comes from the hinge and pivot pin scraping as the door opens.

Rossolino, his hand on the doorknob, stands, held by the sight of Tess's back. He is holding a small bag Tess had left at the desk. Tess knows the bag is hers, but just now what is in it is a mystery to her.

"Max," Tess whispers urgently into the glass. The words float up to the high ceiling. Max lifts his head to see what Tess is looking at in the mirror, his eyes reluctant from sleep ruined.

Tess looks down to the sink, then back up to the mirror, searching for protection. The large white towel is back on the bed. She sees that Max and Rossolino's eyes have met now in the mirror, eyes round, bright, fixed for a second in a languageless stare that Tess both knows and understands she can't interpret. Rossolino's eyes flick to meet Tess's. Her gaze swings to Max. A current flows through them in the glass. Then Rossolino lowers his eyes, places the bag just inside, and pulls the door closed. The question of maps, of lines of demarcation, of how you get where you're going has given way as Tess and Max hold their gaze in the mirror.

———•◆•———

WHISPERS

M ax is sitting in a café downstairs across from the Duomo waiting for Tess. She'll meet him later than he wishes but as soon as he can hope for. He wants to show her something he's found without her this morning on a walk to a part of Padua where tourists rarely go.

It's an austere piazza with only one large tree at the center. The bottom of the tree is painted white to protect it from the sun. The low stone wall around the tree is white too. Along the edge of the piazza are simple shops, a small fruit stand, a housewares store, and one very plain restaurant where the tables are old washed wood with plaid cloth napkins. There are always two dishes to choose from. One is a pasta; the other will be meat or fish.

He shifts where he sits: this damn chair.

That's the right place for today, Max thinks. He puts his book down on the table. Me in an empty chair of love; she purs'd up my heart, as the great man put it. Sometime she's got the temper of a shrew, (he mops his brow) but then sometimes . . . she makes hungry where most she satisfies. And what does she want, what *will* she see in this old coot: my daring (my mischief), my ardor (my histrionics), . . . or my sheer oratorical power? Or . . . the real me. Could she love the real me?

Tess's wariness, her good Italian face, her strong limbs, her intense neurosis embedded in her bossiness all appeal to him. He likes the package. A dozen years older than Tess, Max has been through too many ordinary wars to still have that certainty in his heart or limbs. For Tess it is all still crystal clear. She knows how it is all supposed to go and who is to blame at every turn.

A dry, white heat pours out of the Italian sky. Footsteps are moving toward the indoors—there are fewer and fewer as Max waits.

"I've finished writing to Naomi," Tess says swinging her light skirt under her as she sits down when she finally arrives. The whole town is beginning to close up for midday. "I had to tell her about getting to Padua after all this time and seeing the Scroveni Chapel. She knows how long I've been waiting to see Giotto's paintings." She's explaining her lateness, setting everything right. "It's something that she and I have talked about for years. I had to write it all down before the details slipped away."

"Let's see, Naomi's your oldest friend. She lives on 105th Street. She's seeing a guy you're not sure you like the sound of, right?"

"Well," Tess starts slowly, but Max interrupts. He has very particular things he wants to happen today.

"She's the one you tell everything to, right? So have *I* been entered into the canon yet?" He pulls his shirt away from his skin. He's courting her with his memory.

"No, Max," Tess says tilting her head way over to one side. "I want to keep this for myself. I can't give any of it away yet."

"That's the reason?" he asks reasonably. He looks up into the blue-and-white-striped awning overhead that is protecting them from the worst of the high sun.

Tess turns her head away to watch two young girls walking quietly down the street just in front of their mother. "Look," she says, "American kids would be skipping or running. So Italian."

Max nods and stands. He takes her hand, and they start to walk. His mother said all the time, "*Leben ist mit leute*" (Life is with people).

They walk, turning through many small streets under the unforgiving midday sun, finally arriving at the special piazza. The heat is so intense and dry it has baked Max and Tess back into more elemental bodies.

"Here is the piazza I wanted you to see," Max says with a quiet flourish when they arrive at the low wall around the tree.

Tess stands still, taking in the rough circle of buildings, the single tree, one white building draped with a swag of grapevines over the doorway. The rest, as simple and stark as she imagines towns in Morocco to be. She turns around in a slow circle.

Max watches her. She's not saying anything. She's not leading them immediately to the edge of the piazza that she's decided looks the most interesting or that would be the best place from which to take it all in. The white heat, the stark piazza, the single tree are all colliding in Tess's heart. She's a bit stunned.

Max is pleased. This is the place, he thinks. I've chosen the right place. He hangs his large arm lightly over her shoulder and whispers, *"Questa è la vita"* (This is the life).

———•◆•———

FALLING

After her brother fell off the side of the mountain, little pieces started falling off Olivia. She started losing eyeglasses, wallets, keys, right off the bat. She just couldn't seem to keep things attached anymore. She'd go to unlock the door to her house thinking that the keys were actually in her hand, but when she'd look down, her hand would be empty, waiting for the keys to appear. She took a week off from work. It wasn't as if she could lose her job. She had her brother's death and tenure. She wanted to get out to Colorado to pack up his things, make arrangements for his rent, his bills, that kind of thing. His roommates said they'd do it for her, but she was hoping the trip would help her. She wasn't sure what she expected to find out there.

They couldn't get his body back; it was in a place that was too dangerous to send a recovery team, an unfathomable crevice. She didn't have to go out there immediately, but she had become afraid of what would drop off her next.

When she went to call for a plane reservation, she couldn't find her glasses. She was standing by her desk, bending over, squinting, trying to punch in the numbers by feel. She knew she was hopeless without her glasses. She started to cry, blurring what little vision she had left. She called her friend Naomi who was number one on her speed dial. Olivia knew Naomi was the person she needed tonight. She asked Naomi to call and make the plane reservation for her. As soon as Naomi found out that Tim had died, Olivia knew that Naomi would try to make this into an opportunity to get her to see a shrink.

Naomi thought her own therapist was a shamanic presence in her life. "I tell her a dream leaving out the key detail—like I was nursing one of my students—and she'll get it anyway. 'You're longing for a baby to take care of.' How does she do that?"

What else could Olivia expect of Naomi?

But the way she figured it was that she and Naomi had a deal: Olivia represented the three people still living in New York who weren't shrinks and who didn't go to shrinks, and Naomi represented the rest of New York—the true believers. Someone had to prove there could be mixed friendships.

Naomi came right over as soon as Olivia told her what had happened. They stayed up all night drinking the scotch and eating the Lindt chocolate with hazelnuts that Naomi brought with her. How did she know to bring exactly those two things? They started in the living room hanging out on the couch. Then they smoked some grass and went to lie on Olivia's bed head to toe. They looked at old photographs of Olivia with her and her brother Tim from when they were tiny kids right up to a recent picnic in Riverside Park when he had been in New York. Naomi was all listening utterances—just ohmygod, and an inhaling of saliva that meant I can't believe that, murmurs, and hushed hmms. They fell asleep around three in the morning for a few hours.

The following evening Naomi came right from work with Chinese food, but at 10:30 Naomi said, "Look, tonight that guy I told you about, that carpenter I am considering using to do some work for me in my new apartment—Eliot. We kind of started kissing the other day. He said he'd drop by tonight after he got tomorrow's job ready. I love a man who knows how to use his hands. Then there's the tools. Tomorrow night you come over to me."

Another one of Naomi's ridiculous men, Olivia thought.

The next night when Olivia went over to Naomi's new apartment, Naomi didn't take long to start in with Olivia. She sat down in the middle of the piled boxes, took a deep breath, and blew it out. Then she said, "You know you might think about getting some backup here." Olivia knew exactly where Naomi was going.

"Naomi, don't go there, don't start on me with that. I swear I'll just go home and . . .," the implied threat. Olivia knew she was being manipulative in the face of someone who really cared, but she didn't give a damn. She wanted to stay on Naomi's couch surrounded by the half-opened boxes in the living room and not sleep. Olivia would know that Naomi was asleep in the next room. That was enough for tonight.

Naomi drove her to the airport. Olivia knew that Naomi had to hold herself back from saying, "Just something to think about."

Not really, Olivia didn't answer. She just looked out the window so Naomi would leave her alone. Olivia needed a ride and her friend's presence, but we never get the package just the way we want it. Olivia knew that. But Olivia knew that you can't always help yourself, even when you know better.

"Did I tell you that Hannah Arendt used to live in my new building?" Naomi said to let Olivia know that she knew she wasn't going to go too far today. She was all support.

"Yeah. You did," Olivia said, looking at the water as they drove across the bridge where Naomi wasn't. The water was glass, silver and gold, below the bruised dusky sky laying Manhattan out, it seemed, for Olivia's melancholic pleasure. "What do you hear from Tess? Is she ever coming home?" Olivia asked, clicking the door lock on and off as they thumped over the heavy metal plates on the roadway. Each kthump a punctuation.

"Oh, she's all involved with somebody. Only *she'd* go to Italy for a year and find a guy to fall in love with who lives in Greenwich Village." Naomi said with disbelief and irritation. "Probably pregnant too."

Olivia thinks Naomi will have them all in family therapy in a few years. Then immediately. Why do I keep criticizing Naomi when she is being so helpful?

Olivia's brother's roommates met her at the airport. They were crying when she came through the gate—four guys, in jeans, plaid shirts, climbing boots, weeping over their lost friend. Could there be a more beautiful sight?

They all worked for a small offbeat computer company. Nar,

the guy who was driving that night, was the one who got Tim the job with Neruda—the name of the company. They were all going to be poets before they got into computers.

Nar's the one who designed the way the components fit together—one of those spatial relations genius types—could fix a vacuum, pack a car trunk using every bit of space, *and* design a hell of a computer. But they all worked there. They were tight: cooked, ate together, played Ultimate Frisbee all the time—an incredible bunch of guys.

She ended up staying with them for a week. All of Olivia's luggage had been rerouted to Canada. It didn't matter. It was better this way. It helped her blend into Tim's life. They turned over Tim's room to her, suggested she wear his clothes, loaned her their own toiletries. She slept in his bed. She needed to sleep in the sheets he had last slept in—one of the last places his skin had been. They had that smell of sheets that should have been changed, a faint oily smell. She was so grateful they hadn't been changed. So familiar—him—Tim—his smell. His smell was part leaf dust and his sweat—a clean male smell, just his juices. You know, all the clichés: his voice on the answering machine, games he had saved on his computer.

Nar was the one Olivia felt most comfortable with. Was that just because he had been driving the car that first night? Who knows? He'd cook—bring her food. She couldn't seem to leave that room.

After a few days the bed began to have her smell. Couldn't shower. She only left his bed to go to the john. She still couldn't, just couldn't understand, couldn't get her head around the idea that her brother had taken up mountain climbing. She pulled his laptop into bed with her and spent all her time roaming around in there. Olivia could see him moving through this territory. She started down through the directories. She was trying to find anything that would help her get a grip. She read through his journals, late into the night, entries about someone at work he was trying to get up the nerve to ask out, other ones about their mother driving him nuts. Olivia wasn't sure what she was looking for—at least some hint as to when he had switched from hiking to mountain climbing. We're not a mountain climbing kind of family. He wouldn't even climb the trees in their yard in New Rochelle.

Olivia had been climbing around inside Tim's drive for a couple of days. The further down in the drive she went, the less she found anything interesting. She began to get fidgety. It was driving her nuts that his smell was disappearing under her own.

She asked Nar to stay and talk to her the next time he brought her some weed to smoke. Nar had designed Tim's computer especially for him. Was Nar Indian?

Nar told her they all had been talking about her taking Tim's job at Neruda. She was a CS teacher at the junior high where she taught. She closed her eyes and bit her lip.

He sat down on the edge of the bed and told her that he had been the one who had talked Tim into taking up climbing. Tim was the kind of guy who had always wished he could do something like take up climbing—never felt he had the talent, the nerve. She could see why hanging out with someone like Nar would make you feel you could do it. He'd lead the way—you'd follow. It would all be all right.

Nar had that kind of effect on people. He leaned toward her and ran his finger along the slope of her ear. The sensation brought her up out of her grief.

"There were people watching from the lodge when he fell," he said. She swallowed.

"He left the ridge," he went on. "It must have been getting too steep. It looked like he decided to traverse the scree field. He was heading for the west ridge, but he must have lost his footing; he started to slide. He managed to flatten himself out and stop. He was close to the edge of the field. He had been reaching for a tree, a stump, something, but the next thing they saw, he was sliding. Fifteen feet, off the scree, and then it was all air." Olivia looked down, tried to shake that picture off. He waited, didn't do *anything*. Then she reached over and pulled Nar toward her.

She felt bad that Tim's sheets smelled of their lovemaking. But somewhere in the night she had one of those moments, an intuition, a flash of absolute knowing. Nar's smell was already on these sheets. The sheets had a hint, a trace memory. Olivia had an infallible nose. She knew that Nar and Tim, that her brother and Nar, had been lovers. Now here they were in Tim's bed, where he and Nar had been together. It brought things into focus. Tim had followed Nar up mountains.

She was sure it had brought him a kind of pride he had never had before, until it killed him.

Nar told her he had warned Tim never to climb alone. Olivia knew Tim wasn't the kind of guy who listened to basics.

They spent a week together in Tim's bed. She was sure Tim's spirit or energy or whatever you want to call it—his residue—was there in the room with them, delighted by their lovemaking.

On the eighth day she got up and started packing Tim's things. She gave most of his stuff to his roommates: his poetry books, his clothes, his boots, all the key things. Nar helped her. But she packed Tim's computer herself. Somewhere in the interstices between the hardware and the software, between the root directory and the files, was something of Nar and Tim. She needed to take a piece of them home with her. She had to have something to hold on to.

She held the computer on her lap on the plane all the way home. She wandered around all of the directories of the computer all the way home on the plane. She wouldn't even take a drink from the stewardess. Finally she asked the computer to search for all the hidden files. She found what she knew she would. She read a few lines and then moved the directory even deeper in.

After that she shut the machine down and asked for an imported beer. She closed her eyes, tried to imagine Naomi with Eliot the carpenter. Olivia was reaching for anything to stop thinking about Nar.

After she got home she put the computer up on her highest shelf where no one but she could possibly come upon it. It was an awkward spot to get it down from. She didn't call Naomi to tell her she was home. She'd go into the closet and close the door behind her, sit on a small stool she kept in there. She felt calm, flat as a plate in there. She only allowed herself one or two tokes.

She was going to have to decide what to do. In the closet there was no one but her, the computer, and what she was pretty sure was an embryo inside of her. She was sure Tim would want her to keep this baby. Wasn't this baby his too in a way—what there was left of them as a family now? She knew she needed to write a long journal entry to sort this all out on her own, but it belonged in the directory she buried in Tim's computer. Every time she started to reach for the computer, she pictured it slipping out of her hands.

——•◆•——

LEAVES AND BROTHERS

"I've called you here today to . . .," Naomi says both to mock herself and to make Olivia pay attention. Naomi is beaming at Olivia.

Small yellow leaves drift past them, then scrape along the sidewalk sounding oddly like metal. Olivia is preoccupied watching a single, cupped leaf slip down from the tree nearest to them toward their table.

"Not about Eliot and me." They're sitting at the Hungarian Café across the street from St. John the Divine Cathedral.

That single leaf lands on the edge of Olivia's saucer as if to make a still life. Lately, all small, unusual events like this one seem to be visits from her dead brother, Tim.

Naomi has interrupted Olivia's internal transactions. Before this version of her brother arrived on her saucer, she had been staring at the cathedral and living in Paris. It made her life make so much sense. Why does the idea of transporting ourselves to another place always make one's life better?

Olivia snaps out of her trance. "Let me guess. You're going to become a shrink."

Naomi stares at her. The air between them has only the loud rumble and screeches of trucks and buses on the street while Naomi turns to look at them. "Well, thanks for being so excited for me."

21

"No. It's good. It's just that it's inevitable. It's your only religion. You should practice it. You'll be a great therapist."

Naomi looks back at her friend's hands folded over her only slightly protruding belly. She decides not to be annoyed. "Oh, you're right."

Even Naomi's therapist, Ruth, had said, "I think it's time we got your life up and running. I know just which institute is right for you. You'll be really good at this." That Ruth would say it so clearly was *something*. Naomi had to pay attention. The application had been on her desk for months.

I'll be good at this, Naomi had carried Ruth's words with her for two days. Kept it to herself. Ruth thinks I'll be good at this, Naomi thought as she walked her streets for the recent days. Now she reaches over and picks up the leaf from Olivia's saucer, then stretches up and tucks it into her friend's hair, thinking, my life has been decided. It'll be a good life.

"I'm really happy for you, Naomi. You're going to be a classic."

———•◆•———

NO LONGER

This is what is no longer. In order to get this story straight, let's go back to the beginning.

Tess never cried; she never cried. Max had been crying when they met, but then he had cried almost continuously in Italy, moistening the cool, ancient stones. She had been walking down a narrow, shaded *viale* early one morning when she saw a man slump slowly to his knees. Tess rushed over, "*Che successo? Malatta?*" She struggled for the right words in Italian. A large man's large head looked up at her, the tears streaming behind his glasses.

"You're an American," he announced in English. "Maybe you'll understand. Look. Look at this." He scrambled back up lightly to his feet and pointed past an iron gate to the end of a cobbled drive that opened to a small yard. There was a marble fountain with a carved lion's head circled with a garland of leaves, water streaming from the animal's mouth. Plants, balanced on the edge of the fountain, surrounded its base, shades of greens and pinks flooding the courtyard. A young mother sat near the fountain, nursing her baby. Absorbed with pleasure, the woman gazed at her infant. Two little girls were washing their dolls in the fountain.

"Did you ever see anything so beautiful? *Questa patria, il mio patria,*" he declared, moving her toward a piazza, where there was a bar. A tiger-striped cat leaped in front of them. Startled by both of these creatures, Tess wasn't sure where to turn.

A professor of literature, Max had come to Italy "to kiss the stones of the maestro," he told Tess earnestly, a few days after they met, "and to write a book for promotion." Divorced, he had one twenty-one-year-old daughter, Claudia, who was "beautiful, talented, and always mad at me." He had just finished paying child support. That was why he could finally come to Italy. "I've waited all my life for this."

"Dante walked *these* streets," he insisted, as if Tess disagreed. "He might have stood right here on this spot, had a coffee, a panino, at this bar." Max threw back his head and laughed. "Really. I have to show you something."

Reverently he led her to a spot pictured in every tour book, by a stone wall that guides the Arno through Florence. "Just where we are, Dante stood the first time he saw Beatrice." His eyes shone at the thought. "Cavalcante might have walked here too," he added realistically. "*Non tengo riposta te mis cup se non per dicer poco. I do not keep my heart hidden from thee except to speak less.*" Max gestured grandly to the passing water. "The greatest poet, the master," his voice went into soft contortions, "could have stood right here, as I am standing at this very moment." His chest heaved, his face lifted, and the tears streamed.

Tess looked at Max, expecting him to bend down and kiss the dirty stones beneath their feet while the small screeching cars whizzed by. Instead he stood, eyes raised, not even wiping his happy tears. She looked across the Arno at Florence, then back at Max's wet, rapturous face. She wasn't sure which startled her more. What was she doing standing in the middle of Florence with this . . . this guy?

She'd come to have a long, slow look at the birth of real painting—Giotto, Fra Angelico, Masaccio—to study perspective, not lose it, and to decide what else she was going to do with her life besides loving other people's children.

Before Max, before Italy, Tess had been an art teacher at Emerson, a private school on the Upper West Side of Manhattan. One morning she had been working in her room preparing for the day.

"Tess, Tess, where are you?" Jeff's five-year-old high-pitched voice reached the room before he got there.

"Jeffy, Jeffy," Tess echoed his pitch and style from the closet where she was getting supplies. "Here I am." Small children rarely noticed how they amused their teachers.

Still, she loved their unformed hearts; they looked like eggs, living in the sacks of their uncertainty.

"What is it, honey?" Jeff was one of those kids who demanded unfair amounts of everything: room, materials, attention. So, Tess unfairly favored him.

He had leapt into Tess's lap, "My mom had the baby. It's a yucky baby sister. That's what I am going to call her. Yucky. I told my mom not to have a sister." Now he climbed on the table and swung his legs over the edge. "Mom will be home day after tomorrow." Now he beamed. "I talked to her on the telephone."

"I'm glad." Lately Tess hadn't been able to keep track of the lost dogs, overworked fathers, mothers giving birth. Until recently she would have remembered the due date. Jeff couldn't have known this, but Tess did. He jumped down from the table and ran toward the door.

"Jeff," she called after him, "how did you know I was here already?"

"You live here, silly," he yelled as he raced out the door. He peeked back in the room with a puzzled expression on his face.

By the end of that day she had made a plan to put into action her long-delayed dream of a year in Florence. She wanted to see her beloved annunciation paintings in person.

"I'm going to do it." She called to tell Naomi, her closest friend. Naomi and she can and do talk over anything. If something isn't clear to Tess, and she has a long enough conversation with Naomi, something passes back and forth between them, in their words, in their mirroring looks that clarifies what the central point is. Naomi and Tess turn over every possible consideration even if it's silly. Now Tess has made a sudden and abrupt decision. But Naomi is all approval.

"I'm so jealous!" Naomi said. "You have to go and have an adventure just when I have to buckle down in graduate school. Did I tell you that I got a letter from NYU giving me a half tuition?"

Naomi drove her to the airport the day she left. "Bring me one of those prints from Pompeii, the mosaic of the two doves, and one of those Italian guys."

"Eliot?" Tess asked.

"No, that is just for fun. He'll be gone before you're back," Naomi said.

Tess had arrived in Florence in June. She'd painted small, pleasing watercolors, and she crocheted. She spent time watching the small Italian kids playing soccer in the courtyard below, practicing sentences she would say to them when her Italian got better. She shopped, cooked, wrote long letters to Naomi when she got lonely. Then in September she met Max. He was thrilling, difficult, but company, kind of fascinating.

"You know you remind me of my mother, the way you knit all the time." They were on their way to San Marco to see the Fra Angelicos. Tess thought she knew him well enough to show him the places in Florence that explained why she had come.

"It's crocheting, Max. I crochet."

"That's what I mean. She used to knit, crochet shawls like you do." They had arrived at the front door of the cool monastery.

He was still talking. Tess wasn't listening. She had fallen into the building, its stones and solemnity. Max trailed, sighing. Then he went off to the bathroom and found her after a while in the cloister.

What will Max think when he sees the way the Archangel looked at Mary, arms crossed in a deep quiet, the way Mary looked off, troubled at the thought of being the mother of God, the news held up in the space between them? They were making their way through the solemn cloister to the stairway.

Max was still lost in his comparison, "Her eyes were blue, but veiled like yours. They didn't tell you what she wanted to say. I wonder what you aren't saying." They stopped when they were at the bottom of the long flight of austere stone steps. At the head of the stairs the painting lay waiting like the sky.

They were part of the way up the stairs when Max turned and saw the painting. One hand rushed to his forehead, then his hand fell to his chest.

"Max, Max, what is it?"

"Oh my god," He slumped against the stairwell wall. "The painting. I'm sorry. I can't help myself."

Later that night he explained, "I'm a Jew," he said, "I'm this way. Russian. Things *mooove* me."

Tess never got used to it. She thought he was having a heart attack, dying fast, dying slow, something was terribly wrong. "I've never been so peaceful," Max told Tess later that week. "So much for the heart. The heart can live here. That's why I'm so contented in *bella Italia*." He was in his after-dinner mood. "When the Renaissance spread north, the ideas, the humanism, the aesthetics moved, but the source stayed. I mean the love of art as it begins in life, the way everyone worries when a child cries, the way the antipasto platters set out in a restaurant look like a painting, the way an espresso machine is designed." He sighed, "An Italian's idea of austerity is to have nothing but Fra Angelicos to meditate on in a monk's cell. I've found my home at last."

All her life Tess had been waiting for fate to arrive on winged feet with a whir and a portentous breeze placing before her what her life would be about.

Was Max her winged fate or a disturbance in the weather? Tess wasn't sure. She knew she could not let the winds blow past her this time.

"Max, will you . . . will you marry me?"

"Of course, of course. What do you think I've been leading up to?" He wiped his eyes. "We're going to be very happy."

Tess kept her tears to herself. Should she announce to Max what she wanted most in her life? They'd work it out. He adored her. Didn't he say that all the time?

The day they were married, Max insisted on going by Alinari's after the ceremony. Tess wanted to get to the champagne lunch in Fiesole. As soon as they stepped into the busy print shop on Lung' Arno, a young man stepped up to Tess with a flourish. He had a package and a bouquet of flowers in his hand. "*Signora, mille auguri,*" he announced handing them to her. They walked out to the river to be on the Arno when she opened the brown paper wrapping.

"Tah, dah," Max sang, eyes gleaming. "Our painting. For our home." At the sight of the framed picture of Angelico's Annunciation, Tess leaned into Max's vast chest. A flyer for a performance of *The Marriage of Figaro* blew past their feet on an autumn breeze.

During the first weeks after the wedding, Tess spent a good deal of time wondering who this man was she had married. She had always assumed that after she married, a man would walk toward her down a street, out of a building, and she would say to herself, "Here's my husband." So each morning she recited to herself, "This is my husband," looking at this stranger drinking coffee across from her. That man singing "*La ci darem la mano*" to the man in the kiosk is my husband. That man embracing the waiter is my husband. It was odd. *He* was odd. She became so preoccupied with her new job of keeping her eye on Max, she stopped doing her watercolors, stopped crocheting, stopped writing to Naomi. She didn't want to miss anything. She was trying to get the hang of this. But as dutiful as Tess was, as often as she practiced her litany, what she said when she saw Max by surprise was, "Here's Max."

———•———

AND NOT YET

"I'm not kidding," Max said as he brushed a curtain of crumbs off his sweater on the plane ride back to New York. "We won't be able to open the front door of my apartment. The newspapers are piled to the ceiling. It's chaos." They had decided Tess would move in there for now.

"I'm good at fixing up," Tess insisted in turn.

"We'll have to fight our way in. I'm warning you. Promise you won't leave me."

When they stumbled out of the cab from the airport, it stopped in front of an old building on Bank Street. Tess stood transfixed by wood-burning smoke that filled the cold air. The sun setting beyond the river burnished the streets with umber. The row of dark red houses lining the street looked as if behind the long, curtained windows people were cooking dinner, sipping good scotch, or reading stories to small children. She trailed up the stairs behind Max.

"My husband," Tess said, "You are my husband."

"It's just oedipal. You'll get used to it," Max said, inserting his key in a lock on the fifth floor. "Ready?" he turned the key. "Set," reluctantly he turned the knob. "Go," he swung open the door.

Tess expected the door to stick at least. Instead, they entered a set of small, grayish rooms. There were piles of newspapers next to dirty, worn easy chairs. Like a carpet unrolling, dust balls floated away as they walked in.

"See?" He looked annoyed. "Why did you make me bring you here? We should have gone right to a hotel." Max sat down and hung his head, staring at the newspapers stacked by the couch.

"Max, I forgot to tell you something. I'm a magician. Look!" she threw her scarf over his head. "It's disappeared. Tomorrow the apartment will be transformed." When Max was upset Tess had gotten into the habit of talking like him. It made him laugh. It stopped him from inhaling all the emotional air.

"Do you think it will be okay, really?" He picked up his coat from the floor where he had flung it. "I just have to run over to see Claudia. I'm sorry to leave you with such a mess, but I'm late now."

"Keep your promise. Don't tell her yet. We should tell her together, after she's met me and sees I'm not so bad."

"We can get another apartment. We'll get a penthouse, if that's what you want." He picked up his briefcase and dashed to the door, dashed back, kissed Tess, "I mean it," he said, and left.

Tess wandered through the small, depressing rooms looking out the small windows facing in different directions, at back yards, at the street, out to the river, all at odd angles, none large enough to be the views they might have been. I'll get this in shape, she thought.

We'll have coffee here in the morning, she thought, by the kitchen window. It looked across a courtyard of bare trees to windows that looked back. We'll read the paper; we'll look out and see other people drinking coffee reading the paper look up and see us.

She sat down on the arm of one of the chairs in the living room and looked around. This new husband of hers, this Max person, had made so much of the fact that they weren't going to be able to open the door that Tess had pictured herself pushing a door against a huge pile of papers. Now that she was in the room behind the pile of newspapers, she saw why he hadn't wanted her to picture the rest. She looked down at the dust. The door had opened easily. The apartment was only shabby. She was disappointed.

When Max got home from registration the next day, he found a mountain of green plastic garbage bags out in the hall. "Tess, *il mio tesoro*," he called to Tess in every variation he could think of from the other side of the mountain of garbage. She appeared from behind it, in her hand a plate with some green stuff growing on some cracked dried bits that had once been food.

"Max," she pleaded, "I found this in the refrigerator. And there's more. But it's not just old food. There seem to be dirty dishes, chicken bones, and a shoe too." Could she cope with this? Max's genius for chaos had been disclosed.

"It's the roaches. I don't want the roaches to smell the food. See! I told you this place was no good. I told you." He collapsed onto a chair. "We can't live here like this. What have I done?" He waited for Tess to tell him.

"Apparently, not *a thing* in this apartment, for years."

He glared at Tess, and then a fast chortle came. "You made a joke." He grabbed her and sang, "I'm the most happy fella," dancing Tess around the living room "in the whole Greenwich Village."

Tess had gotten used to the moist eyes. It was steady, consistent. But she still couldn't follow the rest of this fast river of emotion around the twists and turns Max made from one minute to the next. Some of the time, even while she was dancing in Max's big embraces, inwardly she stood off to one side to watch as he leapt deftly from flowing tears into a gorilla ballet, lifting his hairy arms above his large head as he did pirouettes around the room on tip toe, his expansive body held delicately, his eyelashes fluttering. She was fascinated, but sometimes she asked, "Is this guy really my husband?"

"Where shall we eat?" he yelled now from the bedroom where he had rushed away. "The Plaza? The Ritz?"

By the time Tess got around to hanging the *Annunciation* across from their bed, she felt she had agreed to something deeper than marriage. This was her home; Max was her husband.

"Did you see what the bastards did today?" An outburst as he stands in the kitchen while Tess is preparing dinner trying to cut the onions for the salad, watching the evening news. "Did you see

what they did to those children?" He is bereft. It was the terror-
ists, it was the pirates, it was someone, somewhere in the Bronx,
or someone else in Africa. She can't blame him: they were sav-
age, really, whoever they were, those in charge of the blood those
particular days. Max comes over to the counter, sticks his hand
in the salad for a tomato wedge, and then stops and stares at it,
throws it in the sink in disgust, "What are they made of?" He is
beside himself; his eyes glisten. "What has happened to humanity,
common humanity?" He insists Tess explain it to him.

Tess wasn't sure exactly what had happened to common
humanity. She didn't know how to comfort Max, who had to live
in such a world. She stood behind him, put her long arms around
his wide furry shoulders, and placed her face against his back,
hoping this would help.

The third story on the six o'clock news is about a father who
has been holding his eighteen-month-old son over the edge of a
building all day, threatening to drop him. The father is angry at
the child's mother. She won't let him spend the weekend with his
son. This is the father's answer.

"That's enough for tonight." Tess snaps off the television.

"See, see what I mean?" Max slams on the table, making the
tomatoes and the onions jump in the bowl. "This is why we can't
have children. We can't have this going on. Anyway I've tried raising one. And failed." He says it with a kind of relief. "It's over."

"Oh Max, please don't start that right now." Tess has finally
revealed that what she wants is to have a baby. Max keeps insisting that he's a terrible father. He can't do it again. He finds every
opportunity to show her why it isn't reasonable to bring a child
into this world.

"Don't you care?" He cuts vigorously into the meat. "I care
about all this." One hand goes up and sweeps the air, includes the
television, the room, the world. "I'm really worried." He distrib-
utes thick slabs, pours gravy.

"But what does all this have to do with us?" Tess asks.

"We have to take a stand. No more children until the world
shapes up. Go on a children strike." He wipes a wet corner of his
eye and begins to hungrily eat his supper.

Tess told Naomi; Max told Claudia. Separately. As if rehearsed, they both said, "You what?"

But we were madly in love. We are madly in love, Tess thinks sitting at the kitchen window with her coffee, looking across the desolate courtyard.

The pigeons sweep from Tess's roof to the fire escape across the way. They ride the air, making gestures of largess. In a window across the way a couple sits drinking their morning coffee in a way that Tess and Max aren't. Max has early classes. Tess is a late riser. The man across the courtyard is offering the woman some bread. The woman breaks a piece off and leans out the window. The pigeons open into an expanse of reflected light as they fly onto the other woman's fire escape.

Tess, afraid of birds, can only imagine them landing in her hair if they came near. What would she do?

What should she do? About Max? She can't, for instance, get Max to introduce her to his daughter.

"She says she's met enough of my girlfriends."

"But I'm not your girlfriend."

"But she won't come over. What am I supposed to do?"

"Tell her she has to."

"You think I have influence on her? I keep telling you, kids grow up to hate you. You have no idea about children! They don't forgive you once you screw up."

Tess knew where this was leading.

"Talk to her mother. See if she has any idea about why she won't come over to meet me."

"You think either of us can get her to do what we want? You want to know what her mother said when I told her you wanted to have a baby? She said, 'Maxwell, oh Maxwell.' Then she laughed and laughed. *She* understands."

"Maybe we'd be better at it than you two were."

"You're so innocent." Max's chin went into his chest. "You don't know anything about it. My kid hates me." He sobbed into his chest. If in Italy his tears had been an expression of the largeness of his soul, in America they seemed to spill over from real misery.

"I failed the folding test again," Max explained to Tess's friend Naomi, when he met her for the first time. The three of them were waiting on line to see a movie. He meant the bath towels. "And I studied all week too. But when laundry day came, I couldn't get those corners to stay lined up." He put his arm around Tess and squeezed her close to him. "I'm taking the refresher course next semester." He twisted his mouth, pushed his chin forward, as if to say, what could he do?

"What a charmer," Naomi assured Tess the next day on the phone. "Good for you for grabbing him."

"You think?" Tess asked.

"What about his professor friends? Are they all married?"

When Claudia finally came over—she called one day to say she'd drop by on her way to a rehearsal—a young woman wearing ripped boots with tape wound over the tears, jeans with patches sewn over holes, rhinestone earrings adorning an elegant head that should have ridden on top of a Persian statue stood just outside the door. She was here with her offering of her own sullen beauty, and a long young man encased in black, "Dad, this is Mickey."

"How'd ya do young man?" Max smiled briefly at Mickey then turned his excited attention to his daughter. "Poopsie! How's my darling daughter? Come in! Come in, the two of you." He vaguely included the young man, grabbed Claudia's arm, and pulled her inside.

Then Max dropped Claudia's wrist and rushed over to grab Tess's elbow, "Claud, this is my Tess." Tess moving forward to shake Claudia's hand, stumbled a little on the corner of the rug.

Claudia refused to notice Tess stumble and stretched out her hand rather formally, "It's good to meet you," then turned to sit on the arm of the chair where Mickey, his full length stretched out in the most comfortable chair in the room, waited for her.

Max darted back to his daughter. "Look at her! Just look at this face." He pulled her chin up, showing her face to Tess and Mickey. "Gorgeous, right? She looks just like her mother did at her age. Her mother was a world-class beauty." He called on Mickey and Tess to applaud the praise of his first wife.

Max reached over and tousled Claudia's carefully arranged tousled hairdo. "Oh Dad, stop it." Claudia smiled, tightly pursing her lips and shaking her head, pleased and annoyed by this display. "He always does this," she explained to Mickey, who was indifferent to this spectacle.

Now Max rushed back to Tess's side. "Tess taught art at Emerson."

"So you told me," Claudia said glancing briefly at Tess, then said firmly, "Sit down Dad."

Max, obeying his daughter, stopped his darting between Tess and Claudia and sat down primly on a small desk chair a little off to one side. He looked down into his hands and stopped talking. Claudia and Mickey held on to each other. A sodden silence filled the room.

Tess broke into the quiet too cheerfully, "So you're a musician? I really admire that kind of bravery. Performing in front of people."

"Mickey too. We're in a band together." Claudia turned to Mickey, "Did I tell you Cat's got a steady stream of gigs now, Shea Stadium, Glasslands, Union Pool, Pete's Candy Store?"

"That's great."

"Wait till I tell you the best. Next month, they're playing at Brooklyn Bowl on Wythe Avenue.

"No! You're kidding. I'd kill for that." Mickey jumped up and stabbed the air. Claudia looked up happily into his violence.

"Damn! We're better than she is. Why can't we get an audition?" He fell back into the chair and waited for Claudia to explain that to him.

"Where are these places?" Tess asked. "Can we go see them play?"

"Couldn't you have joined in a little?" Tess asked Max later as they walked down Bleecker Street toward Sheridan Square to buy the late edition of the *Times*. The streets were filled with the quiet dust of night. It had settled onto the other people walking on the street, all of whom touched by the night, touched each other.

"Did you see that performance of hers?" Max turned to Tess, anger and incredulity filling his eyes. "This kid, *Mickey*—she's so connected *to him*. It was meant to show me up. Something like that. What do you want from me? I don't know how to talk to my own kid."

"Couldn't you even try? She's young. And dumb."

"When you lose a child, you're at a funeral. I've lost her. I'm not up for small talk." After they bought the paper, they walked home side by side, space between them, their bodies unlinked.

"Look, I'm not having another kid," he said with quiet fury the next day when he came home from work. "You'd better figure out what you're going to do." Max sat down on a chair just outside his study and sank into himself. "I can't. I can't do it again." Tess started across the room, but Max held up a hand. "Don't. Please just let me be." He got up went into his study and closed the door. He was determined to be closer to his misery than to her.

"I don't know what to do," Tess confided to Naomi on the phone, "I can't seem to get through to him."

"Have you tried to get him to really talk about why he's so sure it won't work?" Naomi and Tess were trying to make this story come out the way they thought it should.

"He's practically not talking to me at all anymore, much less about that. He's gone somewhere inside himself, and I have no idea how to follow him." Tess was sinking into despair with Max. Even her phone calls to Naomi didn't help her sort this out.

"Would you be willing to give up the idea of having a baby? At least you'd have him. That's something."

"Give up the idea forever? Would you?"

"I don't know. Answers don't come so easily anymore, do they?"

Tess stayed up later and later, looking out the courtyard window. There were no pigeons in flight at night. Max got up so early that sometimes he climbed out of bed as she climbed in. The world was quiet then, not even a breeze rustling the leaves. They didn't call each other Cookie, Honey Lamb, Sweetstuff. *Il mio Tesoro* didn't make a single appearance. It began to seem as if it would take a miracle to bring them back together. Neither knew how to make one.

They moved into the polite stage that a marriage becomes when the fissures have separated into cracks, the cracks have opened into breaks, the breaks about to form into the pieces that will be strewn around when the marriage comes apart.

"Would you like some lunch? I'm making tuna."

"No thanks. I'll grab something on my way uptown."

There were no tears, no fire, no ice; the air was still between them.

"Look," Tess finally said when a premature heat wave took all of New York hostage, draining all the sap and hope of its citizens, "You're right. This doesn't seem to be working. I could ask Naomi if I can stay with her and Eliot for a while."

"If that's what you think," Max spoke briefly from a dark place where lovers didn't go and then turned back and descended further.

Tess didn't know what to think, what to do. She began to pack her things in fits and starts, the boxes piling wherever she packed them, in the front of closets, in the middle of the floor. The apartment began returning to the chaos in which Tess had found it. She had joined Max in something that didn't seem to be marriage. Max stayed out of the apartment or holed up in his study with the air-conditioner on frozen. He was working on a paper about the geography of descent in *The Inferno*.

She began to hate being in the apartment with Max locked up in his study all the time. She couldn't think clearly anymore. She felt like a fraud whenever she looked at the Fra Angelico. One night Tess took the picture down and laid it on top of a liquor carton and went for a walk by the river. Maybe in the open air something would come to her.

In the glowing orange light rising from the blood-black water beyond the pier, couples walked hand in hand, men with men, women with women, men with women, all with each other. A father knelt holding a small boy on his lap. The boy's face was in tears. He had a scraped knee. The father lifted the knee to his lips and kissed it; the father and son were bent together in a reparation that bound them together. She felt her disconnection. It was time to leave.

When she got back to the apartment she realized that she had forgotten her keys. She rang the doorbell to no response. Then she phoned upstairs from the corner. It rang repeatedly to no answer. He would never hear the phone in his study with the air-conditioner on. Encased in ice, he couldn't be contacted.

The only other person who had a key was Claudia.

"I'm just going out." Claudia's voice was cool when Tess called, but a hint of interest was there: Tess locked out. "I have a gig I have to get to. You can borrow the key if you come over right away. And get it back to me by tomorrow."

The conditions were everyone else's. Tess found Claudia, her shades on in the evening twilight, sitting on the steps to her apartment with Mickey. She was working on a song she was writing, playing it for him. He watched her with veiled pleasure. Too cool for joy, beneath the shades, the leather jackets, the torn boots, one still felt the tight bond between them. "I really appreciate this." Tess was always careful with what she said, with how she said it. "Your song floated down the street. It's lovely."

"You liked it?" Surprised. Claudia was careful to keep her distance.

"What's up with you two? Dad says you're leaving him." Claudia, arrested by this possibility, risked a moment of interest.

"He did? I guess. We seem to be screwing this up. Too much fun too fast."

"Nah, he's a shmuck. That's the way it is with him. Everybody gives up on him." She gave Tess permission to join the club.

"There are two of us there."

"Whatever." Claudia turned back to her boyfriend, her guitar, away from Tess and her father.

When Tess got home the phone was off the hook, the air-conditioner was on, but Max wasn't in his study. She went into the bedroom and opened a window. She didn't know what to think, what to feel anymore. She lay down on the bed, legs dangling over the side. She gave up. A pigeon, beating the air, landed on the windowsill. It folded its wings, extended and retracted its neck several times. Tess, drifting on her troubles, felt the stir of the bird's wings as a veil of sleep fell over her.

A set of small clicks, metal slipping against metal, a key in a door, came from the hall, tearing her sleep away. When the door opened a breeze came in with Max, passed over Tess and moved out the window into the trees in the courtyard, the leaves taking the breeze in. Max was sweating, as if he had been running. He stopped near a pile of boxes, then came and knelt down by the bed.

"I went looking for you. I couldn't find you." He held up the Fra Angelico print. A messenger with a message. "Get it?" he asked. His sweat and tears flowed.

"What Max? Get what?"

"Don't leave me Tess." Max teared up and said, "We will have a baby. We will."

"What! What are you talking about?"

"I really think we should. I mean it."

"What? All of a sudden you change your mind?"

"I called Naomi after you left. I was sure you'd be there. She didn't even know we were breaking up. I walked all over looking for you. I couldn't find you anywhere." Overtaken, he couldn't talk for a minute. "I was sure I'd never see you again."

"Oh Max, we haven't figured out how to be married. How can we have a baby?"

"Oh, we'll make a mess. I promise. The kid will wonder how we ever had the nerve to think we could be parents. My daughter will explain what a bad deal it's getting. She'll write a song about it. It'll be broadcast on radio."

"So why?" Here he was again, outrageous, impulsive Max, delivering this news. How could she possibly have a baby with him?

"Because not to is . . . to give up . . . hope," Max said.

Tess considered this, considered the currents of her husband's weather flowing over her. She gazed at the cast of light in his hair. She felt so confused.

Max moved into her confusion leaning over to kiss her belly. "Don't be afraid Tess," he said. "Hello eggs, this is your father talking. I'm sending some guys in to meet you. Any brave eggs in there? Only brave eggs come forward please. All nervous eggs please move to one side. Tess and Max's home isn't for you."

Max looked at Tess, tears flowing as he held his news up in front of him. Tess, full of disquiet and hope, looked off beyond the glow. Fear and aspiration moved on the air between them.

———•——

ASPARAGUS SOUP

Tess lay on the bed. "It's just a state of mind," she explained to her toes. She was trying to talk herself into getting up off the bed to make Max's soup. It was the third day she had promised she would make it. It was the third day it had been in the nineties. It wasn't quite the middle of April. No air-conditioning yet. She was six months pregnant. Too big. Too hot.

She looked down at her belly. "Soup," she asked, "in this heat?" Her body rolled over. Some of it rolled off the edge of the bed, hands dangling down. Her feet refused to follow. They lay attempting to stare up at the ceiling. Her eyes fell on her slowed, throbbing hands. "Do something," she told them, "make soup."

"Could you make this soup for me?" Max had asked the week before, at her family's Easter. It had been his first Easter with her family. It was the first time he was with her family for any holiday.

"Stop it," she'd whispered. "I'll make it for you next week."

"I mean just like *this*," he had insisted at her aunt's table. He grinned with delight at her. This was a city performance in her family's home town. They didn't do this kind of teasing in public. It wasn't their kind of joke.

"Yes," she told him. "Yes, yes I will," she told all the faces at table that had turned toward them.

"Will it taste exactly the same?" he continued. He looked around the large extended table at her people, smiling broadly at everyone looking back at him.

Tess didn't know if she should be embarrassed by this public display or by the fact that he didn't think she could cook her family's recipes. "Of course, Max, I *can* make this soup."

"It will be exactly the same," she told Max. The table knew the answer. They had raised her.

———•✦•———

PASSING HISTORY

David lived at 370 Riverside Drive, a building where Hannah Arendt had lived. David learned this after he and Sage had bought their apartment. Though he hadn't read Arendt himself, he felt sometimes that if one more person referred in passing to the banality of evil—How many of them had actually read that book, he wondered, or even the particular passage that dealt with that idea directly?—he would happily feed them a knuckle sandwich.

Still, he had to admit to himself that he felt some odd comfort in the idea that he was living in a building graced by someone of Arendt's stature. He imagined Hannah Arendt's friend Mary McCarthy brushing past Rafael, before his demotion to the late shift, appraising his long, stooped body with a glance, dismissing his decayed good looks with barely a raised chin of a nod before she made her way regally to their side of the lobby—the side of the building with "the views"—to ascend to talk over with Hannah whatever husband was driving her nuts at the time.

This picture pleased David and helped him put in perspective the welfare hotel across the street with its poverty, drugs, and misery so apparent and so noisy. This is New York, a wild old whore of a mistress, he thought, not the lady that the countryside had been.

This was why they were moving in from the small town in New Jersey where they'd been living: to be back at the heart of things. Arendt's flame might still flicker here. I could catch a spark, even ignite here in the proximity of her spectral fire. He had thought for a while his life was what it should be, with his love for Sage and for history. But his passion for history had cooled. Now only his love for Sage kept him warm.

Richard, his boss, well, mentor really, was the one who had said, "That's a great building. I think that's where Hannah Arendt lived," the night David called to say they had finally put an end to their search for an apartment.

Where does he get this stuff? David wondered, but when he mentioned Arendt, attempting to be casual, to the members of the board the night of their interview, "Yes, yes," all the members of the board smiled, "this is the building." One said, "The Lees live there now—nice Asian family. Isn't that the Lee's apartment, that nice Asian family? The little girl plays the violin?"

But he hadn't asked what he had wanted to ask: "What was she like? Did any of you actually know her? Have you read her stuff?" This was an interview, and even though David knew that this board couldn't ask for better additions to their building, he was automatically nervous in the face of anyone assessing him. He felt being reticent was his only possible stance. So it had taken all his nerve to find out if for once Richard was wrong. No, Richard's endless cache of tiny, but significant details was accurate once again. It was as if Richard opened an ancient velvet bag and took out tiny parts and pieces to hold them out as gifts in the light of friendship. Although it was annoying, Richard was never one to pretend to know something he didn't. He just happened to know which piece of theater was good, which was the newest, hottest restaurant. He should have been a concierge at a grand hotel instead of the headmaster of the Byrnes School for Girls, where David did admissions.

But then just as David and Sage were pushing back their chairs to leave the interview, a short woman, shoulders held back stiffly, a face grey with age and packs and packs of cigarettes said, "I never liked her. She thought *what a somebody* she was. Who are the rest of us? And I didn't like her ideas anyway, sleeping with that Nazi. That's not banal, that's wrong." David turned and looked at her. In her eyes he found a welcome and a challenge. You ask a question, you'll get a response. You want to know what I think? Ask me. He thanked her and thought, This *is* a good building. He felt such an intense burst of pleasure he had turned and kissed Sage modestly on the cheek, saying, "Welcome to 370."

Several of the members of the board had laughed, stopping short of the smattering of applause they felt inclined to make in the face of David's gesture. As David and Sage left the meeting, Sophie, for that was the woman's name, had insisted they come to tea after they moved in. They assured her they would honor this insistence.

"They'll be a nice addition to the building," Sophie told everyone after they'd left. No one would think of contradicting her.

David's life had been sliding around for a couple of years, from side to side, from Sage to Richard, from home to work, from books to cooking. In fact lately he had become quite a good cook. He loved the alchemy of it, turning raw into cooked, the bland into the spiced. He spent long, happy hours in the kitchen listening to Billie Holiday while he chopped and cut, sautéed and braised, setting the gas at precisely the right low flame to simmer.

Admissions he could do while he slept. He had worked at Byrnes for the last four years, since he'd gotten his master's in history. "The most useless degree I could find," he told Richard the night they met at a party." A reason to read. Not that I'm defensive, mind you." He had been trying to decide whether to continue to the PhD as originally planned. The idea that he was falling into being permanently dependent on Sage's money had begun to come over him in places like the shower where his only armor was a bar of soap. History had suddenly become a series of papers to write about ideas that had been flat, without the oxygen to give them life. Richard took to him immediately.

"And you can't get arrested now," Richard announced when David told him his field was the history of science. He had been working on the development of parallel scientific inaccuracies in ancient cultures.

"Work, I mean. Well at least I can help you pay the rent. I just lost my admissions director. Can you talk to people? You look presentable."

Now they had beaten a path between them that had little to do with being boss and employee. Richard never brought up Sage's money, a conveyance of his affection for David. A trust officer at a bank, she made a solid six-figure salary. She had grown up with money too. She inherited money after her mother died. Her father still sent her a generous sum at the end of every year. But it was *still* her salary that they mostly lived on. She knew how to deal with money too, prudently without being tight. She was perfectly fiduciary.

He loved to watch her drink her single glass of really good red wine every night watching the light change outside over the river. Never more than that one glass unless they were out for the evening. Then she had two and stopped.

David, in turn, never asked Richard why he hadn't done more with his education in classics: "Harvard for God's sakes," David told Sage after Richard had let this be known to David. One late afternoon, as they stood on the step of the old Georgian mansion that housed the Byrnes School, Richard explained that he still translated Greek for relaxation on the weekends in the country. He had looked away from David as he said it, giving only a quick turn of his head back to make sure it was having its full effect. Then he turned to look East again, watching the indigo sky come over the city. Even his regret was worn thin. Instead, in Richard's office after work on Fridays they drank a little too much scotch together. "It's a really great scotch," David would say with the perfect pitch of self-mockery, "not just good," when he explained one of his Friday latenesses to Sage, who hadn't asked.

And David tended to the embers of his love for Sage. The way she invested money, her own and other people's money too, carefully and with great satisfaction, moved him. David felt their looks contrasted nicely: he, with his rusty coloring, his pale blue watery eyes; she, with her long, thin body, her quiet sandy beauty, which she took for granted. She had the look of being slightly afraid if you came upon her suddenly that stirred a well inside David he didn't understand but for which he was deeply grateful. It meant a lot that she didn't give a damn what David did with his life as long as he loved her. Sage's center simmered quietly inside him. For David the aura of his love surrounding her gave his life light and heat.

When he had given up on the idea of being a historian, a small light had flickered and gone out inside him without his noticing it. It had only seemed like one of life's small decisions. I can't take any more of this bullshit, he thought, after one too many courses attempting to uncover the truth of one period or another, each professor with his own sense that *he* had the large perspective. Most said the same thing about their material, their period, their tiny postage stamp of the world: "Study me, and I'll teach you how to be a real historian," or worse, they didn't give a damn anymore about history or their special field and certainly not about their students. They were too involved in what grant they might get, so they wouldn't have to teach or who was talking to whom at what poker game. This wasn't a life he wanted to sign up for.

When they had moved to New Jersey the year after David began working at Byrnes, he had thought he might rekindle his passion by the light of the stars. He'd bike on lonely country roads, and the quiet would clear his head. But the stars stayed silently up in the distant sky. The quiet had crept into his senses, the silence of the sky silencing him. Even the working-class neighborhood where they had tried living in Queens, where David's neighbors washed their cars for leisure, had more life than the town they moved to in New Jersey. He had stopped reading seriously, cooked practical, healthy meals, and watched a lot of sports on TV. Once or twice he made love to Sage with a burn of wintry anger that scared him. He kept a careful watch after that for that kind of cold to rise in him and then dug up his passion or withdrew from her.

"You belong in the city," Richard said late one Friday afternoon after more than a couple of scotches. "Are you going to punish yourself forever because of Sage's money?" David was stung that Richard would speak of Sage's money. He'd better do something.

At first looking for an apartment had been a new kind of hobby, a way to see into people's lives, "They actually open up their closets and show you how they hang their clothes, keep their shoes," he said, giggling with high-pitched surprise after the first week of looking. One evening he reported excitedly to Sage, "I actually saw someone's used underwear on the floor of a closet today. The woman showing me her closet simply walked out of the room. I really felt for her. I wish I had loved her apartment. I'd have bought it on the spot." He was disappointed when he looked at freshly painted uninhabited apartments. These empty apartments held no appeal for David, no residue of character to contend with. But after one especially dangerous taxi ride back to work, David felt the cadence of his blood again. It beat to the swerve of a New York cab ride. He had looked at 370 that day. It was respectable without being excessive, doormen twenty-four hours a day, real New Yorkers, full of color, a little crumpled, worn even, but from living their lives. He saw at least five kids in the building by the time he came and went. He wanted the press of people against him. It might not be perfect, but it beat shopping at air-conditioned malls.

Now they were the new people in 12A with four big windows on the river. They slept with sirens going off in the middle of the night, neighbors posting angry notes in the garbage room about not letting doors slam. An elevator ride might include an intense discussion of why no one was to stand in Zekey's corner, a four-year-old who had staked out one of the back corners of the elevator after his sister was born. The tenants honored this possession; they were for people taking over corners. Almost everyone took part in asserting that right for Zekey.

"You know you can't stand there, Eliot," Naomi, one of the neighbors, might pull her distracted husband away when Zekey got on and found him there. "That's Zekey's." This was a place where people put energy into the simple act of coming and going, never mind being there.

"You like living here?" Sophie, the woman from the co-op board, wanted to know the day of the insisted-upon tea. She was fixing the perfect pink tea roses Sage had chosen for her in a small, embossed blue vase.

"Oh we love it," Sage said quietly but distinctly.

"But the question is whether we'll do." David turned the tables on Sophie now.

Sophie threw back her lovely old Eastern European head and laughed without a sound. "You're a card, Duvid."

"And you want to know why I've married a shiksa, right? Tell her Sage."

Sage was embarrassed about this. Technically she was Jewish. Not that anyone in her family paid the slightest attention. But they had immigrated first to Baltimore a couple, three generations back from somewhere in the Prussian Empire, "and when we got to Texas, well, let's just say we didn't talk about it a lot. It was easier. But I have great respect for the Jews. I've been doing some reading. David gave me Paul Johnson's *History of the Jews* to read recently." David knew that Sage was uncomfortable in situations like this. But he wanted to challenge Sophie.

"So are we having tea? Or do you have something like a good sherry for me?"

"Did you have to lay it on so thick?" Sage asked him when they got home. "You put the old girl in a tough spot."

"You don't understand these women. She adores me now that I didn't take any of that shiksa guff. Returning the challenge keeps the game going: without the return there ain't no tennis."

"I guess you'd know. Only don't make me into the ball." And it was true there was no sense Sage getting dragged into this. David began to stop at Sophie's apartment pretty regularly.

Sophie was home for David, only she was smarter than the tough women he had grown up with. He was comfortable in this setting that could as easily have been his grandmother's or one of many similar apartments in Warsaw, Vienna, or Prague. It held shelves of books, an old black, upright piano, many carefully framed pictures of faces with large intense features. Embroidered tablecloths covered the wood surfaces. They passed books back and forth. They discussed religion, but mostly they gossiped about the building.

"What's that screaming I hear coming from the back windows?" Sophie knew everyone in the building.

"I'm afraid we have a wife beater here. Mr. Ash. I personally have called the police three times. And I'm not the only one. But always she sends them away. 'It was just the cat in heat,' the wife says. "Some such nonsense."

"Once I stared him down in the elevator, 'What do you think of these wife beaters?' I asked him. 'Do you read the papers?' You know what the bastard had the nerve to say? 'Maybe it does them some good.'"

"'Whatever God you do or don't believe in is looking down on you,' I told him. Looked him straight in the eye."

David gave her a kiss on the cheek when he left that day, announcing, "I'm going to bring us a really good bottle of scotch."

"No, buy cognac. I like it better. Don't spend too much."

This is historic, David thought. Real history of how people lived their lives. Day to day what people say to one another: or better what people do and then what their neighbors say about what they've done. Aboriginal history, the first commentaries. Never written, but sotto voce, in hallways, by mailboxes, in kitchens. Never mind the fucking Annales school with its baptism certificates and tax records. This was the genuine article.

On his next visit David asked about the afternoon doorman they apparently were stuck with, "What's the deal with Rafael?"

"Him? That no-good-nick," Sophie said. "We got stuck with him about ten years ago when they wanted him out at 375." That was the next building up.

"What's that have to do with us?"

"You know what that creep did?" She was serving them the eighteen-year-old Remy Martin David had appeared with. She paused, holding the bottle in midair over the etched wine glasses that sat on a tooled brass tray that rested on a small piece of tapestry that covered a small, dark carved wood table set on a worn oriental rug that lay on shiny parquet floors.

"He let the door go just at the right moment, so it hit one of

the tenants he didn't like right in the nose. It had been one of the
tenants living in the building because the guy yelled at Rafael to
'open the God damned door.' You know how he moves so slow,
so you'll open it yourself? So that piece of you-know-what makes
sure the door hits the tenant right in the smacker. 'My hand
slipped,' he said. So instead, *we* got him." She sat down with some
satisfaction and lit up.

"Why should we get stuck with him?"

"Well, I guess he had three little kids then. There was sympathy for the wife. The management didn't know what to make
of this situation. Then there's the union. 370! That's their answer.
Who knew?" Her voice slid up high with this question. "He was
just the new doorman. Years later I became friends with a Mrs.
Cominski. She was from 375. She told me. By then . . . my Bernard
was sick. I didn't care." She sat and looked at her handsome husband's photograph in his suit and tie in the etched, silver frame.
"There's some people not worth bothering about. Ignore, I say."

David had the second bedroom lined with green metal, industrial
shelves which he then called, "mein study." Sage joined the choir
at St. John's and went to a yoga class with Leah and Irene three
times a week. David power walked in Riverside; they shopped at
Westside Market, bought their bagels at Lenny's. They had settled
in.

"It's a good life," one reminded the other when they were brows-
ing, say at Book Forum. The promise in the weight of the paper.

"In all of documented history very few people have had it this
good: food, shelter, and books, music, and movies at every turn.
Who has lived like this before? No one. It's more than enough.
It's as good as it can possibly be," David might say, his shoulders
slightly bowed, as he kissed Sage goodbye on a Monday morning
at the corner of 110th Street and Broadway.

"I'm so lucky to have you," Sage might whisper, kissing his
neck just as David was drifting off to sleep at night, his book dropping from his hand to the side of the bed.

David was back to cooking elaborate meals for sport. He had
taken up Thai cooking recently: he spent hours worried over the

lemongrass and coriander, cooking up imported smells in his kitchen.

On a crisp Sunday, after he had walked three miles in under forty-four minutes, he decided he'd pick up J. C. Gregory again on the theories of combustion. He'd start with Gregory and then read from Heraclitus to Antoine Lavoisier. Reading about oxygen might fill up his lungs.

Sophie had told David the vivid details of Bernard's long illness. How many years it had been before she had been able to clear out his dresser. She still had one pair of striped underwear and one pair of socks. The last of his things. "I always bought him the best, never spared the money."

David had spent one long afternoon telling her about falling in love with Sage when he had begun to think he wasn't capable of love. The way she always smelled like sheets dried on a cold day on a clothes line. How her small gestures, the way she cleared her throat when she had something to say she was worried would offend you, the way she brushed his shoulders proprietarily when she found dandruff there. She didn't ask. He was hers to take care of.

'She doesn't want *kinder*?' Sophie was thinking.

"Sophie!"

"Out loud, I said that?"

David ran into Sophie in front of Westside one afternoon when he stopped after work to shop for dinner. They were in vegetables when Sophie surprised herself by turning to him and asking, "Why didn't you go on? To be a professor?"

"In front of produce, you ask me that?" The lemongrass looked fresh. Where did they keep the fish sauce? He couldn't remember.

"I'll meet you by the register," she declared. "I have to get some marzipan. My Sarah's coming, my granddaughter from California. She loves 'grandma's marzipan,' as if I made it."

Could he explain this? Answer Sophie's question? He found the peanuts stored below the root veggies, the fish sauce above the spices, the coriander below the fish sauce. Sage loves this salad. Just the Tsing Tao beer now.

At the register Sophie was asking where Cheik was today. "I haven't seen him for two days now. Is he sick?" No, he was just out because his cousin had arrived from Nigeria. He'd be in tomorrow.

"Good, good. Tell him I'm asking." Sophie had decided to give David a little time. If he wants, he'll tell.

David wasn't sure he understood this business himself. On the way home as they turned West, it was the hour of fine, sandy light. He should try at least.

"I thought the guys I was studying with were jerks, the students and the teachers. I thought that was the problem then. The whole thing seemed so corrupt. How do you say what happened in the past? I'm not sure I could tell you what's actually taking place in front of my nose with anything close to accuracy.

"I'm pretty sure now I didn't think I had the stuff to add anything really important. When I realized that . . . I love to read, to talk. I'm better at small moments. I was ashamed to write one of those books just to stay in the game. It would hurt my pride to write that way about what's important to me.

"I'd rather just do what I do right, make a great meal and eat it with friends, talk to you, read what I want. It was better I didn't."

Duvid, Duvid, Sophie thinks, why do people do this to themselves? They were at their door now. The sun threw up a light beneath the clouds, giving them a crimson undercast, rising to a wild pink coral color.

Sophie climbed wearily up the two steps. "Duvid," she said sympathetically, "take a chance, right or wrong. That's all we get. That, love, and maybe God. About him I'm not so sure."

"I'm better at the margins of my life than most people are at inhabiting their centers," he said to Sage a few nights later, when they were cleaning up after the exceptionally elaborate three-course Thai meal he had cooked for Leah and Aaron, their friends who lived up the street. Sage had only asked when he had started to get seriously interested in cooking. But it felt like everyone was asking him annoying questions these days.

Even Richard had started to say things that David felt were not part of their agreement: "I have to have dinner with Dr. Rodino tomorrow night. He's the real power on the board now. Come with me. I'm not going to be headmaster forever."

"Oh Richard, do you want me to do that to myself?" As soon as he said it he felt bad. "I could never soothe these . . . feathers the way you do."

"Okay, I'm only talking. If I were your age . . ." Richard wasn't offended. He could see David still had fields marked "Prohibited." "Look, take a crack at that history of our school I asked you to write. It can't hurt, and it could position you, if you change your mind. You should be able to do that in a weekend."

"Don't. Listen: I landed the Wood girl today. You have to be nice to me. Her father's a VP at Coopers Lybrand." David tried to make it right again.

"All right, all right. Can I take the two of you to dinner? Call Sage. Tell her I need to congratulate you on your coup. Why are you so good at this, admissions?"

The next time David visited Sophie he brought his own building gossip. She was getting better. Maybe he'll walk her to Broadway over the weekend, take her out to a café.

"Did you hear that Naomi has a guy?"

Sophie was impressed. "Who told you this?"

"Well, I see them everywhere in the neighborhood together. I asked. Naomi said, 'This is my friend, Eliot,' the last time I was with them in the elevator. She was lit up. You could tell she just had to tell people. I think . . ." Was it his business to speculate about this?

"You think . . . ? What?" Sophie lifted her glass to be refilled.

"She looked, I'd say tired and different, but pleased with herself." David hesitated, the bottle in the air, poured, and asked, "Could she be pregnant?"

"Why not her?" Sophie sniffed the air between them. She paused, then, "So you two? How come no children?"

He sat brushing the crumbs from his slacks.

"Is there trouble there?"

"No, no, that's not it." He picked the last crumb from his pants, rolled it around between his thumb and one finger, popped it in his mouth.

"I'm not sure I can tell you, Sophia, my dear," he said using the full formal of her first name only when he was being completely serious. Once before, he remembered, when they had had a long talk about God. David wasn't sure why they didn't have kids. They hadn't so much decided not to have children as the decision had crept over them like moss the longer they put it off. They had talked about it for a while. They had even tried briefly. Even now it wasn't out of the question. He just knew it wasn't going to happen. "We're just not going to have children." He felt damp and sweaty; his shirt was sticky.

Even Sophie seemed out of pronouncements. They sat there quietly. Then Sophie rose and kissed his cheek. "Come by soon. I'll make a bundt." It was sad. It was wrong, but he was forgiven.

That night, after David and Sage had been in bed reading for a while, David turned to her. "Richard wants me to write a pamphlet on the history of the Byrnes School." Sage looked especially beautiful. Her hair shone against her white nightgown. She wished Richard hadn't asked him to do that. To write that kind of history would make David feel bad. Sage wondered if she could call Richard and talk to him about this. David didn't tell her about the other thing.

"Honey, why do you think we decided not to have kids?" David asked her now.

"I'm not sure. I don't really need to. And you always seem like you're waiting for an urgent telegram or an alarm to go off. I didn't want to interfere."

"I guess. So why is it bothering me?"

"Something's missing, David. You thought when we found each other that feeling would go away, and it hasn't. Then once you were earning money, once we had a home." She turned and sat cross-kneed facing him. "For me you're enough."

"It's not that you're not enough. I'm not enough for myself. Sometimes I think someone else is living my life while I'm playing hooky. Maybe it's this guy," he said gesturing with the book his fingers held open. He looked at the stack of books at the side of his bed. "Maybe it's all these guys."

"What are you going to do about this? It sits in the middle of our life, but only *you* get to do something about it. I've played my hand. I have what I want."

"What happens if I can't play my hand?"

"I don't have anywhere else I want to be."

"For how long?"

They both looked out the window where a narrow view of the river could be seen between the buildings. They slept deeply that night, their windows open to a spring rising up from the river, the filmy curtains blowing up, lightly, into the room. On that kind of night it was hard not to sleep like a child or a person of virtue, someone who has worked hard all day.

He finally got around to the conversation that had connected him to Sophie in the first place. "What was she like?"

"Her Highness Arendt?" Sophie knew who he meant. "'Dr. Mrs. Neighborly Love?' She had no use for us. What she meant by her neighbors was, I guess, the neighbors of the mind. Her mere real neighbors were not worth attention. Did you ever notice how high-minded types treat us ordinary ones bad?" That another Jew who had lived through the war, had family who died, and who had had to leave the world of her childhood should have been contemptuous of her? Sophie left them both in a wash of annoyance that comes only from humiliation. He changed to something that had only just floated through his mind.

"Richard seems to want me to be his successor."

"You want to be Richard?" She served them lemonade. Already the temperature had hit ninety-five. It was only June, but it was one of those short spells to remind New Yorkers of where they were headed. The air-conditioners weren't in yet.

"That would mean I've decided to give up for sure. I don't think I can bring myself to do that yet."

"Sage? What does she think?" Sophie rubbed her knee. The humidity always made her arthritis kick up. She felt old today.

A siren burned through the blue dusk.

"I didn't tell her yet."

David felt bad. He was disappointing another person. He scanned the hot room, took a long cool drink of the iced lemonade. The outside of the glass coated with condensation dripped on his damp skin. David sniffed the overheated air. It had a corrosive smell.

New York at the end of August is permeated with a thick, sweet smell of decay. Summer vacations which have been filled with light, air, and movement are immediately corrupted by coming home to that smell. Thomas, who was usually the midnight-to-morning doorman, helped David and Sage carry their luggage in from a taxi when they arrived home from two weeks on Martha's Vineyard. As Thomas set down their bags, he said, "Mrs. Schreiber isn't well. Her daughter came in from California last week," nodding his head confidentially. That's what Thomas always called Sophie. A Seventh Day Adventist minister originally from the Caribbean, he had no use for unearned intimacy.

"Where's Rafael, Thomas?" Sage asked.

Thomas raised his eyes to the ceiling, shrugged his shoulders and held them there. "I don't know Mrs. He not around. Something happened." He closed his eyes, lifted his shoulders. It wasn't for him to say.

Sage checked their messages. David called Sophie's apartment. Her daughter answered. "What's up, Lisa?"

"My mother just got home from the hospital yesterday. The heat was really terrible. I think she was trying to save on the bill—wasn't using the air-conditioning. She had a kind of stroke. Come down. She needs to see people."

When David arrived at 4D, Sophie's granddaughter was playing on the living room floor, knees splayed reading *Harry the Dirty Dog*. Sophie sat on the couch watching her. Her proud head sagged. She looked like someone had beaten her. When she saw David, she clutched the top of her bathrobe, embarrassed to be seen like this, no makeup or girdle on, undone.

David looked tan, healthy. His eyes seemed darker blue. "I leave you for a couple of weeks, and you go and do this to yourself? I thought I could trust you."

"It's just age. I haven't been watching lately like I should, my sugar. It's just an ischemia—something, they call it.

"A stroke."

"All right, a stroke. But I'm tough. Just I have to watch. Take medicine. They want me to walk. I can't stand."

Then distractedly, "Look, my Sarah's learning to read." There's a smile more on one side of her face than the other as she gazes at her granddaughter who's making up the words to go with the pictures.

"Don't listen Grandma Sophie." Sarah looks down at the book, refuses to look up at her grandmother.

Sophie knows that Sarah doesn't want her grandmother to know she was making up the words. Sophie remembers with Lisa too, the same thing. If these kinder knew it's one of the secrets to everything: instead of being ashamed, her grandmother thinks, make it up as you go.

"Sit, sit." She pats the couch beside her.

David sits down by this smaller, lopsided Sophie. He moves closer to her, picks up her crumpled hand, and holds it in his. He sees on Sophie's face, I'm that bad? I'm scaring you?

David fills Sophie's living room with words. He talks about crab soup, dawn on the porch of the house they had rented, the accident they saw on the highway as they came home on the Merritt Parkway. He doesn't tell her what he brought back with him.

"I don't think I'm going to be Richard." David has a burnished glow from the sun. His auburn hair gleams in the dusty room.

"*Vu den*? A banker?" Sophie pushes the dull clouds in her eyes away for a moment.

Something hot flickers across David's brain, flaring then dimming. David wants to tell Sophie about the big barn full of books, sitting out over the brook, where they served iced tea and lemon tarts, where he'd come upon a copy of *For Love of the World*, a biography of Arendt. He had found a picture of her with Jaspers from the sixties. Jaspers looks at her with tender devotion. Arendt looks off into the lens with eyes that are certain and veiled. When that photograph was taken she had long since reconciled with Heidegger. Why? David had stood there by the buckling shelves made of old barn wood, trying to imagine their reunion.

The picture made no rational sense. Arendt's former professor, her former lover, older by seventeen years, stands outside a hotel door in Freiburg; when the door opens, Arendt's piercing, intelligent eyes look into his. Arendt reaches out her hand; then, chin raised, she looks away and gestures him in. David could see Arendt looking up after they are seated. She finds the eyes that had understood something about consciousness that no one before Heidegger had. Did they hold each other's gaze or look off into their own knowing? Arendt knows that Heidegger had not been able to see what everyone else understood about him. *Stuff*—hope and memory—from the *no longer* stirred.

David had thought, Still she made her choice. Maybe she was wrong. For us, for the world. Not for herself.

He could become a history teacher at Byrnes. Maybe he'd run for president of the co-op board. But one thing would continue to hold the center for him: when he holds in his hands the accumulated weight of thin pages bound together, a spark bursts against flint, flames smolder, a small fire crawls along his veins. Now is not the time to tell Sophie this.

Later, David would find out why Rafael had finally been fired. Later, Sophie will tell David how frightened she was when she couldn't find any feeling on the left side of her body, sitting alone in her hot apartment. Much later than that it will be to Sophie's specter that David will explain that, sometimes at sunset walking down Riverside Drive, he sees the *no longer and not yet* glinting side by side for seconds on the horizon.

David and Sophie both look down at Sarah, who is pretend reading the last page of *Harry the Dirty Dog*, saying, "After dinner he slept in his favorite place, the um, on the pillow. He slept so soundly he didn't even . . . he didn't even . . . he didn't even see the scrubbing brush under the pillow. He didn't even feel the scrubbing brush under his pillow." Then Sarah closes the book, looks up at her grandmother. She has gotten pretty close to what is on the page.

———◆———

BEBOPIN' BABY

Naomi is making the case for Eliot to her friend Tess. "I do love, yes, him, yes. I think I do. He's so energetic—you should see him in bed. Even after all our on again off again when I finally said I am going to have a baby. I had actually made an appointment to start insemination the last time we broke up. What a mess that was when we got back together. Sneaking thermometers. He's using a condom; I'm running off to mysterious appointments. I had to tell him. When I did, he was right there with me. Right away said, 'If you want to have a baby, let's do it.'

"Now I actually am pregnant. By him. And he's happy about it. He works, makes money. Not a lot, but . . . He can be weird. But who's to say? Hey, he even cooks."

The women are on one of their walks in Riverside Park. They walk briskly, briskly in the cold, crisp dusk. Then the words they are saying make them hesitate so that they can consider Eliot. They pause and stare off into the cold, bright sky and wait for it to reflect back what they think. Should Naomi marry Eliot?

That's astonishing. "Men never say yes right away to the baby question," Tess says, watching the slow surface of the water turn a dusty paprika as the sun slips to sit just exactly into a burning orb on the horizon before she turns her head back to her friend. The dark orange light melts long across the water, paints the buildings up on the drive the color of transparent curry. At this hour, in this light, everything is made right. All will be well. The sky is speaking to them. Tess moves one foot forward. Then they start walking fast again to take hold of this.

"You should do it," Tess says certainly.

"I know. I know. I think I should. If it were one of my patients, especially you know that one, I'd be thinking, How many chances does she think she still has? Grab it while you can. I've been watching people dither all the time like I used to do. I have work I love, a home. It could even work out. I'm ready for this."

Something has shifted against the sky—the low, bruise-colored clouds are lit from below now. In this glow, with her friend Tess, walking so close to the water, almost on it. Are some cells beginning to split into new configurations in her womb? Is the zygote attaching itself to the wall more firmly? This baby is not just a possibility any longer. It's a certainty now. She has a baby inside her, a person who will exist. Naomi will be the mother. Eliot will be the father. The baby will be the baby. There's no going back now.

Naomi and Tess both stop and look at each other. "A baby, a baby," they sing to each other, stunned by what has just happened. The women lift their arms and embrace; then they do the bebop lightly, foolishly along the water's edge; this moment is at one with the beating heart in Naomi because Naomi is going to have a baby.

My baby, Naomi thinks looking at the sun slide quietly down behind New Jersey—a completion to this astonishment.

———•———

SYNCHRONICITY

Paul is the dawn on his mother's horizon; he is the stars in her dark night. He has large, dark olive eyes set against golden hair and skin. A current runs through him, quivering along his wires, whizzing, whirring as his strong legs carry him along. His small, sturdy body moves before an idea has finished leaping across the synapses of his brain. The salt shaker sitting next to Tess's glass of wine rains salt into her glass, white crystals falling into the rich translucent red before Tess's chin has the chance to drop, long before she has the time she needs to reach out her hand to stop the salt from raining down. He is three, and he is still getting up two, three, four times a night. Tess longs for sleep the way she had once longed for him.

His first year, he got up three, four times a night, nursing quickly, desperately, and descending back into a deep sleep. Tess tossed for an hour or more; then just as she was being smuggled across the simple waters into sleep, he'd wail into the dark. Although he had long been weaned, in addition to still waking several times during the night, however dark or light the season, however blind to light the shades on his window, however calm or frenzied the previous day's activity had been, Paul wakes twenty minutes before dawn. Some mornings the soft rising glow of light on the horizon wears away at Tess's tired skin like sandpaper.

"I've got him, Hon," Max would say most mornings, ,but not before Tess picked Paul up from beside their bed where he had stood waiting, pulling the soggy weighty bottom, his smell, the tiny musty puffs of breath into her body. Then Tess would pass him to Max and sink back into a headachy stupor. A rage of exhaustion and an aboriginal passion for her son were always at war in Tess.

This morning, she is awake anyway. Max might as well get some sleep. Paul stands by the bed, his eyes wide with an eagerness to begin. "Wanna play Mama?"

"Yes, Mama wants to play with you." And she does. The puffiness about his eyes and the simple longing in his request push Tess's sleepiness away. There is only a call to answer his eagerness when she first rises from her warm bed. Tess watches the light come up behind the buildings outside her kitchen window with something like calm while she and Paul mess around in the kitchen. She makes the coffee. NPR is on the radio. Paul climbs up and down, on and off her lap, running matchbox cars over her various limbs. It is only after a couple of hours and at least two cups of coffee that her body starts aching, usually about 7:30 in the morning.

Tess remembers getting up in the middle of the night the first months after Paul had been born. Nursing him, she felt as if they were the only two creatures awake on a large, rusting boat crossing a wide, black sea under a starless sky. It was up to her to carry him fearlessly across the night waters, after his mouth had shuddered into quiet, sucking, then whimpering a quick complaint, then sucking again, then whimpering, finally settling into a steady suck, suck. It had been just the two of them facing the dark, filled with invented danger, yearning for the sun's rising, for the warmth of daylight. She'd drink a large glass of water, as satisfied as she had ever been.

But as the first year had turned into two and then three years of sleeplessness, a terrible misery had overtaken her. Most days passed with Tess feeling achy and miserable. On those days she thought one of them might not survive Paul's raising up. Motherhood was consuming her brain, her flesh, her spirit. A gray presence had taken the place of her once vibrant self.

"I have a idea," Paul's dark eyes shining says now. "We could play . . . play . . . do play dough."

"Okay, let Mama finish her coffee, then we'll make it. Okay?"

"Where's the powder machine?" she swigs down her last half-cup and washes out the grounds from the coffeemaker, "that goes round and round?" Paul is standing on the small step stool, next to Tess at the sink. He means the flour sifter that he was playing with the day before.

"Let me clean out the sink, then I'll get it for you."

"Where's that powder Mama?" The flour. Paul has already knocked over the step stool, which has banged into Tess's ankle in his haste to look for powder and powder machine. Tess knows this tempo. He's moving faster than Tess wants.

"Wait honey. Let's get out all the ingredients, the flour, the salt, and the big, big bowl. So we'll have everything we need," she says, bending over to rub her ankle. She's trying to manage this the way she always imagined she would when she had been a nursery school teacher, longing to have a child to wake up with. She had pictured making play dough with her imagined child; that child had stayed at her side, moving at a pace she had generously accommodated.

"Here's a gooder powder bowl Ma." There are several pans on the floor, two pan covers. Proudly, Paul holds up the bowl that he went to find.

"That's a good one, pumpkin." Tess doesn't want to suggest that maybe they need a bigger bowl to contain the mess that will soon be rising in her tiny kitchen.

"I, I, I got it my own self."

Tess quickly puts away the pans and covers, hurries to get the flour and salt, and then measures it herself so that it won't wind up on the floor. She puts the water into a pitcher so that Paul can pour the water in himself. She can't remember where the cream of tartar is. She sets up the "powder machine" in the bowl so that Paul can begin to play with the flour. This, she knows, is the main inspiration for this request to make play dough.

He begins to pick the flour high up above his head. Then he opens his fingers and watches the flour rain down, soft, loose, powdery. Some of it goes into the bowl; some of it lightly covers the sink and the counters. Tess looks at his sturdy male body enveloped by this silky cloud. A floury pleasure rises in the air.

"I like this powder Mama," he says, with a big, sloppy grin. He's coating his arms with it now, carefully patting it on, and carefully watching it fall off.

"I know, honey." Not all mothers would let their children play with flour like this, Tess thinks virtuously. She hears Ginny, her neighbor, saying, "Flour is for cooking, not for playing with," in her ever-certain tone. She's so angry all the time, Tess thinks. Some of the flour is in the sink; more is on the counters. There's only a little on the floor in front of the sink. Tess is opening drawers and cupboards looking for the cream of tartar. She's sure she bought some the other day. Here's the food coloring. She doesn't want to go around the corner to the pantry to look for the cream of tartar; anyway, she doesn't keep it there. Paul has just dumped the water all at once into the too shallow bowl. The flour goes up into a spray; some floury globs spatter the rug by the sink. Tess bends to wipe it up with a sponge.

"Be careful honey," Tess can hear the hard edge of Ginny's voice coming into her own. How does that happen? Whenever she congratulates herself on not being like some other mother of whom she disapproves, within seconds she says exactly the kind of thing that mother would say. It seems to be a secret rehearsal, concealing from Tess that she's about to behave in a way she hates— concealed until Ginny's high pitch emerges from her mouth. So what if some of the flour is on the floor? Enjoy your kid, Tess commands.

She finds the cream of tartar in with the vitamins. Paul's arms are deep into the gooey mess. His gluey fingers are trying to open the food-coloring bottle. "Red's good, right Mama?" he turns toward his mother, his floured gooey hands dropping some more blobs of play dough on the floor. His powdered face looks earnestly up at Tess for approval. Flour fills the air like chaos; it falls covering the counters, the floors. Little bits of wet and dry dough stick to Paul's face and hair. Tess sighs, releasing her distress into the space between them.

"Be careful about where the powder's falling, okay?" Her voice is rising. She looks at the clock. It's 7:50. Tess has been bending down wiping up the worst of the mess with a wet sponge as it happens. This is what you waited for all those years. Why spend it on cleaning up when it finally arrives?

Paul is going at the mixing, kneading it intensely. "Good job Paul. You're just like the baker, making his bread. Good kneading."

"I'm a gooder baker, right?"

Tess is using all of her self-control not to start putting the ingredients away, when the phone rings, a loud demand into their floury disorder. It's the building management. Tess has been trying to reach them for weeks to come and inspect the water stains from the leak.

"Ma, I have to clean my hands now." Paul is tugging on her nightgown with his doughy hands. Tess is trying to get him to knead some more so she can deal with this phone call. "Just a minute honey, Mama will be coming back to the bakery."

"Look, you said you'd come and see them last week." As Tess turns to get her appointment book to write this so-called appointment down and the name of the person calling, she sees that Paul is shaking his hands now trying to get this goo off. The pink dough splatters around the tiny kitchen, on the toaster, on the walls, on the light fixture over the sink.

"I'm not going to be able to match your paint, you understand?" the man on the phone is saying. But Paul has climbed down from the step ladder, and he's racing toward the living room, gooey hands out front. Tess drops the phone on the floor and races to get Paul. "Just a minute," she screams. "We're not going to do that." Who is she yelling at? She marches Paul back to the kitchen, and holding one hand around his middle she places him back on the step ladder. "Look, just come and look at the damn stain," she says to the guy on the phone. "We'll talk paint later."

Paul has squirmed away; he's racing toward his father in the bedroom, "Papa, Papa, I'm a bakerman."

By the time Tess gets to the bedroom Max's eyes are flaked with dried bits of Play dough. "Jesus honey," he says looking up at Tess, "what's up?"

As filled with turmoil as the dark hours can be, waking into life with a toddler feels more bizarre than a dreamscape. "Oh please," Tess says, suppressing her sympathy for Max. She's afraid to give her sympathy to Max now, or all the sympathy in the house will be used up; there will be none left for her. "I've been up since five thirty. I've had too much coffee. We've made some play dough. The building management called to harass me. I'm exhausted, and your son's ready to rock and roll." Paul is watching his mother from his perch beside his father's head, one leg casually over his father's shoulder. His hair is standing up in several doughy peaks. "We going to dance Mama?" He's waving his hands above his head, moving his bottom to his own rhythm. Should she hug or strangle him?

"Jeez, is there any coffee left?" Max says now, shaking his head.

Tess looks at the clock. It's eight-thirty now. The long day stretches out in front of her. She lies back on the bed. "Please tell me tonight's not your graduate course."

"No not tonight; just a departmental meeting. I'll be home by five. I'll cook tonight, okay?" He bends over and kisses her. Paul is soon poking his nose into the small spot where their mouths are meeting.

"I'll kiss," he's saying. "I'll kiss too." Tess looks up to see his dark olive eyes. Swept off the roundness of his cheeks, the dry play dough in his hair, the confidence that he is wanted in their kiss, emotion floods into the smallest cavities in Tess' body; how could she have yelled at him before? It's not even nine o'clock in the morning.

"I'll kiss a Nuggins," she says lifting him above her head and then airplaning him down to her mouth. Max has wandered off to the kitchen. I'll drink some Coke, she vows. Today I won't let myself be exhausted, today.

Fuck the house, cooking, everything, and no TV either. The day stretched out generously in front of Tess and Paul.

"*Il mio tesoro, la mia regina,* my treasure, my queen," Max is yelling from the kitchen.

"Sesame, Sesame," Paul is chanting, bouncing up and down on the bed. She hated when Max reduced her name to flatness and added *that* endearment—she pictured an old, fat woman in a heavy brocaded dress with a weird hairdo. She snaps on the TV before she goes out to the kitchen. She has to have a minute with Max before he leaves.

"Don't call me that horrible name," she says coming into the kitchen.

"Look, I just remembered I've also got a poker game tonight, but I'll cancel." He is looking at her, firmly committed to his winning the Best Husband of the Year award. "I mean it."

"You'll just make sure everyone knows what a devoted husband you are, what a good guy, how I couldn't get through the night without you. Go to the goddamn game." She isn't sure who she hates most at that moment. It is definitely someone in this apartment.

Tess in a furious whirl has picked up the house, made the beds, taken a shower, made Paul two snacks. She feels calmer because the house is picked up but depressed because what she wants is so minimal and so hard to come by. Triumph for Tess these days consists of a bed made and a shower taken. She's broken all her earlier resolves. Paul's been watching TV steadily, and she's yelled at him for cleaning the jelly off his hands on the couch and for rejecting the second snack he promised he would eat. The atmosphere crackles with the tension and disappointment she feels.

She gets him ready for the park. They'll be the first ones at the playground. She can't seem to get the hang of her new neighborhood on the Upper West Side. Tess has different rhythms than the other mothers: they come out after lunch. Paul can't wait till then. She longs for Abingdon Square Park and the mothers she knows downtown.

"Where's anybody?" Paul often seems surprised when they arrive at an empty park. Today he wanders over to the sandbox and starts digging in what seems to Tess to be a desultory way. Tess goes to sit on the bench and read her *New Yorker*. It is cool out this morning, so Tess sits down in the sun, hoping it will take the chill off. She is always cold when she is this tired. She starts to read "Talk of the Town," but soon her eyes wander back to Paul; she is inextricably drawn back to watching him—a planet circling the sun.

He loves the sand, holding it, feeling it, watching it fall in streams from his hands. Sometimes he lies down in it and rests there, then he pushes some of it to one side with one foot, then the other. If he moves, it moves; if he slides, it slides. It is one of his mediums: stuff that moves when he pushes. Water and snow are the others. Just now he was brushing it back and forth with his fingers, quietly moving it one way, then the other. The sand is completely accommodating, completely accepting.

I should be his sand. That's what a mother should be, Tess thinks. She had wanted to be a mother all her life. There has been no other constant in Tess, as old, as utter, as this longing for a child. It was with Tess through all the girlish years: when she piled small red berries on maple leaf dishes for her doll babies to eat; when she daydreamed as a teenager what it would be like to lie on a cool bed and make love to Donny—that could lead to making babies, she'd thought in those days, with delightful anxiety; when it became a real possibility in her twenties and then began to look as if it were going to slip away from her—she didn't seem to have the ability to make men want to stay and have a baby with her; until it finally accompanied her as she fell in love with Max, and he said yes he would carry in his arms what she would carry in her body.

Now here she is with her baby, and her lungs are filled with a tight uncertainty. The sun hits her full on her shoulders now. Paul is singing some phrase over and over to himself. "I like a blue play dough. I like a blue play dough." Tess walks quietly near, hoping he'll keep singing. He's turned away from Tess and doesn't hear her coming. "Mama don't like a blue play dough. Mama says no blue dough." His voice is small, high, sweet. It's filled with a yearning that matches Tess for something inexplicably not this.

The emptiness of the swings, slide, and benches fills the park with absence. A confusion that is with Tess all the time crawls up the muscles of her larynx, fills her sinuses, crawls into the spaces around her eyes; it burns in her, in her face, in her neck and shoulders, in every crevice of her understanding, with sadness at what is wrong and unchangeable in her life. She is always tired, worried, and miserable during this—the most longed for—time of her life.

Tess bends down and pours some sand on Paul's belly, "Hi Mr. Nuggins."

"Hi Mama Nuggins." His dark eyes light up, beaming up toward her face and resting there for a minute. Then he jumps up, throwing sand in every direction. The sand goes all over Tess, on her hair, into the pocket of her jacket, down the neck of her flannel shirt, into her eyes. "Could I do swinging?"

Tess is not going to let the sand bother her. She stands up and shakes off the sand, blinking her eyes, scraping it off her neck, jumping up and down to get it out from under her shirt. "Let me think. Can Paul go on the swing? I don't know." He stands in the sand looking up at her. The anxious blur between teasing and reality has his face puckered, waiting for the relief of the not teasing. "Mr. Nuggins can go for a swing."

"And Mama will push?"

"Yes, yes, Mama will push."

"Up high, high Mama."

They walk over to swings sitting still in the thin fall sun. The diagonal metal poles feel damp in their hardness. Is there any object as still as a swing with its inherent need to move? The metal jangles as Tess lifts Paul into his swing; he has complete faith that he will get what he wants. She is determined not to let the ache in her muscles, the boredom of the repetition, the necessity of surrendering any wish or need of her own cut this swinging short.

First she plays the I'm-going-to-eat-these-toes-for-lunch game from the front. Each time the swing comes toward her she pretends to catch Paul's sneakers in her hands as if she's going to munch them. Sometimes she says, "Sooo delicious," and sometimes she says, "Uh oh this food's getting away from me. And I'm hungry!" He flings his head back in abandon, thrilled when the lunch gets away.

"From the back Mama," he says.

"Okay Button." She goes around the back to push. Each time her boy's back returns to her she gives it a definite push back into the flying future.

"Higher Mama." She paces her shove to meet the back of the swing just before the peak of the return comes toward her. She receives it and then gives it a thrust for height.

"More Mommy, more." Paul is laughing. The swing is in its rhythm. Tess pushes each time with just the right amount of energy. Her arms still have their morning ache, but something else is there too, a pulsing to the rhythm of her task.

Paul seems to be mesmerized by the swinging. He's stopped shouting for more. I'm going to give him all the swinging time he wants, she thinks. This time.

The emptiness of the park has only the sound of the swing moving through the worn fall air. The sound of the brushed air has moved inside them. They seem to have entered into the trance of the swing and release-return and go away.

A silence has descended. A current runs between them. They're deep in the back and forth. She's intensely gauging how much harder she can safely push. The metal swing is received easily into Tess' waiting hands, then swing and hands continue to move backward through the last piece of the sweep; with hard control she pushes it forward, and it flies forward out of her strong hands with the force of certainty.

He is really moving now. Tess pushes hard for catch and return, balancing the hard shove for speed against the need for control. She knows if her pushes get even a little off center the swing will easily jerk out of synch twisting in that abrupt violent way, then shiver to a halt—a perversion of swinging.

She begins to feel as if they've arrived on another plane where nothing exists but them and the swing, as if no one else ever came to this park, Paul is the only child who's ever swung on this swing.

Paul swinging and Tess pushing him: the tepid sun falls across their sweaters, on their bones, young and younger, tired and more tired—they've entered a world they might not be able to come back from—as if she'll have to go on pushing him forever if she doesn't stop soon. No one will ever come down the hill yelling. Max will never come home from work. Everyone and everything has disappeared but them and the swing in the park.

She decides that she'll count to one hundred and then stop so that the endlessness of this strange moment will have shape. She counts quietly in her head. When she's up to eighty she reconsiders and thinks that maybe she shouldn't stop. Why would she take them away from this strange synchronicity they're in—this stretching, this elastic silence, this coupling and uncoupling?

This then is mothering—this tearing apart, this ripping and rending, and then the return, the coming back together, the inexorable giving in, the yielding—the terrible surrender at either end, the flight in the middle.

For the moment, the battle has quieted, and the war in Tess has subsided. There is no her, trying to keep her identity separate from her husband and son, no husband for whom she has too little to give, no son who asks more than she can give. There is only this, aboriginal love—mother and child.

Inexorably she counts down the last twenty swings. As Tess pushes her son off on the count of one hundred Paul speaks for the first time into the quiet—"That's enough Mama. Stop."

Tess lets the swing go, and it moves back and forth each time a little more slowly, in shorter swings until it wiggles to a stop. Tess lifts Paul out of the swing, and they walk side by side up the long hill home in the thin warmth of the fall air.

———•———

NEWS AT 370 RIVERSIDE

David had just heard the news from Angel, the doorman. He brought it right to Sophie. "Naomi and Eliot are breaking up." He hadn't meant to stop by tonight, but now David and Sophie were sitting having a before dinner tipple.

"You believe everything they say? Who told you this?" Sophie wasn't sure she liked this news. Her skin looked dry today. That always meant she had had a bad night. She kept rubbing her eyes.

"First, Angel. But I ran into Eliot, and he looked so glum I asked him. And he said that it was true. They were trying to do the best they could for Mia."

"And what about the baby?" Sophie asked. The baby was Mia, Naomi's two-and-a-half-year-old daughter.

Sophie liked Naomi. She looked liked her cousin Eva, killed during the war. "Think of that baby, torn between."

"Well actually that's the *real* news. Naomi bought one of those small apartments off the lobby so that Mia will see her father every day."

"Good." Sophie declared. "She's smart. Doesn't know how to pick a husband maybe, but smart. Wants to protect her girl. Okay." It was settled. Naomi had done as well as she could with bad material.

"Naomi looks like she could use some real cheering up," David said. "The kid looks upset. I watched them leaving for Mia's school the other day. Naomi had to carry her."

David felt for all of them. Eliot made a point of looking cheerful. But the only time Mia seemed to smile these days was when she was fooling around in the lobby with Angel, the day doorman.

"Mia's a sweet kid. When the time comes I'll see if she wants Byrnes." He was gazing into Mia's future, which apparently rested just then over Sophie's piano.

"Such a nice girl," Sophie added. Then she gave David a peculiar look. He took another Pepperidge Farm cookie and ate it slowly.

———◆———

TWO LATINS

When Naomi left to take Mia to school that day, Angel was on the door. He was a young, good-looking Latino with eyebrows arching wide over his deerlike eyes, a short trim body, and a gentle, luminous smile. The children in the building all thought he was their special friend. "Hi, You-a," he said this morning, a typical teasing opener for Mia.

"I'm not You-a. I'm Mia." Her long legs hopped, then she stamped one foot to make her point.

"No. I'm me," he said. "You're you. I told you that yesterday."

Mia was giggling, her hand resting on her mother's pocketbook. "No you're Angel. I'm Mia. That's my name."

"Oh, I forgot," he said. "I don't know what's wrong with me."

He never went too far. "Goodbye, You-a. I mean Mia. I think I have it now."

Naomi, frazzled, always rushing, never failed to stop and enjoy her delight in these interchanges. She delighted even in those she wasn't present for. She knew, for example, that in the afternoon when Mia returned with her father, Eliot, Naomi's ex, Angel would play this silly game again, or another one. Occasionally, if Naomi was running late coming home from work, she'd pause and imagine the encounters she missed between Mia and Angel and smile, knowing her daughter lived in a world where she was loved by everyone who came upon her. If Angel should happen to be busy carrying packages for another tenant in the building and not notice Mia, she would stand there saying, "Angel-a," until he turned back to her like a dancer, easy on his feet, bringing the full light of his golden attention. "Where is that package I left?" he might say, picking her up, pretending to carry her to the mail table with the other packages. Then he might peer into the perfect oval her face was, into her large black eyes, and doing an unmistakable double take, he would say, "But you're not a package," as if he were surprised that he was holding Mia. "What are you doing sitting on the mail table, I'd like to know?"

Mia would then throw back her head and laugh the full laugh she had had since she was a baby. "*You* put me here!" Mia threw herself into being played with. Filled with a kind of longing, she waited for anyone to say anything to make her laugh and then rolled ahead of them in the joke, laughing her deep body laugh, anticipating that there would be more. It inspired anyone who played with her to go to extremes. Angel was a perfect match for her wishes.

But that morning Naomi wasn't really paying too much attention. Angel fooling around with Mia was something she could take for granted, while she worried about what to do about this other business.

Naomi usually had a pretty good idea about how she wanted to handle things. She was one for making decisions that really suited her—no matter how unconventional. She told herself she was too busy to find conventional solutions. She just didn't have time for the fussiness of ordinary convention. In fact she was kind of famous in her circles for coming up with unique solutions to painful modern problems; like when she bought her ex, Eliot, the apartment underneath hers so he would be sure to see their daughter regularly.

He had already let his original family slip away. Not from meanness, but from some deep inability to stay connected. She had worked with him on this in the beginning. First Naomi thought she had gotten him connected to herself, then she got him reconnected to his parents and his brothers and finally to

Mia, whom he seemed to like more than anyone—grateful he had gotten the hang of how to love someone. Although he seemed almost to hate Naomi by the time things broke up between them, she couldn't get him to move out. First, he couldn't find an apartment. Then he didn't have time to really look thoroughly—he had that big job on West End Avenue, then the one uptown. Finally, she bought him an apartment on the first floor in her building, small but nearby, wiping out the small inheritance she had gotten when her father died.

Most of her friends were shocked. The members of the board in her building, all of whom knew what she was doing, were aghast. Should they let her do this? The president of the co-op board took her out for coffee and spoke to her confidentially. But Naomi stuck to her guns. She had her priorities. What mattered to her was her daughter and getting out of this fucking marriage.

"Thanks, Dad," she had said privately to her father in the dark on the night she thought up this solution, lying next to the lump Eliot's body had made. She had lain there thinking, "This way he'll see Mia every day, and maybe he won't be able to ditz out on her if she's right here. And he'll get out of my apartment." Mia saw Eliot most evenings. Naomi cared about getting things right. That money had been put to good use.

But this other problem stumped her. And it bothered her that she was paying tens of thousands to be stumped. Private school. She was glad Mia was at Children's Garden School. It had a great reputation. But this year, the second year Mia was there, this teacher she had—whew—she was something. It wasn't going the way Naomi had assumed it would, when she had been negotiating with herself the year she made the decision to send Mia to private school. "Of course it's too much money. It will leave us really tight. We practically won't be able to go to the movies. I don't believe in spending this kind of money on something like a school. There are perfectly wonderful less-expensive alternatives that plenty of people use. Linda Wolcott across the street, the super's wife of that building, for instance, takes in children. Those children that she cares for aren't less interesting than Mia. Maybe they're more. "Probably they're even livelier," Naomi explained to Tess, a friend she often talked to about this kind of problem. "Their mothers aren't in a panic about their 'reading level preparedness.'"

Naomi was all for lively. Lively is my middle name, she sometimes consoled herself, when Eliot seemed to resent her doing the rumba with Mia in the aisles of the West Side Market. Why would he hold that against me?

"Who doesn't like lively?" she had asked her women friends. "I thought that was a given on the Upper West Side."

It was just that when Naomi thought about Mia being with Linda Wolcott every day, she knew Mia would spend more time watching soap operas than playing in the park. It was funny. In a way she thought hanging out watching soap operas with a housewife who loved children would have been exactly the kind of thing she would have wanted for a daughter of hers. She had spent long hours fantasizing about just that when she had decided she would be a mother. She wasn't going to go down that automatic middle-class journey, all books, blocks, and private schools. She was going to teach her child about life, real life as it was lived by the people on the other side of Broadway.

But Naomi, a therapist, often had to work later than she liked. And she couldn't count on Eliot consistently. Who knew when he would have to fly off to see a client, one of his kids, his mother in Florida? Linda's brother, Harold, who lived with the Wolcotts on and off, and seemed like a nice guy, drank on the stoop with his nattily dressed friends after work. Naomi was glad it seemed to be only booze they did. They'd sit on the stoop holding small brown paper bags sipping and chatting. But Naomi wasn't sure she was up for that.

I guess that's what middle-class life is about. You can almost be sure that if you spend an amount of money that in the past would buy three houses, your kid won't have to smell liquor on someone's breath and wonder why they walk funny sometimes.

But now it turned out that the cost of three houses a year didn't protect Mia from what sometimes seemed like a private school specialty—sanctimonious teachers.

Flavia was head teacher this year: a large beauty of some Latin heritage, she had been a teacher's assistant last year. South

American, maybe, Naomi thought, not an island Latino. Now she was head teacher in the 3-4s. The Children's Garden School was thrilled to add to their "diverse" faculty. And by looking at her you thought she'd be wonderful with kids. She had warm brown skin, glistening black eyes. Everyone had been happy when she was appointed head teacher. She'd be the perfect head teacher.

On the very first day when Mia had arrived all full of excitement ready to start the new school year, she had burst into the room and hugged Billy, one of her best friends from the year before. They had fallen to the floor in their excitement, laughing and rolling over with soft awkward thumps while Naomi and Pat, Billy's mother, hugged quietly in the hall. "So glad to see you again."

"How was the summer?" But before this could go any further, Pat and Naomi could hear Flavia saying in a loud serious voice, "We're all glad to see our old friends. And we'll have a hugging circle later this morning, when everyone can meet their old friends, but right now we're having a quiet circle on the rug."

Pat and Naomi had exchanged a glance that included slightly raised eyebrows, shrugged their shoulders, and followed their children into the room.

"What do you think this is about? You think she's just new and scared?" Tess wanted to know a couple of days later.

"I don't know. Neither Billy nor Mia seemed to mind too much. The first day they ran over to the rug, holding hands, and sat down with their arms around each other. But every day there seems to be a new rule about skipping down the hall, about laughing during 'reading' hour, about kissing in the house corner. These rules were announced at *quiet* meeting time in the cozy corner *and* sent home in the notes home which are supposed to be filling you in on your child, not on the teacher."

"Have you mentioned this to Rose?" Rose was the director of the Children's Garden School. Tess had taught nursery school with Rose a long time before. Wasn't Rose supposed to handle things like this?

"Pat and I went and stood up at Cooper's for a quick cup

this morning after we dropped the kids. We decided we were being over anxious. We should give Flavia a chance. We shouldn't pounce right away, like a couple of over anxious mothers."

Tess was for pouncing. She remembered the first time she had a classroom of her own, how many hours she spent fixing up the rug corner. How important it had become to her that the shelves lining the sides were filled with the right materials, how important the pillows were she had spent late nights sewing. She knew that you had to watch out that the cozy rug corner didn't become a throne room—for the teacher.

"I wouldn't let it go too long, Naomi. These teachers have their own laws when they're new. They're so proud of the fact that someone has made them head of anything, all they can think of is that they have this one corner in the world that belongs to them."

Naomi had more faith in people. In herself. She'd wait and see. "Anyway, Mia's okay. When I picked her up today she said, 'We went to the playground I played in the sand, and, Mom, I ate all my lunch. Flavia says we eat all our lunch in *her* room. Mom I missed Billy in summer.' She doesn't seem too upset."

When Naomi got off the phone she was wondering: Is Tess right about Rose? Maybe it just annoys her that Rose is head of the Center. She probably thinks she could do a better job, if she hadn't left teaching. Naomi decided to ask Eliot what he thought when he brought Mia upstairs that night. He's not always wrong.

"Flavia seemed a little structured," Eliot said when Naomi asked. "But frankly I'm not sure these Upper West Side *pishers* don't need a little of that. Sure she makes them walk in a line from the room to the door. No talking. But what's wrong with a little quiet? I like her."

Naomi thought that sometimes Eliot would like it if everyone would just shut up more or less permanently, except for, "Pass the lotion," by which he meant pass the catsup, so he could go on thinking about the cost of the next renovation he was doing. Mostly these thoughts were about the money he wasn't making. But did he "like her" like her?

He looked so soulful with that thin, poetic face of his. He wasn't typical. He loved going to the opera. But he wasn't a talker.

His work was important: Naomi knew that. It made it possible for people to have someone they trust to work in their homes, redo their kitchens. It was just that he barely broke even because he made it about his perfect work instead of about money. I fell for him, Naomi thought. So adorable.

"Where's that Mia?" Angel was looking all over the lobby for Mia as she clung to his pants leg, "Naomi do you know where Mia is? I don't think you should leave until you find her."

"I'm so worried," Naomi said. "What do you think I should do?" she asked Angel, with her most worried look on her face. Mia giggled. Angel pretended to be looking under the mail table, out on the sidewalk, looking for Mia everywhere, while Mia followed him wherever he went.

"I think we'd better call the police. We can't lose that girl. We'll be too sad," Angel said to Naomi, who sat down now on the step and pretended to be crying, as happy as Mia to be playing this game.

"Yes, Angel," Naomi said, through her pretend tears, "pleeeze call the police; tell them I lost my beautiful daughter. Where is she?" Naomi asked, sobbing wild sobs, enjoying this descent back into the world of children, the thrill of easy exaggeration.

"Here I am," Mia announced, throwing her arms around her mother. "Here I am."

"Oh thank god!" Angel said.

"Cry Ma, cry more." Mia loved her mother's part in these games. "'Tend you're worried."

After two weeks of the Flavia Talks, as Tess has come to think of them, she can't help herself. She asks again, "Have you talked to Rose yet?"

"Every time I went to see her she was shut up in that tiny office of hers with one or another desperate-looking parent. When it was finally my turn to be the desperate parent, she pushed those sincere wire-rimmed glasses of hers up on top of her head and took me into her confidence. 'Flavia's just getting her feet wet. If I go in and start criticizing her now it would just make her defensive. Give it some time. Please.'"

"I guess I have to," Naomi says. "I don't know if she was just being slick or what."

Tess was more or less annoyed at this sensible position. "Well how *is* it going?"

"She's okay about getting ready for school, and she's fine on the way. But when we get near the room Mia gets very quiet, no matter what she's been doing on the way. This morning we were singing, 'I don't want to go to Macy's,' as we came down the hall. Then she looked at the door, looked up at me, and said, 'No singing Mom. Singing at singing time.' And walked very quietly into the room. Her whole face changed as if she was walking into a courtroom or the doctor's. Actually she loves going to see Dr. Garwood, so that's the wrong comparison."

"What about the other parents?"

"Emily's mom says she's crying a lot these days. But honestly that kid cries all the time. It's horrible not liking a kid."

"One of Sam's fathers, the beautiful black guy, Nat, seems to be taking a turn for the worse. I'm not sure if he's actually dying. I just can't bother the other father, Brian, right now."

"What's Billy's Mom say?"

"Oh. He's waking up in the middle of the night again, after a year of sleeping through."

"You know," Naomi continues, "Billy's Mom, Pat, and I spent hours discussing it so far this past week. Two professional women, a teacher and a therapist, and we're both stumped. After a while one of us has to race to a staff meeting, or to see a client or a patient, and we still haven't figured out how to handle it. You know, we have to go off to the world to pretend we're grown-ups." Both women laugh merrily into their phone receivers. Tess and Naomi delight in the opportunity to think of themselves as ridiculous.

"I have to go. Max and Paul are home. I've barely seen them since Monday. Are we swimming this week?"

Angel wasn't on the door the next morning when Naomi left to bring Mia to school. Rafael was. He hated kids, hated grownups. Hated. Once when Mia found a long stick in Riverside Park,

Naomi had dropped it off with Rafael on their way to the store. "Rafael, would you hold this for me, until we get back?"

"Sure, sure," he said, a tall handsome man, who seemed to have been ruined for life by this single advantage, his large handsome face. He had gotten up slowly from the couch, barely looking at Naomi, Mia, or the stick. When they got home from the store carrying two large bags Naomi had asked for the stick.

"That thing? You don't want that."

"Yeah, I do." Mia looked very serious.

"I threw it away." Mia's face was starting to pucker. All the way home she had been planning how to make the stick into a wand. "I could glue the star, right Ma, from Billy's birthday, right?"

"Where is it?" she said, controlling her voice. Naomi wanted to know what Rafael had done with the stick.

"It's in the garbage downstairs." Naomi had barely been able to hold her temper, but she'd grown up on the left. Socialists didn't yell at working-class people. "Would you go and get it please?"

"Nah, you don't want it." When Naomi had insisted, he had returned with three broken pieces: "Someone must have broken it."

Naomi and Mia walked past him where he sat on the couch without even saying hello. This was an extreme measure on the West Side, an even more extreme measure for Naomi.

"Mom, stay at school during circle?" Mia says, as they head across 110th Street. Naomi has a patient in forty-five minutes. It was Wednesday, which invariably began with Caroline, a patient who was just starting to get somewhere in her treatment. Naomi had an idea about something Caroline had said a while ago. She had been looking forward to spending a few minutes looking through some old notes that she thought would help her with this patient.

"Well, I can only stay for a little while. I don't know how long." She's working on making sure she's really listening to Mia, "Is there a reason you want me to stay today?"

"Billy says Sam is his friend now. Flavia says in circle that we're all friends. But I have to sit next to Emily. She cries."

Even though Naomi took a cab, something she had vowed to

do less of since she'd bought Eliot his apartment, her nine thirty, Caroline, was actually waiting outside her office, the door locked. "I'm sorry," Naomi said struggling to get the key in fast, open the door and flip the light on all in a series of hurried jerky moves, "One of those days. Go right in." Her mind was still back at the Family Center as they settled into their respective chairs across from one another.

Flavia had asked Naomi to sit in a chair, not on the floor with Mia, after Naomi explained that she was staying a few minutes, "Mia is a little needy this morning."

"Floors for children, chairs for grownups," Flavia said firmly, as she sat on her own chair in the middle of the rug.

"I don't mind," Naomi had said, plopping herself down on the rug, pulling Mia onto her lap.

Flavia had pointed to the picture on the wall covered with contact paper of a teacher sitting on a chair, ringed with children. "We're all working very hard to learn our rules, right children?" Flavia said carefully, looking now at Naomi's knees revealed by Mia's sitting down on her mother's lap. Naomi scrambled to her feet, blushing. Mia clung to her skirt. "Maaa," in a whine.

"You sit right here at my feet Mia, and I'll hold your hand." It was funny how teachers have a way of asserting their authority over the parents too. Even when you are older than they are, and you are the mother. To take Flavia on now would be to make Mia's life even more confusing. Should she try Rose later?

"Are you even *here* today?" Naomi's patient asked.

"What makes you think I'm not?" Naomi hated when she tried to fake it with her patients. She knew she was trying to deflect her distraction, because she was feeling guilty, because she wasn't supposed to invite her patients into her life. Why couldn't she just say, "I'm sorry I'm just not really here today—something sensible"? "Because I started throwing in nonsense syllables just to check. That's why."

"Do you think you have to speak nonsense to get my attention?"

"What does that mean?"

"Well I wonder why you feel you have to use nonsense language with me." Naomi didn't believe the words even as she spoke them. She just didn't know where to go with this now that she had started it.

"Don't give me that shrink crap." Caroline started to rise up off the chair. Naomi could see Caroline's blood rising.

She was losing her, maybe even permanently. "Look, I'm sorry. I'm very worried about my daughter. It's nothing serious."

Naomi didn't want to do this. They'd spent weeks on the fact that Naomi was a loving mother who brought her daughter's problems to work with her, unlike this woman's mother who ran a girdle shop in Queens who never even noticed when her daughter was suicidal. If they went back to discussing Naomi's devotion to her daughter it was sure to be a long detour in Caroline's treatment. It wasn't worth it. It was going to be a long, whiny waste of time. Naomi had heard stories about the mother for almost three years before they finally started to dig at something deeper, odder, the fact that the woman's father was always fingering the girdles. The mother was always distracted by this, trying to keep her husband from walking past the dressing rooms. Was he just restless? "I like to pace," he'd say. "Go pace outside on the sidewalk," the mother would respond. But it was always too hot, too cold, raining, humid, reasons to stay inside, rearranging the girdles, greeting Mrs. Cohen too enthusiastically. But Caroline had actually worried as a kid that her father had wanted to wear them. It wasn't clear that he hadn't.

"Look, I apologize. Please let's not get distracted from you."

"That's my point. Would you mind going over that apology thing again a little more slowly?" When this patient wasn't whining she was funny and sweet.

"I'm sorry. Let's both stick to you."

"Mia, mia bo bia, fe fi fo fia, Mia." Angel was on the door that day. Mia giggled happily.

"I'm a big girl, Angel. I can't wear my shoes at nap time any more," she announced proudly.

"Is that right?" He knelt down to listen.

"Flavia says big girls don't wear shoes at nap time." She looked down at her new pink Velcro sneakers.

"Those are beautiful Mia. Maybe someday I could borrow them."

"You're too big. You'll big them up on me." She skipped out the door. "Hi Linda, Inda, Bobinda," she called to the neighbor from across the street who was sitting on her stoop rocking a baby carriage, who waved back cheerfully and absently at the same time. Two other small girls were sitting on the sidewalk rolling a ball back and forth. Mia stopped and looked at them. "Can I play?" The girls stared at Mia and then moved over to make a space for her. Mia sat down on the sidewalk and started playing. The new guy from 5B walked out of the building just then. He was handing a briefcase to a tall, elegant red head. Naomi could tell they were definitely a couple. The air between them held.

"Mia, you know we have to get to school." It was Wednesday again, Caroline's day. Of course. Naomi was thinking to herself, I can't be late for her again. She could feel another cab ride coming on. She looked in her purse to see if she actually had the cash to pay for one. She had deliberately left her credit card home lately.

When Naomi had rented her office one of the things that had really appealed to her was that she would be walking the thirty blocks to work. That was just a few months before she and Eliot had decided to have a baby. So many things in her life had been on track. She and Eliot had really seemed to be working things out. She had walked calmly to work thinking things through. It'll be fine, and this way I'll still get my exercise even after I have the baby. Like all pregnant women she had worked out many sensible ideas before the baby came, which had nothing to do with babies, nothing to do with anything resembling sensible once the baby came.

"Come on Mia, we really have to get going."

Mia pretended not to hear her mother. She was doing this a lot lately. Was this because Mia was three and a half? Was this because she and Eliot were separated? Naomi started to sweat. "Mia, I'm going to have to count to twenty, and then we have to go. I mean it." At twenty Mia sat there doing and undoing the Velcro straps on her sneakers. Naomi had had to carry her the two blocks to school. Mia wandered in listlessly to the classroom. The circle was already singing, "This land is your land, this land is my land." She put her lunch box in her cubby and sat down on the rug. Naomi didn't know whether to be relieved that Mia was taking this quietly or to stay here with her daughter and lose Caroline. Why did Mia always pick Caroline's mornings to act out? It must be that she's picking up my anxiety. Naomi thought. Oh God, I hate being a therapist.

"I don't suppose it would do for me to put the make on my doorman," Naomi mused that night on the phone with Tess. "He's so cute. How come working-class guys are so good with kids?"

"I know. Kids are part of their lives. They love to play around because they're not always at meetings, afraid someone's getting the edge on them. So they play with their kids, the ones that aren't out drinking with the guys at some bar."

"This Angel guy is so nice. In fact he's just the kind of guy I wish I could find. He's the reason Mia gets up and gets ready to go to school, which she does more and more reluctantly. But when I say, 'Angel is waiting for you,' then at least her face brightens up. Once we're out the door, she kind of drags her feet. It's getting worse. She used to love going to school."

Tess stops herself from asking the Rose question. "Have you tried talking directly to Flavia?"

"I don't know. Yesterday Flavia asked to speak to me outside the classroom when I dropped Mia off. Then she said to me that she thought Mia was troubled about the separation. Mia's hit a couple of kids recently. Sometimes she refuses to sit in circle." Naomi started to cry now. "Maybe she's right. Maybe it's too hard on her. Maybe it doesn't have anything to do with Flavia. Am I screwing up my daughter's life?"

Tess wasn't sure what the perfect truth was, but she knew that when any friend of hers felt bad, it didn't matter, the other person was wrong, the teacher, the husband, the other friend. "No, she's not right. She sounds like a sanctimonious shmuck. Don't let her do this to you." Tess decided she was sick of this Flavia.

"I was the same when I was first teaching. She thinks if she arranges the room right and draws bunnies and flowers around the rules, covers the sheet with contact paper, and hangs it in the quiet corner she's all set. She's young and stupid. Think of her as one of your really immature patients. But please don't let her do this to you, on top of messing with Mia."

Naomi cried quietly into the phone. She couldn't stop. "But my daughter . . . What if I'm ruining her life?"

"Do you want me to come over, Naomi?" Tess asked hoping Naomi wouldn't really want her to come.

"No, no, I'm too tired." Naomi sniffed. "I just want to go to bed." She was surprised by what had poured out of her. She didn't even know she had felt anything about what Flavia had said other than annoyance. "What makes you think it's not the separation?"

"Because you're a good mother. You love your daughter. If you don't believe me, ask Angel."

"I'm not going to school this morning." Mia announced one morning when Naomi woke her up. She had been saying this every morning for a week.

Naomi had bribed her with promises of Italian ices, with pizza after school, even candy. She had tickled her and let her wear her party shoes to school. She had even been reduced to granting permission for a middle-of-the-week movie night. She was out of bribes. She was tired and she was still stumped.

"I don't like Billy anymore." This was a new twist.

"Why don't you like Billy anymore? Did he do something to you?" Naomi sat on the side of the bed, stroking Mia's hair.

"He says girls are stupid. Only boys know how to play running." She turned her head into the pillow.

Mia was much taller and stronger than Billy, a much faster runner. Naomi couldn't quite figure what this was about. "What did you say to him?"

"Nothing," Mia looked intently at the fire escape outside their window, then, "Flavia says, 'no sticking tongues out allowed,'" Mimicking a quiet, severe tone that could only be Flavia's, "'especially girls.' I don't want to be a girl." The phone had started to ring in the middle of what Mia was saying. Naomi let it ring. It went on and on as if there were an emergency. Naomi wanted to scream. The phone always rang into the most important moments of her life.

She picked Mia up and held her close. The soft young skin

of her daughter's arm, so tender under her hand, brought up in Naomi a sudden sweep of love for Mia that rolled them both over onto the bed. Sometimes words failed. This was one of those times. Sticking your tongue out might be just the ticket. "Flavia's wrong. If Billy says anything like that to you again you stick your tongue out at him for a long time."

"But Flavia will make me do a timeout," Mia said.

"If Flavia gives you a timeout for sticking out your tongue when someone hurts your feelings, I'm going to give her a timeout."

Mia's eyes widened with shock, then pleasure. "Will she have to sit in the chair in the book corner?"

"Definitely. In the timeout corner. No talking for Flavia."

Mia wasn't sure her mother could mean this. She tried out this crazy idea and stuck her tongue out at Naomi. Naomi stuck hers out at Mia. Naomi knew what she had to do.

When they went downstairs Mia stuck her tongue out at Angel. "That's the prettiest tongue I've seen this morning," Angel said, holding the door of the building open as if it were the entrance to a theater. Mia skipped off to school.

"I was ready by the time I got to the Family Center. I stretched myself out as tall as I could and walked right up to Flavia and said in my most la di da voice, 'Mia has my permission to stick out her tongue at people when they hurt her feelings.'" Naomi had called Tess later to fill her in. "She looked at me dumbfounded and said, 'But that's bad manners.'"

"Then I said in a very loud voice, my Aunt Sarah's voice actually, 'I think you should sit on the rug with the children,'" Naomi was giving it a full dramatic reading.

"Go Naomi," Tess murmured, cheering her on.

"You know what she said?" Naomi's voice pitched up. Tess could tell by the incredulous tone that this story wasn't going to come out the way it should.

"She said, 'You're ruining your daughter.' In front of the children! Can you imagine?"

"God," Tess aspirated the word.

"I kissed Mia and whispered that she should stick out her

tongue whenever she felt like it. Then I walked out of the room before Flavia could say anything else. I was afraid of what I would do. I wanted to slap her. She makes me feel like I'm one of the kids."

"I waited a couple of minutes trying to calm myself; then I marched into Rose's office. I was still roaring. She practically jumped off the phone. And after about a half an hour of talking to her—of course, it took her that long—she took off those glasses of hers, and sort of admitted she'd made a mistake. 'This job has turned into taking complaints about Flavia. All the mothers are calling and driving me crazy,' which is of course great by me. She was smiling that professional parent-handling smile of hers. Then immediately she says, 'Flavia told me yesterday that Mia's sticking out her tongue. Are you sure that's healthy for Mia?'"

"They can never just admit it out loud that this one's a lousy teacher!"

"She actually had the nerve to say to me, 'We have to accept reality, sometimes.' Twenty thousand dollars of reality, mine, not hers. 'It's good for the children to learn that there are situations that even grownups can't control.' I wanted to take Mia out of the school right then. But where would the kid go to school for the rest of the year?"

"Could it be a contract issue?"

"I doubt Flavia will be back, if I'm reading Rose right, but she's not going to fire her now. Who knows?"

"So what are you going to do?" They both knew there was no winning these fights. "Bank Street should hire your doorman. What's his name?"

"Angel?" Naomi said horrified. "Oh no. Then Mia would only have him for a few months. This way we see him every day, for years I hope. You know, you go to college, go into analysis, work your ass off, pay gigantic amounts of money for this middle-class life—schools, camps, toys. And then fate delivers a gift to your door, a doorman your child is glad to see every morning, just before you plunge out onto the sidewalk."

Both women stared into space, each into the air buoying them up invisibly in their kitchens, the phones dangling from their ears.

All this struggle, the best stroller, shoes from Harry's, the right books, these expensive schools and then life brings a young Latin man with a smile that glows and a quiet voice. And life on Riverside Drive, on the West Side of Manhattan, seems blessed for a while, until fate decides to lift him up and set him down in someone else's life. Maybe by then Mia would be in public school, Naomi thought.

———•◆•———

FRAMING DARKNESS

Tess, Max, and Paul live in a dark apartment even though it's on the tenth floor of a building on Riverside Drive on the Upper West Side. They are on the back side of the building surrounded almost completely by other buildings, except for a few openings where slivers or small frames of light appear.

What did I do?

In many ways Tess prefers the dark: She is more at home with shorter, darker days. They hold a comfort for her: a good rainy day, cups of tea, books piled, three pillows. When the sun pours itself all over her world, Tess feels she has to be outside, about her business, at the very least to be moving, to stay above the waves of the should. On an ordinary day the approaching dark signifies the luxurious end of duty, a return to her inchoate, darker side—the night woman.

What possessed me?

The winter solstice is her season: twilight at four in the afternoon, a time to collect nuts and burrow in, curl up against the dusk.

The everyday has an ineffable goodness at that hour. The radio is on in the kitchen, news of misery on other streets, of peace summits in faraway cities, where not much peace will be planned, of tribal peoples in fierce battles. She is heating olive oil in a hot pan, peeling garlic cloves, cleaning vegetables. Her son arrives home from school, rumpled, dirty, laden with too many books. He's hungry, has too much homework, but for a brief time they'd be in the kitchen—in respite. He tucks their cat, Katrina, on his lap. He settles at the kitchen table, reading an *Archie* comic. She puts on a pan of water to boil for the macaroni. Her friend Naomi calls. They do the news of the day in review while each clatters their kitchen gear. Max arrives. She hears him thump his heavy bag down in the foyer. His day, too, was too long, filled with meetings where there was more conflict than agreement. Everyone is tired, but home. The world is at bay. They're in their dark kitchen where the "not world" is stored.

I have to tell Max that I signed the lease.

This sense of sweetness at this hour has its origins in her father's coming home from work. An ironworker driving his clanging truck, her dad always came home at twilight. He'd slam out of the driver's side, hungry, tired, smelling of dust and sweat just as the sun went down, the color, a pink sandy glow, the night arriving like pleasure.

This will change everything now. It won't be the same.

For Tess the dark and the night offer a time of grace. The larger dark interests her too. There's the dark of swimming deep down in a cold summer lake or sinking into sleep next to the warm body of her husband on a cold night, the sinking into dreams.

So if anyone can live in a dark apartment with comfort it is Tess. And mostly, it is. Her home is colored by reds, intense greens, rooms covered with books, filled with reading chairs, pillows, blankets—a place to be when night is here.

But maybe it's the small frames of light that render this lightless enclosure so sweetly held—the little light that does slip in.

Here is the light their apartment does get: In Max and Tess's bedroom there is a slender opening between two buildings. That opening is too narrow. She keeps the shades drawn—too many windows surround her on either side of the narrow opening.

In the store she signed the lease for she'll be exposed all the time that she's there. Graduate school would have been safer. She had to do something, but she hates going to school.

Her son Paul's room has the only real light—: in the mornings his room is flooded with golden, eastern light, while he is at school and no one else is in the room either.

There is only one other room that gets any light and air in this apartment: their bathroom. The window is almost always open. When Tess stands in the shower and looks out across several rooftops, her eyes come to rest on Upper Broadway and 110th Street. To stand in this shower with the window open, looking out onto Broadway makes a rare sensation. It's a corridor to the world outside.

A few blocks up she's going to do something bigger than she's ever undertaken before. Max said it was up to her. But it's his life too. And Paul's.

Within the glistening white porcelain tiles the water pulses, the soap slides; she is naked, warm, wet. Outside lays the exuberance of modern urbanity.

Loud metallic trucks blast their way down Broadway. Large, dented livery cars with luxurious, upholstered interiors charge through the traffic. People cross the intersection with light, perfect attention. A mother crosses holding her child's hand to her left and a grocery bag in the crook of her right arm. Three teenagers run and push each other. Everyone moves, carries stuff, backpacks, gym bags, but mostly some idea of themselves.

In every extreme in that shower she feels its privilege— obscured and protected she has light and the world framed.

"Max," Tess yells. "I have something I have to talk to you about. Pour us some good red."

———•———

PASSED OVER AND PASSED ON

"Richard's dead."

"Nooo."

"He's dead. Helena called."

"What?" A whine trailing off. "What happened?"

"I'm not sure. She just said she found him dead. I guess he died in his sleep. 'Would you come over?'"

David was standing in front of Sage, who had just picked up a cup of coffee and settled back against her pillows, the newspaper lying on the bed. It was Saturday morning after a week that had been so frantic at the bank where she worked she hadn't had time to read the newspaper. She had to suppress a feeling of annoyance now because this moment of repose she had held out to herself all week had just been taken hostage. Richard was dead.

"I can't believe this." Her wide mouth was slack, her hazel eyes dull.

David often slung Sage's tall quiet beauty onto his pride, but as he looked at her taking in this news, he thought, She looks old. She's tired, he corrected himself immediately—twice bitten by his own disloyalty. Why am I thinking about what *her* face looks like?

It never makes any sense, Sage thought. She watched David's ruddy coloring slip away. He stood there as pale as if the news of Richard's death had pilfered some of his blood as it passed.

"What did Helena say?" The paleness of David's face hanging in front of her brought Sage up out of the warm, wrinkled sheets, her arms circling his neck, so she could bring her blood close to his. Even his auburn hair looked drained. Breathing him in, there was the smell of a body relaxed from sleep: under that the acrid smell of anxious sweat.

"She didn't say much. They were supposed to go over some tax material this morning. When he didn't show up at the coffee shop where they were going to meet, she went over to his apartment and let herself in. She still has keys." David was grateful that Sage had brought her body near his, but to his touch she felt like something with measurements and angles—a piece of furniture— not the body he knew intimately. Sage's sweet, he was thinking.

"I'll come with you," Sage said, glancing down at the newspaper lying there. She wished she could climb back into bed, pick up the paper, with death distant where it belonged. We learn early to lock one arm stiff and hold death off on the long loose horizon.

David sat down on the bed and stared straight in front of him. There was no need to hurry. Unless it was to hurry out of this room, away from the place where the news had arrived. Richard would be dead for a while. David didn't feel like crying. He felt, what? Arrested? He looked up to see if Sage was still there. How did she happen to be wearing that ripped green plaid nightgown? Plaid was such a homely pattern.

"You can stay home, you know. It would be all right. I'm just going to jump in a cab. Help Helena make arrangements."

"I'm coming with you, David." Sage, still standing, looked uncertain.

Relief washed through Sage that she and David were still okay, alive; shame flashed behind that relief. The shame pushed her out of the bedroom. She said again from the hallway, "I'm coming."

David found himself brushing his teeth in the bathroom where he was surprised to find himself thinking that he still brushed his teeth exactly opposite from the way dentists insisted you must, bristles at an angle against the gums. Their way was just wrong.

When they got downstairs Thomas was on the door. He leapt away from the desk, leaving the phone to open the door for them. "Good morning. It's a perfect Saturday." David almost told Thomas about Richard dying. Someone should be told. He could see that Thomas was on the phone with one of the members of his congregation. From his post on the door, Thomas spent hours ministering to the members of the Church of God where he was deacon. A lot of people in the building resented it. But David often found himself imagining how he would do standing at the door eight hours a day, waiting as other people came and went. David knew he would need at least God to keep him company. The brilliant light of September rushed them as they left the building—it was not the right weather for a soul to empty its skin.

Out on Broadway they hailed a cab; David watched Broadway spill past them as they were driven toward Richard's body.

Sage stared at the back of the driver's head, the shine in his black hair becoming the location of a very early memory rising there on his pelt: She had been in a small sailboat with her father off Rehoboth Beach. "Do you see that line there? It's called the horizon," her father had said, pointing out the faded line between water and sky. "No matter how close you try to get to it, it always moves away from you."

"Go just a little farther, Daddy. It's not that far."

"You want to go a little farther?" Her father had been laughing. "Look where Mommy is. Do you see her?" Sage had turned toward the shore to see where her mother sat on their red blanket, in her white two-piece bathing suit trimmed with the blue and red embroidered tape marking an X in the middle of her chest. Her father's strong arms handling the ropes and rudder put more water behind them; then he had asked again, "Does it look closer?" gesturing toward the blurred line at the edge of the water.

"A little," Sage had said, unsure of herself.

"Look behind you. Where's Mommy now?"

And where was Mommy? Far away now, Sage couldn't see the X marking her anymore, just a tiny smudge of white against some red.

"Just a little more please." And a couple more times, he had, as Sage urged him, until he finally said, "It's so far away we can't reach it. It just looks like we can." The distinct turn of the boat toward the shore made apparent that all those on the beach were specks now. Her mother was one of the specks. It had been an immense shock to see how far they had gone, to be swept to this understanding. It was the shock of life not being what it seemed certain to be. A first time Sage understood that.

Death, when you weren't actually faced with it, was something like that. A small boat in a large body of water going toward a vague line that never came closer—death always the same safe distance from your boat. No matter how long you moved toward it, it continued to move off ahead of you. Then when someone you knew died, death appeared in your boat, and you were supposed to contend with its abrupt, confusing arrival, for which you had no talent, no gift. It was never as if you came to believe it. You were just very confused. Full of refusal. After a time of stunned confusion it moved back out there far away where it belonged. And wasn't considered again until it had to be again. The horizon: what is not yet.

The back of the cab driver's head, where Sage's eyes were fixed, was slipping back into hair. The cab driver turned to listen to David ask, "What are we doing *here*?"

The cab had pulled up to the Byrnes School. He looked up at the raking cornices above the windows of the Georgian facade and realized which address he had given the driver, was the place he thought of as Richard's home. Even now he had an impulse to go inside and sit in Richard's office for a minute before he went to deal with his remains.

"What's wrong?" He looks like my grandfather. David noticed the cabby's deep-set, dark eyes, the shiny, black hair. Josef Ibrahim was the driver's name.

"No, it's okay." Nothing about this was explainable. He gave the driver the address of Richard's apartment building.

Helena was waiting for them in the lobby. Helena had been married to Richard for ten years before they had finally given up.

"I called Jack. He's on his way in from Connecticut: he was in the country." Jack was Dr. Rodino; although not the chair, he was the real power on the board at Byrnes. Helena had the same emptied look on her face that David and Sage had.

Where does the blood go when you find out that someone you know has died? Does it collect inside to cover the core, so death won't collect you while it's in the neighborhood? Sage put her arms around Helena. Sage's willingness to feel sorry for someone else gave her back some vitality.

Helena was weeping small, hiccupped sobs. "It was awful—finding him." David and Sage could only bleat and purr back to her. Sage reached behind David to rub Helena's arm.

David walked numbly in between them. Helena reached back to respond to Sage. In their solidarity they guided David into position: he was to be in charge of Richard's death. Either of them alone was more capable than he of dealing with this. But David could see that neither of them was going to accept that arrangement. Some time between when David and Sage had entered Richard's building and this short walk toward the elevator, the two women had elected David presiding chair over Richard's death. Why had he been elected?

It was simple. A heart attack in his sleep. Richard was seventy, exactly the same age at which Richard's father had died—one of the many small, odd things that David had come to know about his friend after he died. Like the fact that Richard had lied about his age. He had never actually said, but he had allowed it to be deduced, dropping just enough careful hints, David realized looking back, so that you came to think he was sixty-five. "Class of sixty-four was an especially bright bunch at Harvard." And it had been. It just wasn't the class that Richard had been in. Why had Richard lied about something so trivial?

Richard had been blessed in his health and in his looks. A long body, topped with white, wavy hair, an easy banner of his good looks. He had the natural elegance of someone who enjoyed moving because his legs were long and worked well—loose joints propelling him easily forward. It had seemed at times as if his pleasure in his body's grace was what moved him to say just the right thing to a distressed young teenager of the Byrnes School. His body had prepared his populace to have confidence in the arc of his attention. And in the deep flow of his blood, he knew that when he rose from his chair and strode across the stage, people would so enjoy seeing that long, easy stride, that their pleasure in watching him, and thus in waiting to hear what he had to say, pulled up out of him exactly the right words, and his speech followed inevitably: natural, graceful, and to the point. The inherent grace in most things—no waste.

Perhaps Richard had thought if he lied about his age, he might confuse death's pursuer long enough to get, if not the day wrong, then at least the split second, and that then his death would have to be rescheduled. Richard always counted on having just enough edge to make the difference. Who knew when the next slot would be free? But records had been kept, apparently; the moment so carefully recorded on his DNA had ticked off, and Richard had died.

"Passed over" was the expression Thomas, the doorman, had used the day of the funeral when David and Sage had come home in the middle of the day dressed in dark colors. "Your face brings to mind something wrong. Did someone pass over, Mister?" He knew it was David's loss by the way Sage had held his hand, hers in front, as if she were the adult leading a child. Thomas never called David "Mister," but Thomas was one who understood occasion and searched for small ways to mark ceremony. He had nodded his head solemnly to indicate respect for the one who had passed.

"Yes, Thomas. My boss, my friend, my dear friend died," David had said trying to match his dignity to Thomas' that day. "Thanks for asking."

A week later David found himself sitting at Richard's desk. There were files everywhere. But David was still experiencing each of his senses separately, each one uniquely impressing itself upon him—each heightened in its disconnection from the web of ordinary meaning—a miasma of sensory data in a world that no longer held events in sensible order. He'd stopped trying to make anything behave. Instead he stuck to his tasks. Whatever Mrs. P. (his assistant now?) told him to do. One by one.

He could hear the students arriving, hurrying into the building filled with the urgency of their own bodies. The noise of their arrival broke these unanswerable questions up into the dusty particles these questions become in the face of young feet moving.

It looked as if David was expected to step up and be Richard at the Byrnes School. At least for a while. Everyone seemed to assume that David would be acting head, "At least for now, David," Dr. Rodino had said. Dr. Rodino was Jack. The person Helena had called after she had called David.

"We know you can't be expected to make a decision right away. Just keep us on course for a while. We'd be grateful." But did David want to be Richard—even for even a little while?

Throughout the last few years when Richard had tried to get David to consider this, David had steadfastly refused. Now there was no Richard to say no to. His long, casual body wasn't there sinking back into itself as it absorbed another of David's ironic, self-deprecating remarks.

"I'm not as tall as you; I'll confuse the parents." That kind of remark from David made it clear what a ridiculous idea this was. To David. Since no one was actually asking, the question had become whether David could say no to himself.

Mrs. P. came in now, her eyes glistening. A small, neat woman, she moved briskly, withholding any inclination toward flourish. For several weeks after Richard died, her eyes had teared when she entered Richard's office, her normally efficient, bleached hairdo falling into her eyes. Lately, she just looked surprised to see David sitting in Richard's chair. David stood up quickly now, his arms dangling loosely at his sides. At those moments David was sure he had no business trying to be Richard. Mrs. P. belonged in the skin she inhabited. Even her grief was a kind of home, a location she knew how to populate. For David, these days his skin felt only rented.

"Dr. Rodino's on the phone," Mrs. P. said. "He said to tell you he can call back." But the look on her face said, Take this one

"Oh please, put him on." David was relieved that Dr. Rodino had called. He didn't know if he should be calling him regularly or figuring things out for himself. Dr. Rodino was the man Richard had always been trying to get David to meet with, have dinner with, so that David would want to join the club, become the heir apparent. David had resisted. He felt sure that whereas Richard had loved him for his combination of smarts and confusion, Dr. Rodino would see through him immediately. But men like Jack and Richard—was it Princeton and Harvard, their respective schools that made them seem to always know what to do?

At the funeral, Dr. Rodino had said, "I'll let you catch your breath, but if you need me just tap me on the shoulder." Now Dr. Rodino had made the first move.

David was invited to dinner at the Princeton Club. Did Rodino know about David's reluctance to follow Richard's carefully planted footsteps? Maybe it's all been settled with a phone call or two between a few key board members. Perhaps this dinner is to let David know they were grateful for his stepping in to keep everything going, but they thought his real assets were his ability to bring in a solid class of students.

Dr. Rodino had been on the board since his first son from his first marriage had come to Brynes. He was the one who brought Richard to Byrnes. He knew the school at least as well as Richard had. What did he expect of David?

When David arrived at the Princeton Club he found Dr. Rodino sitting in a chair fairly close to the door of the lobby reading a newspaper, sipping a tall glass of something with bubbles and a slice of lime. He had the look of one of the many conquerors who passed through his ancestors' Italian peninsula: blue eyes, a receding white hairline, swept confidently back making his Teutonic jaw prominent. The jaw had a solid edge to it, until he smiled, which he did as he pushed himself up from the low, comfortable chair. His body didn't respond the way it once had. He was tall, maybe even taller than Richard's six feet one. David was a respectable five ten and a half. He prided himself on the fact that he never mentioned the half inch beyond the five ten he could claim. "Thanks for coming, David. I've always hoped we might have the chance to get to know one another better."

"I'm glad to be here . . ."

"I'd be grateful if you'd call me Jack," Dr. Rodino managed in the crack of hesitation that David had left.

"My pleasure, Dr. Jack." He felt a clouding, a softening of his confusion.

"And he laughs out loud and long, like a mensch. Then he laid out everything for me." David was at home, recounting the evening for Sage. She was in her old pajamas—flannel, worn thin with washing, as soft as fabric gets. Her briefcase was on its side on the floor. The flannel rubbed against the blanket as she adjusted her position on the couch in order to turn her attention to David and what he was saying.

He was wired. Sage could feel electricity coming off him. She couldn't tell why yet. Was it because something exciting or terrible had happened? Does he still have a job? His facial expressions were more mobile than usual, as he stood in the middle of their living room delivering the stuff. He wanted to make sure he was unloading the whole MacGuffin. He wished he had taken notes when he had been talking to Jack. He wanted Sage to tell him what to make of this. He didn't know if he'd been through a hall of mirrors, or if he'd just met a decent man.

These last weeks, she'd given herself over to Richard's death and David's dealing with it. Before, David had usually cooked their meals. Now she was the one who brought in salads, soups, bread, occasionally a treat—once even Saint André cheese after a really low day—and wine. We only have sex and food for physical life in New York, Sage thought, justifying these indulgences. She was waiting for their lives to get back to normal. She could see another piece of Richard's death had arisen. It filled the crevices of her husband's psyche and crawled in the spaces between blood and bone.

"What is Rodino like?" Sage asked, waiting for the positive and negative charges to work themselves into what David wanted to say.

"He said that he knew if he lost touch with Newark, his family, he would lose his way. So he's always worked hard to stay in touch with both worlds. Medicine is the combination for him. 'Intellectual plumbing,' he called it. I thought that was kind of elegant.'"

This was what David told Sage. What Jack had said to David.

Jack had grown up in Newark when it was still an Italian ghetto. He had been the only surviving son of a couple who had poured all of their love and hope into this one son. Three other children had died. So the obsession was not just with the first son but with the only son, and it had made him flourish instead of breaking him. He had gone to Princeton on a full scholarship. When he met Richard as a patient and Brynes was looking for a new headmaster, he had become his backer and made sure he had gotten the job. Richard was so smart, elegant, and confident it seemed as if he were meeting one of those young men he first met at Princeton. "At the time I had no idea why he'd want such a job," Jack has said. "But I knew he'd be perfect for it. So I made it happen."

"You think Jack sounds real?" David asked, after he had laid all of this out. He'd finally sat down across from her, one leg flung lightly over the other, waiting for her response.

"You're the one who's been with him all night. He was Richard's friend. He must be a decent guy. You just said they go way back?"

"Yes. But listen to what Jack told me about Richard. Richard," he paused, and stared at Sage, a little wild-eyed with the surprise of someone else's life, ". . . never went to Harvard. He went to a small college out in the Midwest. He studied classics, but at a really second-rate place out in Springfield, Missouri.

Sage was suddenly exhausted. She wasn't sure she wanted the detritus of Richard's privacy flung around her living room. What about a little dignified looking off into the distance? But she saw on David's face a slightly silly expression, almost a little vacant, the way he looked after sex, stupefied, happy.

"That's true?"

"He said he found it out after he'd gotten Richard the job at the Byrnes School."

Jack had said, "Richard had been a friend for years by the time

I found out from someone I work with at the hospital. I told him I knew about Harvard. I felt I owed him that. It put a distance between us. It didn't have to. He was a real authentic, with fake credentials—which is pretty much what any private school has to be—all that promise that a school can't possibly deliver. It could have brought us closer. I've always had a soft spot for a con man— my Newark days on the streets. But naturally it embarrassed him. We never mentioned it again. Richard had that kind of effect on people. You took him as you found him. I never told anyone. But I always thought he might have told you."

"Do you think Richard wanted me to know?" David asked Sage. He stood up quickly and started toward the kitchen. "I'll be right back. Do you want anything?" His knees had a lightness to them, giving way to his feet as Sage watched him clicking away from her down the hall.

Maybe I should read some Henry James, Sage thought, looking down at the *New York Review of Books* lying on the floor next to the couch. For the duration. I could start with *The Ambassadors*. I promised myself I would someday when I passed that American Lit. exam without cracking it. Sage was the kind of person to honor promises to herself. *The Golden Bowl* waited for her at the end of this idea.

What was Richard up to? And who was he cheating with these lies? David asked himself, as he opened the fridge looking for a piece of Saint André—he needed something to celebrate. But what was he celebrating? "I'm not sure if it's just the excitement of a secret or what, but I feel as if I want to toast him," David said, back in the living room, and he lifted the piece of cheese into the air. If only I could talk to him about this. What a time we'd have, he thought.

"Very good Richard," Sage said to the ceiling. "I have to say in a weird way I admire him."

"And I thought *I* was hiding out at Byrnes. No wonder he loved me. I was merely shadow to his blinding light."

Sage and David sat in the fading light of these words.

Mrs. P. was teaching David how to be headmaster. Up until now he had steadfastly refused to stay up on what made the school run. Mrs. P. told him which parent calls he had to return. Mrs.

P. explained to David that he had to have lunch with one young teacher. "He's young and needs the moral support, but he'll make a fine math teacher in a year or two. They are the hardest to hold onto." Every day around three thirty, after the students left, Mrs. P. let David know that there were certain things he'd have to take care of before he left.

Mornings, he felt a relief when the students arrived: he was allowed to let their noise and presence pull him into the hourly life of the school. Another kind of relief came when their voices faded from the sidewalk as they left, and he tried to concentrate on making sense of all this. But often it was then, too, that he noticed the empty place where Richard had once been.

In one corner of the headmaster's office was a decorative, tapestry chair—the kind of furniture meant to give the room the feel of old money and stability. In fact, Mrs. P. had found it in a yard sale out in Jersey. She had known Richard would love it and that the school's petty cash could handle it. It was only ceremonial, very rarely sat in. Until now. After a couple of months David had come to realize that whenever he thought about Richard, he saw him, sitting in the high-backed chair, his long back bent over, elbows resting on his elegant knees. Usually he wasn't watching David but rather looking out the window onto East 92nd Street, watching life pass by. Occasionally, when David was facing a knotty problem, he thought of Richard as turning around and watching silently whatever David did.

David met with Jack once a week. Dr. Rodino really was Jack now. On Monday morning the last thing Mrs. P. said at the end of their weekly meeting was, "I'll call Dr. Rodino at the hospital and set up an appointment. Give me a couple of times that would work for you this week?"

"How did you get to be this good?" David looked at Mrs. P. with gratitude.

"I'm a mother." She breathed expansively, gathering into herself the fact that another person who had seen her as part of the wallpaper for years was noticing who she was. "I raised my three children by myself after Mr. P. died. You have to be efficient."

Mostly people understood after they'd worked with her for a short time. That was enough for her.

"Should I ask him to my house for dinner?"

"Not yet. You'll know when the time is right."

"Sure, if you tell me."

David got to be familiar with the Princeton Club, its comfortable upholstery, tables of just the right height, placed at perfect angles to the chairs, with good reading lamps on them. As close as I'll get to Tolstoy, David thought. These days, he didn't even think about reading anything other than stuff related to Byrnes.

Jack didn't ask David if he wanted to be Richard. He didn't even seem to necessarily assume David wanted the job. He just believed that as long as David was doing it, he'd want to do it right.

"So have you arranged for the history teacher, Amy is it, to take over your job for the rest of the year?"

"She's thinking it over. I'm pretty sure she'll take it. I sweetened the pot as you suggested. Mrs. P. explained to me that I should give her the extra money but that the most important thing to do for her was to give her Fridays off for now. Her mother's dying in Massachusetts."

"How is Mrs. P. doing? Richard was her number one fan. He knew what a gem she was."

"How could have I misjudged her until now? I used to make disparaging remarks about Richard's need for cripples like me and Mrs. P. around. I feel like a complete fool."

"That's the way she likes it. She seems to only want a couple of people in close." Richard would probably have explained the nuances involved with Mrs. P. to both of them with a subtle humorous commentary. But Richard wasn't talking.

Everything unspoken between David and Jack, between David and Mrs. P. flooded out of David at home.

"So what do you think is going on here? Do you think Jack is grooming me, managing me, checking me out, what?" His shoulders normally hunched over, leaned forward, making small wings on his back ready to flap or flutter.

"I can't figure this one," Sage said simply. She wasn't one for saying anything until she was sure of the ground under her feet. She was worried about a kind of mania eddying around in her husband. He couldn't be only fascinated by the work after all these years of pushing it away, she reasoned, especially since it had risen from Richard's death.

"My first board meeting is coming up. So mostly I work my ass off on the mechanics, getting the budget organized, the plans for the new stage in the gym, the bids for the plumbing that has to be done. Jack says that I should stick to old business for now. This isn't the meeting to try to impress anyone with anything other than the basics. But this approach could also just be a way to contain me."

Sometimes when David came home from these meetings with Jack, he didn't get to sleep until two or three in the morning. Instead, he sat in the living room reading files, smoking cigarettes, sipping wine. This was where Sage found him when she made her way to the bathroom late one night. "It's awfully late,and you said you had to be in early tomorrow. What are you up to?" she asked.

"Just trying to get myself to unwind. This seems to relax me."

Sage was wondering whether she should ask David if he had returned Helena's last call. Helena had gradually slipped to the periphery of their world. Sage felt guilty about this. But David didn't seem to have noticed.

Is he even thinking about Richard these days? she asked herself, as she left him reading in the living room. For her the unanswerable "why?" still slipped across her synapses, breaking up into the same rush of incomprehensible static.

Maybe he'd found the right conditions for him: he'd come to be in charge of something, without having to commit to it. I guess this is a kind of a solution. Cold November night air came from behind her in through the small open window. She had to climb into the bathtub to close it. The residue of icy water in the old porcelain tub seeped through her warm sweat socks, hitting her skin like dread. She slammed the bathroom window down, and on the way back to bed, passing David, she bent down to kiss him, making silent reparation for her silent criticism. Sage had always

been the one more absorbed by work; now she was held in the pull
of her husband's currents.

What David found in one of the files chilled him more than the
November rain outside would have if he had been out in it. He
didn't know what to do with this information—left as it had been
in an odd file. "Richard's Business" was scrawled across the top
of the folder. It didn't have one of Mrs. P.'s neatly typed labels. It
held an odd assortment of receipts, memos, and notes—one from
the sixties on an old, stained napkin—"have a cocktail gather-
ing in my office with $$ied parents." A more recent Post-It, the
glue end folded under, so it sticks only to itself: "Cancel meeting
with Judith. Mention cancellation—Jack." One or two restaurant
bills.

But why did Richard leave this stupid piece of evidence
behind? It couldn't have been a legal issue. And as far as David
could see from the letter, Cross wanted Richard to know that
he was on to him and "his ways." Cross had called on Richard's
honor: "Be a man among men."

Then there was a letter from a board member, one Mr. Cross,
outlining very specific accusations against Richard. David remem-
bered when Cross had resigned abruptly, years back, just after
David had been hired. "Someone I just never got on with," Rich-
ard had said at the time, "but a good man in his own way." How
diplomatic, David had thought at the time. It seemed odd, since
Richard got on with everyone.

He must have resigned when Richard wouldn't. Scrawled
across the bottom of the accusing letter was a note—"Speak to
(there was a single letter that had been scratched over)." Speak to
. . . Was it an H? An X? No an A? Why did you leave this hanging
around, Richard? What missive was this from the dead?

Who was speaking to whom? David wondered, cold in that
late night.

Over the next weeks, this news rolled around in David's head—
though he could barely allow words to take shape about this latest
piece of Richard's legacy. He had something like an idea about

what this could have been about. He considered talking to Jack about it, then Mrs. P. He assumed he'd talk to Sage about it as soon as it got sorted out a bit more. But the way that David felt about all this never rose and fell into strings of words, so he couldn't say anything about it. This was Richard's bequest. Didn't that obligate him to keep it?

After David read the file, he had carried it around with him for several weeks. He'd put it in his briefcase and came upon it as he went about his business. He began to feel as if he were carrying around a decaying body. Finally David put the file where he had positioned Richard: he lay the file on the tapestry chair in the corner of his office by the window, as if he were placing it in Richard's lap.

One morning as David left 370, he saw Angel, the doorman, leaning over talking to Zekey, as the little boy waited for his school bus. "What happened Zekey?"

"It's just 'cause I'm the assistant babysitter—I had to. Jessie wouldn't listen. She has to when I'm the assistant babysitter. She's just the princess. Mommy said."

Angel nodded and nodded.

"But she's a liar. She said I hit. I told her to sit on the chair. She's supposed to listen to me. Now Mommy said I can't watch *Simpsons* tonight."

David walked quickly past the pair and thought, If I say something to Jack about this . . . Do I have the right to do that? Richard left it there. Left it there to be found? By me?

Richard, Richard. Who were you, my friend? David asked the emptiness his friend made in his life as he walked to work.

At their office Richard gave David a wry smile, something like, So you found me out. So? Why ask me? I'm dead. Other things on my mind.

David often stayed late doing a dog paddle through the files. There was nothing else like *that* file. The school's money was in order. There was just the ordinary chaos of one person's eccentricities adding up over a long period of time, a foolish personal filing system, a closet filled with dead tennis rackets, one old cardigan, dust between papers on the shelves. David couldn't find much of

Richard in this dust. What was he supposed to do with this estate? Sage could tell that something was wrong. As they were eating dinner on a Wednesday night at Fish, a local restaurant, after what had been a long, difficult staff meeting for David, he sat staring out at the fall rain that glazed the sidewalk's dirty surface.

"You don't have to take this job if you don't want it," she said.

"I know that," he said in a dull, annoyed tone. Then he went back to eating his monkfish. "Let's go to a movie. Something dumb. I can't think straight to follow a real movie."

"I told you I wanted to go home after dinner and read some more of *The Golden Bowl*."

"What?" he had an incredulous look on his face.

"I'm reading Henry James these days. Remember I told you?"

He burst out laughing, "You meant that. I thought you were saying that metaphorically."

"David! Are you paying any attention? What's going on here?"

"Give me some time. I can't talk about it yet."

David was pacing back and forth across the faded rug. He looked with a kind of longing over at the tapestry chair. The file wasn't there anymore. Mrs. P. must have done something with it. What? I really don't like this chair, he thought, looking down at the arms of Richard's desk chair—its springs still sag to his shape, not mine. In fact, David got up as often as he felt he legitimately could without avoiding the business he had to attend to.

Mrs. P. came in to say good night. Richard always looked at home at that desk, she thought, when she saw David curled over the pile of papers on his desk. She decided not to put the small list she'd just written on his desk tonight. "Do you want to walk out together?"

"No more jobs, Mom?"

"I'll have a full list on your desk tomorrow."

"Are you sure you want this job, David?" she asked him quietly.

David looked up at her neatly coifed blond hair, her white silk blouse. Does she know something?

"No, I'm not sure," he answered flatly. After she left the room David realized that he wasn't sure which job they were discussing.

He wished he could sit on the other side of the desk and talk to Richard about what he'd found in the files. He walked around the desk and sat in "his own" chair opposite the desk imagining Richard rising to the occasion.

Richard would have looked casually out the window and then ambled over to the desk chair David found so uncomfortable and sat back like the aristocrat he had always been. He would have reached down to his bottom drawer for the bottle of scotch and the two glasses that were always there.

"What would motivate someone to do that?" David would have asked Richard?

And Richard would have stretched his long legs out under the desk, one heel out of the back of his shoe hooked over the toe of the other, and his most humane, most expansive self would have emerged. "Who knows what was haunting him? Once you find out, it's all true but banal. Why go there?"

"You're right of course; those aren't the satisfying answers. Let's make up one that suits the crime." It had always been David's job to say something, anything, to keep the scotch coming, the conversation going. The late gold of afternoon would have slipped away between them.

When David got out of the cab at his apartment building the rain had the smell of iron filings.

Thomas, 370's afternoon doorman, held the door ceremoniously open for David. "You still missing your friend?" It was said with the pitch rising as if it were a question, but turned at the end so that it was a comment. "It takes a long, long time—a good friend like him," his hoarse cheerful voice was used to pouring out ordinary wisdom. Why is it that everything that's true about death is so ordinary? David wondered.

When Sage opened the door to let David in before he had a chance to turn the key, whimpers of defeat and confusion fell out of him—primal disbelief—a pouring of tears, queer sounds, the ancestors to language, spilled out.

Sage closed her body unto his.

David sat deep into that night with the emptiness where there had been a skin filled with a man. Into that absence he poured longing for his friend who no longer was. Just before dawn he crawled into bed. Death swam the night waters alone back to the line between water and sky that only it could see.

"Tell me what you think, Jack. Why?" David said to Jack late the next Friday afternoon, when Jack dropped by his office as David was going over his recommendations for the bids for the new theater that he'd present to the board at the next meeting.

"Do you mean the trouble with the board member? What was that guy's name?" Jack asked.

"It was Mr. Cross. I guess. I mean all of it." David leaned back in the chair.

"I never knew details. Just that things happened with Richard that shouldn't have. I used to think I knew him as well as anyone knows someone else. But I learned his passions went where mine didn't. This is what being headmaster means sometimes—things like this. Should you call the Cross family up at this point? Probably. You should know that the board put money into that situation, rightly or wrongly. But if you become headmaster it will involve you having to decide what the right thing for you to do will be. It will be this kind of thing sometimes. Mrs. P. might be of some help. I often had the feeling that he held it against friends like you and me that we loved him for his obvious gifts: his brilliance, his charm, his ease at being himself. It may have been as an illusionist that he wanted to be known. Not mere love."

They sat in the expanding silence. It's not satisfying, but probably something like the truth. David was pretty sure they're talking about all of it, the lying, scandal, the unsayable stuff.

"So have you decided if you want to be Richard?" Jack asked David.

He looked up at Jack's length, gestured to him to sit in the chair he used to occupy across from Richard's desk all those years. He looked around at the beautiful room filled with the glass-fronted bookcases, the worn oriental carpet, the empty chair in the corner. Nice, he thought. He looked down at the spreadsheets, the architectural plans underneath for the theater that would cause David endless problems as it was being built. Nicer. He placed his palms together in front of his face; his thumbs lightly beat against his lower lip. "I thought I'd be David," he said.

"Good." Jack sat down in the chair across from David, leaned back, pulling his arms out of his coat sleeves, letting his coat fall back over the chair. "In that case, as far as I'm concerned, you've got the job. Here's what we do about the votes on the board."

———•———

HAWK IN THE CITY

A hawk is sitting on a fire escape across the courtyard. It's such a strange combination of wild on rust: The hawk's feathers overlap into benevolent curves of whites and browns, the eyes are vigilant, the beak is predatory, and its red tail is folded back.

Tess is watching this from her kitchen window.

The bird sits there. Small, white feathers blow up into the air around the bird. One feather is stuck to the top of his head.

"There's Mr. Hawk," her father had always said, respectfully, whenever he spotted one in flight. The elegance of their flight made him reverent. Tess starts weeping again. Her father died two months ago. She has been walking through a fog since. Nothing makes sense these days. What is that hawk doing here?

The hawk is pausing, preparatory to that high, controlled dive with his legs outstretched behind him, riding the winds up from the Hudson, searching. The loose rust of the iron flutters in the winds flakey under the hawk's claws.

She turns her back to the window now.

She's about to make her Saturday morning call to Naomi, to do their news of the week in review.

"You first," one of them will say.

Or, "What did you decide to do?"

The winds have picked up off the river, and twisting up into the tall narrow alleyway outside of Tess's kitchen window the sound twists into a wild whine as if she lived in the heights of the

119

Caucasus. Tess loves this feral sound; it makes her apartment into a haven against what is outside. It causes the river to make itself known in this tall brick cavern through these strange calls even though she can't see the Hudson from here.

What led that hawk into this dark alleyway? Tess has never seen one in this enclosed back courtyard.

Naomi too is looking out her kitchen window a few blocks down river with its view of the street. She picks up her cup of tea. Either she'll call, or Tess will call. She settles into her small table by the window.

Naomi sees her neighbors hurrying down the street against the fierce winter winds. She feels her own body pushing past against the freezing winds into the warmth of their doorway. Only litter blows along the sidewalks.

"Something's just gone out of me," Tess says as soon as they've settled in. "I've lost my way. I hate teaching now. I don't want to get out of bed in the morning. I don't cook. I know it's about the fact that my father died. It's as if there's a whole country I can never visit again. It was one of my favorite countries, and it's disappeared beneath the earth."

"What does Max say?" Naomi asks.

"Max hugs me and weeps. But he's been doing all the cooking, everything. This is going on too long. He doesn't complain but . . . I'm not any good with Paul. I'm always breaking down and crying when I'm with him."

Naomi sighs and then plunges. "When I'm like that it doesn't matter what I do as long as I do something, anything. I have to make a move in some direction. See a psychic. Quit your job. Do something. It will help."

"I need the name of someone to talk to. I don't know how to get through this one." Tess starts to tear up. "I don't know what to do. I don't know what to do."

"I have a really good person for you Tess. She's brilliant and so down to earth. She was one of my supervisors at the institute. Honest and just a good woman. She may have some openings.

I wish I could use her as my therapist, but because we have this other relationship . . . I'll get her number for you."

Tess wanders back to the window. There are some small, white feathers left on the fire escape where the large bird has been but Mr. Hawk is gone.

———◆———

TAKING AN INCOMPLETE

Esther decided she'd have to take an incomplete in her analysis. She was forced to conclude that she couldn't see a way for this to come to an end. She had been coming to her sessions four times a week for six years. She had been first desperate, then serious, and finally obsessed. Her analysis had become the center around which the rest turned, the locus from which she rose in the morning, the flux of consciousness she walked through in the day, and the well of unconsciousness she descended into at night. But it was only once analysis had become the complete focus of her life that her analyst suggested their work together was coming to a close.

"It sounds like we're beginning to talk about completing our work," Dr. Colangela had said, her discreet, reasonable voice rising from inside her small body, fixed neatly to the chair behind Esther. The shaped air resonated out into the space between them.

When those waves of sound funneled their way into the small corridors of Esther's ear, transformed themselves into electrical impulses in her brain, and lit up her consciousness, Esther was stunned.

She means termination. How can that be? It sounded like a death sentence or an execution. The only thing that's changed is that I understand more why I love doing this so much. It's the only place Esther knew where her irrational side—the part of herself which she trusted most, was most at ease with—was accepted as the vortex from which she emanated. But her analyst, whom she admired, respected, loved really, was suggesting it was time for this to stop.

I guess she's done. I'm not sure I am. Esther thought. She wanted to think, pause, consider, before she stepped off into the abyss of a postanalytic life. She might have to take another incomplete.

As an undergraduate she had a rolling record of incompletes—making sure she had acquired some new ones before she eliminated the old ones. One summer when she decided to go to graduate school she had talked to a professor of hers. "So you think I could make it in the big time?" Professor Mann—her Contemporary Drama teacher who believed in her utterly—asked the admissions people to extend the deadline for her application while she quickly finished up the last few papers in order to enroll in graduate school in the fall. This professor had been happy to oblige. In fact she was the most brilliant student he had ever had. He had spent most of the last two years, except for when they were in bed, trying to convince Esther that she must go on to graduate school. And she almost made it without a single incomplete, but at the last minute she got wistful about leaving her desk so wiped down, so harshly cleansed of books, notes, ideas. How would she start up again from so stark a setting? So she left her last paper, "The Sound of Silence in Minimalist Drama," sitting there in the center of her desk. She was pretty sure she'd left it without the footnotes (which she promised herself to do the following week).

In graduate school she got deeply involved in understanding the historical evolution of the drama from classical to modern. Staging, especially, became her corner of the world. And although eventually she went on to become an ABD in her doctoral program, not everything was left dangling in her life.

She married, became a mother, nursed her babies, changed dirty diapers, and cooked meals that arrived at the table pretty much on time. Her children had secured her and set her free. She liked the idea of being totally committed to her girls, the way the day rambled around without deadlines or fixed schedules.

As time went on she considered the possibility that she might be using her children for cover. She drove her children to their dance classes and piano lessons. She managed several love affairs that for the most part were pleasing to both parties and came to more or less mutually agreeable conclusions.

Jay didn't take Esther's flirting seriously. He thought of it as her way of dealing with her lack of a career. She adored him; he knew that. She was only deceitful by omission. She did all of her initial seducing in his presence. It simply never occurred to him that she would follow up. She wasn't sure herself how she managed the discretion so that she didn't hurt Jay. Hiding things was one thing she was good at. Her instinct for real secretiveness probably came from hiding food from her mother in her room. She never once left crumbs around or an empty bag of chips. It was part of the pleasure, not just eating the food, but keeping something entirely for herself. It had been established early in Esther's life that whatever she accomplished belonged to her mother, especially and including the career as writer she was to have, the PhD, and definitely the slim body she would attain some day.

Recently, the guys she flirted with hadn't flirted back. Esther wasn't sure why. She called Leah, her college roommate and friend, to discuss her confusion about feeling bereft of the attention from strangers. Who were these men to think they could refuse to take her up on her beckoning? Leah lived in New York on Riverside Drive right down from where Esther had carried on that affair with Rubin Mann, her professor. By the end of the phone call she had almost dealt with the fact that her body's sags and pulls might be looking less inviting, but that didn't mean her sexual life was over.

Leah had reassured her, "I know, men don't look at us the way they used to. That doesn't bother me. It's the ones who look through us. The young ones simply don't see us anymore."

But the next phone call to Leah was to say that she was pregnant again. All that stretched skin, another shoe size, bottles to sterilize, nights without real sleep. All that unbounded emotion. It was too much. She couldn't do it again.

After the abortion, Esther shut down. This was the incomplete that really got to her. She stopped cooking. She stopped making the beds. She stopped combing the girls' hair, until finally her easygoing husband said, "Well, what's going to happen here?"

"I don't know," she said. And having said it out loud like that to Jay, "I don't know," so unadorned, made Esther realize she had to do something. What's going on here? That is the question. I'm closing in on forty, and I still don't know what time it is.

That was when she had discovered her ultimate course of study—the seminar—a study of herself—psychoanalysis. That way it became clear to her. The reason she had taken so many incompletes before was that she had been studying the wrong subject—not herself.

And Esther had taken to it as if she were a creature dislocated at birth to the wrong climate and finally returned to her own weather. She loved floating on the airy fluids of her memories, coming upon a fluttering image that she had been bumping gently into every day for years without paying it much attention. In one she was walking with her father in Riverside Park watching the Hudson sweep out to the ocean. Her father was a short distance off, his small body hunched into its own worried attentions, looking off at the river, smoking a cigarette. Why would such a simple image slosh around in her mind all this time and each watery ride around a sensation of pleasure? It was the clarity of the words matching the picture that made analysis the plain astonishment it was for her. Sentences that cut through encrusted ice like an act of nature. Things fell to either side, and words were being said that made her see what she had been perceiving without language for years.

"You didn't have to talk to feel connected when your mother wasn't in the picture."

She began to read the literature. For high drama, Freud was better than Italian opera. She read indiscriminately, voraciously. She stumbled onto Levi-Strauss and started a degree in Boston— she got them to agree to an interdisciplinary degree, a psycho-analytic approach to the anthropology of theater—she wanted to focus on the psychological underpinnings in celebration and grief rituals, in matrilineal societies. She drove up and down happily on her own a couple of times a week, feeling more alert, aware of the sound of cars she was passing on the roads, the colors of trees, or the look of passengers in other cars flashing into her consciousness. Studying psychoanalytic material from inside and out, she gave herself over to the pleasure of this material, as she had previously only given herself over to her children, to food, and sometimes to sex.

The rest had been filler. Now the filler became the stuff she was most interested in; it was the filler that revealed the real.

An only child, she had been the object of the frozen attention of her mother, whose only major accomplishments in life were as she repeated often, "I never had any true failures in my life." She'd look at her husband and daughter triumphantly. "And I kept my figure through pregnancy, nursing, and menopause." She didn't seem to notice she hadn't attempted anything beyond these. That was Esther's job: to try to fail for both of them. Anything that Esther managed to accomplish would naturally belong to her mother, who waited at home standing sideways, chin up, head twisted, sucking her tummy in tight in front of a mirror. "Murray's still mad about me," she'd say to her daughter, as if she were the friend her mother had never managed. "Never looks at another woman."

"Of course, Pussy Cat." Murray somehow always arrived on cue, now in from the bedroom. "You're my beauty."

Then to his daughter confidentially, "You should have seen your mother when she was young." his head shook from the wordless wonder she had been. "She was in a class by herself." Her parents embraced, joining tightly.

In the third year, Dr. Colangela and Esther had started to go deeper in, past the family weather to her own natural climes. It was Monday morning, nine o'clock—her hour. After the long break of the weekend she came back usually with a reservoir of dammed waters and flung herself down onto the couch—it creaked under her weight. I've got to start exercising seriously, she'd think each time the noise of her received weight emerged from the joints of the couch—relieved each Monday to be back home in Dr. Col-angela's office.

"Remember last week when I was talking about being stuck out in Madison"—she had gone there before she transferred to Barnard— "hating the cold winters, hating school, but certainly not wanting to go back to my parents' apartment in New York. Something came back to me this morning as I was showering to come here. Standing there with the hot water beating down on me I remembered how much I hated showering out there—the tiles so cold under your feet in the common bathroom. You know how I got through that last winter before I dropped out?

"'I can't deal with this frozen tundra,' I said to Leah, my room-mate—you remember. 'I'm going to bed.' Everyone thought I was very funny. I meant it. I skipped classes, stayed in bed reading whatever I could reach without getting out of bed. Leah brought me food from the cafeteria. And it was usually something of Leah's that I read too. Whatever she had left on the floor. Mysteries, plays, novels. 'Now this is a world I can deal with—the world made just of words,' I announced one night.

"'And donuts,' I remember Leah said to me when I announced this.

"Every day I thought, when I finish this book—whatever book I was reading—I'll get up and leave. I wasn't going to pack. I wasn't going to write a note. I was going to walk out of the room, out of the dorm, off the campus and just keep walking—out of my life. I'd go somewhere—anywhere that wasn't there or home."

"What happened when you finished reading something?" Dr. C's voice seemed to arrive after a long journey from somewhere else that Esther wasn't.

"I probably picked up the next one. Moved on. I even started to read psych texts; that was when I started to be intrigued by this stuff," she gestured into the space around her.

There was a stillness, a stasis, a deadening of sound behind Esther. No small waves of noise rose from the well that Dr. Col-angela made. Esther looked into the still air in front of her.

"Can you remember one of the books you finished?" Dr. Colangela's quiet, reasonable voice asked her.

"Well, that was the first time I read *Anna K.*"

"Why didn't you walk out when you finished reading *Anna
Karenina*?"

"Let's see. A lot of what I read was trash." Esther was back
into her saga, rolling around in her words, her memories. "But I
read *Anna K.* Maybe that's where the idea that being unfaithful
was full of passionate drama began for me. It was the best thing
I read that winter. I had really settled in. Before that I used to go
to an occasional class but by now I felt terrible. I knew something
was very wrong. I actually asked Leah to hand me *Anna K.* Can
you imagine? I wouldn't get out of bed to take the book off a shelf.
It was on my bookshelf! Three feet away. I had been meaning
to read it for years. My mother said you weren't a real woman
until you read *Madame Bovary* and *Anna Karenina*. So I made
up this idea that I would start to do some serious reading. For a
few days I managed to push away again just how bad things had
gotten.

"I remember it was late at night, I'd been reading day and
night, sleeping on and off, eating whatever Leah brought me from
the dining hall. I was in some kind of suspended animation. For a
few days I was happier than I had ever been out there, just reading
under the blankets, climbing out of bed just to pee, always more
waiting for me, then Anna K. went under the train—the little man
who had haunted her was near her when she died . . ."

Esther was quiet staring up at the molding at the corner of the
ceiling. "I started the last chapter, and I realized at some point that
Tolstoy simply abandoned Anna after she died. I flipped through
the pages, looking for the right names. Nothing about the son,
Serezha or Karenin. Tolstoy's writing about the war in Serbia at
the end—I was furious. I couldn't read it. I put it down. I, I, I . . .
didn't finish it."

Air that hummed filled the room.

"Did you finish any of them?" Dr. C. asked very quietly.

A stilled breath rose and seeped out of Esther, poured out of her lungs in a rush.

"No. That was how I got myself to stay. I'd read them until almost the end and then I'd find something terrible in them. I could predict what would happen; the writing was falling apart. I'd take a nap and pick up something new. Halfway through the semester I dropped everything and came back to New York in disgrace. I couldn't have any F's on my transcript—even my mother agreed to that. Naturally I had missed the tuition rebate deadline."

"What do you think prevented you from finishing any of the books?" Esther could feel her analyst's psyche settle in—anchoring herself for this material.

Heat rose around Esther 's neck, her esophagus started to constrict. "There," the tears rolled slowly down her cheeks, "was nowhere to go."

For a while she couldn't speak. Her throat had tightened further—she'd have to cry to loosen it before she'd be able to speak. Pictures floated in and out above her—a dirty snow-encrusted walkway on campus, stubborn snow, herself scurrying from large class to larger class, then her mother waiting at home, and there some words rising, her mother's, "You're even bigger. What have you done to yourself?"

"I had waited all my life to leave home, and when I did I hated my life even more than home. There was no way to go forward, no way back.

"I wanted to walk away from the whole thing—my parents, my friends, school. I wanted to just keep walking," her tears welled and spilled, "out of my life."

Inarticulate sounds spread outward from her body, rising, the room filling with the sounds of a squall. Then the storm subsided slowly towards quiet.

Into that quiet her analyst floated a life preserver: "You wanted to walk out of your body."

Then, "Even there it didn't belong to you. In the bed reading you were a consciousness, not a body."

This was what made her so passionately committed to this stuff. She had been listened to. She had been heard. After she had been heard, and this was very important, she could listen instead of talking. Then words came that described to her what she had said in a way that released her.

That session moved the next six months along. She had walked lighter on her feet. She had started taking a dance class. She didn't lose weight, but she liked how she felt. She got a part-time job, teaching introductory classes in anthropology at a local community college.

Over the next couple of years she made "progress." She fell in love with her students. She got them to fall in love with her. She seduced them with her assurances that they could investigate another world and really understand it, with her carefully worked-out assignments, her conferences with her fine attention focused on them in a way that these working-class kids had rarely experienced. She worked with them on their ethnographies with an intensity that gave her almost as much satisfaction as a reading about object relations or Freud, or analyzing a complicated dream. She noticed how much of what drove her students' presentations was what wasn't articulated, what was hinted at, left hidden behind some skimpily phrased, half-baked idea about the differences between the groups they were studying and the places they came from; their neighborhoods, their families, the streets they left behind them when they came to school. She began to write papers about the unconscious material in her students' work and sending them off to journals.

These papers were published almost immediately. She won several prizes for this work. She worked on ideas about the culture of the college classroom and the phatic classroom rituals between teachers and students. She did her course work. She loved her husband more. She was kinder to her children, while hovering less to see how much television they were watching, how many cookies they ate. Having affairs with other men stopped. She was having an affair, with her analyst, with herself.

One summer, Dr. Colangela and Esther realized that in the fall the only time that would work for both of them was five in the afternoon, because Esther had been given a nine o'clock class. Esther was really upset about it. She was a morning person; she needed the light to think. She didn't do well with dark coming over her. "I'm not at all sure this is going to work. Not at all."

"What might happen?" Dr. C. asked Esther.

"I'm not sure I can do this. I might have to leave."

When she came back in the fall and walked into Dr. Colangela's office, she stopped just inside the door. The office looked west; although in the mornings the windows had real light, in this late afternoon bronzed light the place was transformed. It had a kind of glaze, as if everything had acquired the tint of old brass. Even Dr. Colangela had a patina. The room was warmed with heat from the past. There was a breeze coming in the windows. Esther felt she was in a different room.

She lay back on the couch and didn't say anything for a little while.

"What are you thinking?" Dr. Colangela asked. It almost sounded as if Dr. C. was happy to see her again.

"Trying to figure out just where it is that I've arrived."

The change in the hour over the course of the fall had a real effect on Esther. Deep yellows reflected on the walls, the red in the carpet was richer, and the office had a gloss. Esther was somewhere else. She didn't know where it was. An older place. Whereas in the morning the office had looked pretty much the same in every season, in this new hour it had seasonal moods; as the sun set earlier and earlier the light changed over the course of Esther's sessions.

Esther began to check the newspapers for the changing time of sunset. She began to daydream about what the office was going to look like at winter solstice. "I'll bet it's really beautiful here then."

Dr. Colangela put up a new Indian print filled with tiny gold threads; a woman with her arms raised and gracefully twisted at an Asian angle was hung just above the couch.

"Are you doing this on purpose?" Esther asked the air.

"What am I doing?"

"Creating this new effect in this room?"

The quiet rose and fell and rose and fell again. Why did Esther always think, this time Dr. C. will answer me?

"Keep going," Dr. C said.

"I'm talking about the new picture, and you changed my hour too."

"Didn't your schedule have something to do with the hour?"

"Yes, but this hour, these colors, they're changing my mood, my way of looking at things."

"How does the room affect you?" Dr. C.'s voice lifted soberly at the end of this question.

Is she pointing out my narcissism again? Esther wondered. I'm not at the center of her attention when she decorates her room.

"I don't know. It's weird the effect it's having on me. I'm dreaming in dark colors. It's almost as if I expect you to have candles lit when I come in now. As if I'm entering a church or a temple."

Esther found herself wearing looser clothes in darker colors, especially earth reds, mauves, and deep pumpkin. These clothes suited her. She looked larger but more at ease with her size. Long pendants made of primitively smoothed stones hung from her neck.

In December, as the solstice approached, they spent several sessions just talking about the colors in the room, the quality of light, Esther's anticipating what the winter solstice sessions were going to be like. One afternoon close to the shortest day of the year, Esther decided she was overinvolved in this. It was getting silly. She wanted to move on to other things.

"Other things?" The Voice said.

"You know, real things. Like the fact that my children have grown up while I've been living in this office. They're twelve and fourteen now. I haven't been paying attention. I have to figure out what I'm going to do when my course work is finished and I have to face completing my dissertation again. Like the fact that I'm still overweight."

Dr. Colangela's silence was asking her to pay attention.

Sometimes Esther simply longed for sounds of any kind to rise behind her.

"What would you like to discuss?" Dr. C. asked.

"I don't know. Why am I so obsessed with the quality of the light in this room?"

"It seems to put you in a different mood. Perhaps there's a place that goes with it."

"Some room, quiet where words can be heard, breathing listened to, an internal life."

"Who's in the room?"

"You know there was this one day. That was magical. I was with Professor Mann, the professor I had the affair with in my senior year at Barnard—on Riverside Drive when I was finishing my bachelor's. It was one of those large, cluttered apartments filled with comfortable ratty chairs, bookcases piled one on top of the other all different sizes. It looked out over the Hudson River. He was the guy that got me so interested in drama and the theater. I had been sleeping with him for a while. But the first time I went over to his apartment it was a weekend—his wife was away, his second wife I think—she was in applied linguistics. She took the dogs and went to Chicago to a conference. We spent the whole weekend inside. I went over to his apartment on a Friday afternoon.

"When I walked in the door he put his hand over my mouth, saying, 'Shhh, shhh,' and started to undress me there in the foyer, very slowly, one layer at a time. First he took my hat and scarf. Then he'd take a slow sip of his scotch leaning against the table there in the foyer—except for the morning he drank all the time in those days. Then my coat. I just stood there. I loved the fact that I wasn't expected to say a word, do anything. I was in his hands. He handed me a glass of scotch. Then he took off the dress I had on. I stood there in my slip. He'd brushed his hands over my breasts, my nipples, then my stomach, sliding the fabric of my slip against my skin. The light outside the windows in the living room was changing slowly. I was getting more and more aroused, and he was slowing it down, saying, 'Shhh, shhh,' kissing my neck then standing away from me again. He got drunker and drunker. The sky got deeper and deeper. By the time we went to bed, he was too drunk to make love. It didn't matter. I had had some kind of strange high unsatisfying orgasm sometime out in the foyer; it was the most exciting and least satisfying sex I've ever had. All hot and discontinuous." Esther was wondering why she'd gotten off onto all this.

"Like here," from behind Esther's head the words floated over to her on small bobbing waves. She almost thought she heard ice clink against glass when Dr. Colangela moved, squeaking the spring in her chair. Esther wished she would keep talking.

"What does that mean?" Esther's voice was hushed.

"Some of the most exciting things in life don't lead where you expect them to. You thought maybe here you'd finally find someone who would touch you. Sometimes it seems as if that *is* what's happening here and then I make you leave—as if you were just anyone—instead of a someone precious." The words reverberated.

"Could you say more about that?" Esther used words that had been used on her.

"Why don't you try to talk about it?" Dr. Colangela asked.

That was the wrong answer. That wasn't what Esther wanted to hear. "How about if you took a turn for a while. Where am I going with all this stuff? It's so intense and then the hour's up and I have to go home and make dinner. It leaves me crazy, and I'm not sure where it's getting me. I know I'm not going to do that goddamn dissertation. Or lose weight."

That session ended badly. All Esther wanted to do was to get home to make love to Jay before the girls came home from soccer. Someone else was on pick-up duty today.

Jay was in the shower. Esther came into the bathroom and opened the shower curtain. Holding one finger up to her mouth, she undressed looking at him. Then she took the soap from his hands and started to slide her soapy hands down from his torso. She joined him in the warm shower, Esther insisting there be no talk. They moved into the bedroom—Esther drunk with sex for that hour.

"What was that?" Jay asked afterward. A hot wind from another continent had just blown through their bodies.

"Something came up in my analysis today." From another country, she lay there thinking. Her mind wandered off to the question of how often Dr. C. and her husband made love. She'd dug up that much—Dr. C. had a husband.

"How about you stop your analysis right here—go for a little arrested development right at this stage." The trembling in their bodies didn't change the fact that it was dark outside, and Esther knew she still hadn't uncovered what that session was actually about.

They heard the door slam open downstairs. Wasn't it too early for the girls to be home? Laura was racing up the stairs, "Mom! Mom, I need help with my Cultural Studies paper. It's due . . . Mom!" Esther was out of the bed slamming her door shut. She could feel the winds of the sirocco slipping out the window.

Rosie, who had looked up the stairs and intuited what was happening, was yelling, "Get down here nitwit." For a while that night no one in the family wanted to look each other in the eye.

She was coming to the end of her course work. But the real locus of her life was her complete absorption with Dr. Colangela. Though she still continued to threaten to quit, almost by reflex Dr. Colangela didn't comment anymore when she brought it up. So Esther pushed, "I think it's time we set a date, don't you?

"Well, tell me what made you think this?"

"Well, I guess I'm thinking about ending. I have my two kids. I'm not completely depressed anymore. Don't you think it's time?" The air hung with weight. What does Dr. C. want from her?

"Don't you think I'm ready?

"I think it's time to talk about this. I'm not entirely certain. Let's just explore it."

"Couldn't you just have given it one of your famous 'Uh huh's?'" Why couldn't she just have said it's not time? That's what I want to hear.

"You seem to want to write a script for us," Dr. Colangela said. More and more it seemed to Esther that the doctor was a little impatient when Esther got fresh. Wasn't she supposed to be able to let loose in here? If not in analysis, where? She left her session feeling dissatisfied. For an ending this was a bad beginning.

This was how the sixth year came to a close. But typically Esther picked a fight at the end of the year. Even I know that, Esther muttered to herself, as she walked out the door to the parking lot that day.

"I think I'm going to terminate; it's time." Esther called Leah, thinking about how cute Aaron, Leah's husband, was. I wonder why he and I didn't go to bed that time? We were close."

"Really? That's a big deal," Leah said.

"Even Dr. Colangela is getting disgusted with me, I think. She made this terrible remark last week just before the summer break, 'Do you think you're ready for closure?' she asked me. As if how could I dare to think that? Baby me."

In the fall, they started up again, back in the golden hours watching the sun's movement. These were Esther's hours. The idea that anyone else had once had these hours with the doctor was a horrifying thought. It was that thought that prevented Esther from making her routine remark upon return. "I think this year should be the last."

Each year for the past three years, upon resuming her analysis in September, they had spent several weeks on Esther's need to punish Dr. Colangela with her threat to leave, and each year they would come up with the same understanding: she was furious because they had been separated. Esther wasn't going to waste time on that this year.

In the second week, Dr. Colangela said quietly. "I think it's important that we look at the fact you haven't felt the need to punish me for leaving you this summer."

"You mean I'm growing up. Are we talking termination here?"

"I think you're considering."

Esther was stunned. "*Now* you think it's time?"

That was the famous day when Dr. C. had said, "It sounds like you're thinking of termination."

"When you bring it up, it's time? All the times I brought it up the subject sort of dropped. It's not until you produce the words that anything has any legitimacy in here."

"What bothers you about this?"

But instead of the possibility of ending treatment bringing the deepest stuff up so that they could work toward the end, it brought everything to a halt. She stopped working on her dissertation even in fits and starts; she stopped going to her dance classes, even once a week; she wasn't able to bring her usual delight to her teaching. She tried to turn her attention back to her girls. But they didn't want their mother in their lives much anymore. "Mom, you've got to get a life."

Esther began to bake elaborate desserts. And she took up embroidery, again seriously. She found herself completely gripped by the tiny patterns, the muted colored threads twisted and bound to fabric to make words and pictures. She liked the fixed nature of this threaded world. She'd spend hours looking over pattern books, deciding which of these worlds she'd live in for the next weeks. She loved hanging out in the shop where she chose her colors with women who spent their nights in front of the TV. Women all over the world had always spent this kind of time together deeply embedded in some female art. Only in the middle class in America had these rituals lost their ability to validate. I could write about that, she thought, but then a purply-wine-colored thread caught her attention.

The samplers became a calling, a preoccupation, an affair of the heart. She had to find something that was only between her and her—the needle going in and out, in and out.

She'd get going on these stitches and find herself standing in the middle of a room, completely absorbed by this needle rising and sinking through the cloth—this slowly emerging picture of a house, letters—the smaller and the finer gauge of the linen, thirty-six count, the better she liked it.

"Sit down, at least," Jay would say when he found her there for the second time standing in the middle of her living room, when he went to get a second beer from the fridge. "Yeah, I will when I finish this stitch."

"Mom, you're weird, you know?" Either Rosie or Laura began to say as she passed them on the way upstairs. "Would you please sit down?"

"There," she plunked herself down. "Are you happy now?"

"Yeeeees," Her girls said in unison. "Act like a normal mother." They'd roll their eyes to one another. But unlike most mothers who might have been annoyed with them for this eye rolling, Esther wouldn't have noticed. She was too absorbed in her needlework.

Esther's friend Olivia announced that she was pregnant with her third child. She and her family had moved to town pretty recently, so she had become one of Esther's projects. It was a lovely way to pass the afternoon and revisit her girls' earlier days. She and Olivia would talk over coffee in the afternoons waiting for the evenings and their families to arrive.

Esther wasn't convinced that her new friend really wanted another baby just now. She had a complicated history with her babies. The first was from before she was married. She had it right after her brother fell off the mountain. She was kind of nutty around her eldest daughter. Then she had a second baby right after she got married. Then she had a miscarriage while she was trying to decide whether she was going to keep that third baby. She had been really depressed for a while. Now she seemed to have decided she couldn't face another undone life.

Esther knew Olivia was still blue, so she thought she'd make a really special birth sampler for the baby. She worked in a frenzy in the weeks just before the baby was born so that it could be finished and framed by the time she went for her first visit. And Olivia *loved* the present when Esther brought it to her. But when the baby whimpered, she turned quickly back to the bassinet to pick up her new son, Christian Abramowitz, and had somewhat carelessly tossed the embroidery down on her living room couch. Esther had to force herself to admire the baby. She was shocked when she realized what she had thought this present would mean to Olivia.

My god, Esther thought, I spent weeks on that thing. Why

did I think it would be so important to her? More important than her baby?

"I think you wanted to be able to look at the smallest threads, not the whole canvas," Dr. Colangela said when Esther described how frightened this episode had made her. "Maybe if you'd been able to think about what was going to happen to the piece when you finished you wouldn't have completed it. Does this bring anything to mind?"

This was a long speech for Dr. C.

Esther hated these loaded questions. This wasn't really meaningful. I was just distracting myself. Even I know that, Esther thought. Is she losing it? "We're not doing anything in here anyway, except for me spending my husband's money. I thought I might as well get something done—at least an embroidery. Jeezus! You know it's awfully cold in here. Don't you have any heat on today?"

"Aren't we getting anything done?" Dr. Colangela wanted to know.

"There's nowhere to go. How can we bring this to an end successfully?"

"Why, nowhere to go?"

"What's that supposed to mean? What?" Esther knew the answer was going to bring her somewhere she didn't want to go. She almost sat up and turned around.

"I don't want to leave. I know. I know. This is about not finishing anything. Again. Right?" Reluctantly, she allowed this thought to register.

"If we talk about the real stuff you'll have to leave me. You'd rather stay in suspended animation, not going forward or backward. It's Wisconsin again. Don't finish—don't have to leave."

"You think I'm stalling."

"Let's just say you don't want to look at the whole picture. It's better just to concentrate on one stitch at a time than to look at the whole canvas. The pleasure, stitch by stitch, is what interests you.

You don't know that there's real pleasure in finishing and standing back and looking at what you've done."

There were six years of analysis behind her. She had to set a date. She could sense this expectation rising, like a fever, from Jay, from Dr. Colangela, from her calls to Leah. They were all poised, waiting to see what would happen. Esther waited with them.

More than anything, what Esther fantasized now was just listening to Dr. Colangela. In the fantasy, she was in a Roman ruin. Dr. Colangela would be on the proscenium talking about Esther. Esther would be the only person in the theater lying against the hot, white stones. She would lean back on a pillow and listen. Dr. Colangela was talking, explaining something to her calmly.

"If I were talking instead of you, what would I be saying?"

"Oh, that's not it at all. It's the hum of it, not the content. I'd sit there and listen."

"You want me to talk, but you don't like what I say."

"But you only want to talk about termination."

The silence was complete. Esther looked at her watch. Hour was up. She gathered her bag and her sunglasses; she got up and left the room. She couldn't nod, "Hum, goodbye." She was being forced out.

At her next session, she talked about Jay. "I ran into Jay one Sunday night at Chock Full o' Nuts on Broadway and 116th Street— they made the best coffee. It was after I left Rubin's—that weekend I told you about. And I thought to myself—look at this lovely guy. He had been in one of my lit. classes the previous semester even though he was in law school at the time. He had talked the professor into letting him audit—that's the kind of thing about him I just love. He just does what he wants without worrying about whether it fits together perfectly. And he was smarter than anyone else in the class, too—except me, of course. He really knew how to argue his point. I thought to myself, This is the kind of guy you should be with. I could barely talk. I was in some kind of a fugue state. But I managed kind of an enigmatic smile—my forte, the meaningful look covering the meaningless.

"'Did you ever finish that paper you presented in our seminar on the use of lighting in . . ., was it modernist drama?' he asked simply, as if he wanted to know. 'I liked the way you talked about color lighting replacing sets as a declarer of time and place in contemporary theater.'

"This is the kind of guy I should marry, I thought. Within six months we were living together. Rubin and I had been drifting into strange places. He had been taking over my psyche. I had listened to Rubin as if I had never heard anyone talk before."

She paused, drifted.

"Go on," Dr. Colangela said. There was concentration in her voice.

"I remembered something the other day about that weekend that brings me back to it over and over." They had already gone over—several times—that weekend in Rubin's apartment.

"You know it wasn't really the sex that turned me on. It was listening. Listening to Rubin."

"I thought the rules were clothes off, no talk."

"Partly that was true. We never left the apartment all weekend. We ordered in Chinese, ate peanut butter and jelly. Mostly me. He drank much more than he ate. I ate and drank.

"On Sunday when we got up, it was about one o'clock, I wanted to leave. I had some papers I had to get done. He asked me to stay just another hour. 'Get me through my morning hangover,' he said.

"He sat on one couch against the windows. I sat facing him on another. He had a bottle of scotch, and he was smoking cigarettes, one after another. I was sipping coffee. He started talking, and he knew the talk would keep me there.

"He talked in these low tones, these cadences. Sometimes I imitate him in class when I want to get my students' attention, very slow, with emphasis every once in a while. I just sat there, knees curled under me on the couch facing him. The light had changed slowly over the course of the day; first the blinding glare was behind him, enslaving everything to its charge.

"He talked about himself—about why he loved to drink, what happened to him when he drank, how the world looked better, 'the way when you look at the street reflected in a window shop and it all looks more interesting than reality. That's the way the world looks when I start drinking. So I drink some more, so I can enter the picture in the glass. Then the picture shifts, and I see the people behind the glass, and I see them looking back at me. It's a two-way show. I'm the one on the outside, looking in. What do they see?'

"Then he'd do something like strike a match and hold it, pausing to look at it before he held it to the end of his cigarette. 'I have no idea what they see, only what I see.'

"We both knew I didn't care what he said as long as he kept talking. The radiating, yellow sun was slowly lowering itself over New Jersey. As the afternoon went on it lost its domination of what lay under it, as it went down toward the horizon. He talked into the dusty air between us. He talked about being taken to the opera by his mother when he was a boy in Europe, how much he loved the craziness of a ship being on a stage, immense women playing delicate Asian girls singing those poignant songs. He talked about how his father realized that they had to get out because the Nazis had just won their first election. 'So we came to America where I watched wrestling on television, trying to learn to speak English, and it was as sensational as the opera. You want to learn something about the spectacular, watch those guys—they know how to get you involved.'

"By then the sun was a pure red sphere gaining color, losing control; it was a burnished red then, as if it were being slipped behind a piece of paper as it went down. I wondered how many of his student-lovers had seen this performance.

"There was the smell of overflowing ashtrays and empty cartons of Chinese food, the smell of sex and sweat on me. Listening to him talk was what really drew me to him. It freed me of everything else. The rest of the world disappeared behind the mutations of light and his words. The sky in the distance had become this weird pink. The clouds near to the sunset were turning the colors of bruises, reds like stains smeared across the horizon. I couldn't bring myself to leave until the horizon turned from that gray skin into black; the river flowing by taking the colors with it out to sea. I'm not sure I've ever had a time like that."

"A time like what?" Dr. Colangela's voice broke the clouds of memory.

"It wasn't good or bad; it was outside the moral, outside the normal; it was where I wanted to be more than anywhere else." She started to cry. "Except here." In that session, Esther had gotten somewhere; she just couldn't say where. She only had a few months to go.

She was crying when she left that session. She put her head down so that she wouldn't have to give even a friendly distancing nod to the guy who came after her, always waiting in the ante-room. She called him the night man. She just blew her nose loudly as she left, looking away. The night man looked away in sympathy.

"I don't want to leave," she told Jay. "I can't leave."

"I don't know what will happen," she told Leah on the phone. "Who wrote this in stone?" she asked. "I just want to keep having this relationship with Dr. C. Just go there and talk and be listened to."

"But Esther, why do you have to leave?" Leah asked, one phone call.

"I asked for an extension. She said, 'No!' Can you imagine? I asked for another half a year. That's all. I'm sick about this."

"She must think it's the right thing to do. Don't you trust her by now?"

"I do, but what can I tell you? Nothing has ever been this right for me. Analysis is what interests me. There's no way for me to end this. I think I should just get out."

"Taking an incomplete?" Leah asked.

"Yes! That's the idea. I can't bring this to any end that would be successful, so why not take an incomplete. At least it won't have a terrible, false, let's pretend this is all neatly wrapped up to make Dr. Colangela happy, finale. What a farce."

"My life seems to have gotten more confused, instead of clearer. One minute I seem to be looking at the solid physical reality of my life, wondering why Jay and the kids seem like the sibs I never had. Then that surface sends us into my parents acting like children fighting for control over me. Then we drift far away into a fleeting image of a small child sitting alone under a tree, a world that doesn't really have light, or shape, or only in some distant way. Then there's my life in here, which has come to seem like the most real of all to me, but now you're telling me it's over."

"Listen to yourself—what you've just said," Dr. C. said with emphasis.

What was she wearing today? Esther asks herself. Was it that black mini suit? She even has to have great legs. Fuck her!

"Just because I'm articulate doesn't mean I'm better. I'm not sure what I know anymore. At least I used to know I was messed up. Now I'm analyzed and more messed up. I don't know what we've done here or what we haven't."

"It's true." She spoke slowly. "With you the articulation often disguises what's not being said." Dr. Colangelo's tone was speculative.

"You've always been more interested in consciousness than doing the actual work of analysis." She continued. "You have an exquisite consciousness. Let's use it to look at your issue of completion, completing this. Or you'll leave in the state you arrived in only this time much more disappointed. You've put a lot of energy into both solving and not solving this." The pause that followed seemed this time to move back and forth between Dr. C. and Esther with the pitch of a power line whining.

"What do you mean?" Esther had to fight against sitting up. She wanted to turn to Dr. C. and look at her. Have Dr. C. look back at her.

"Look, this is the stuff you came in with. You're bright, very bright, nothing if not a consciousness, but every time it comes to using that bright consciousness, to do something with it, instead you want to go into another round of metaconsciousness.

"I guess only your thoughts belonged to you. Everything else was your mother's. Maybe you think if you expose it to the air of the actual, you'll expose it to her too. Then you won't even have that."

The words held the air. Esther's eyes were wide with concentration. The room froze in its light. She gazed at the light coming through the white silk on the lampshade, incandescent. She gazed at the room, letting each piece of it hit her eye as a virgin experience. What had they been talking about? Something she should remember.

The next session when Dr. C. brought up what they had been talking about, Esther waved her words away. "Look, you want to talk about my exquisite consciousness. What my consciousness is telling me is that this termination isn't working. I know this isn't going right." The room looked dim today. "I want to talk about the fact that I'm not ready to terminate."

"That *is* what I am talking about," Dr. Colangelo said." I want to see what we can understand about why this is so difficult for you. What does it bring to mind?"

"That I can't bear not to see you."

"So you're going to miss me. Not the analysis?"

"Yooooou," Esther's mouth was a small hole pressing the sound out.

"You always knew this was analysis." A temperature instead of a voice arrives at the couch.

That's how she talks to me now, isn't it? Esther thinks.

"We still have weeks left. Why can't we use the time to look at this?" Dr. Colangela's voice came from where she had placed herself, away from Esther.

"Why have you gotten so cold?"

"Can you say more about that?"

"*You're* the one who seduced me into utterly believing in this idea that I should stick with this inner self. Well, I do believe in it. More than you do. Why should I want my analysis to end?"

"You're acting as if you didn't know analysis ends." The exasperated virtue of her words was useless. It made sense as a technique, not as a reality.

Esther hated it when Dr. Colangela used reason and logic

on her. To Esther she seemed to be fighting dirty. She felt Dr. Colangela was always inviting Esther to take long trips into the unconscious where reason didn't hold, but when it came to dealing with things like schedules, fees, and now termination, suddenly the priests of the irrational became the models of common sense and reason.

Esther found herself crying almost all the time. It was hydraulic. Raw disbelief welled up from her belly, her womb: she found herself pulling into gas stations and running into the ladies' room; the tears, snot, poured out of her; an animal function, like sweat, like blood, sobs tore out of her body. She'd be hanging curtains in the living room, not even noticing the flood when Laura walked in with a friend, "Mom! What's the matter?"

Esther left a message on Dr. Colangela's phone: "This is getting worse, not better. I think I should simply stop now. A few more weeks can't change this." They had a month to go. When Dr. C. called back, she said quietly, "These are your hours."

Esther felt her heart soften momentarily. Then Dr. Colangela went on, "It's important that we work until the end."

"For whom?" She agreed to a final session.

"What exactly has happened here?" Esther wanted to know the day of that final appointment.

It seemed to Esther that Dr. Colangela was trying to give the whole of the last session some formal closure.

"We've done some work. It hasn't been perfect. It's been a difficult and painful termination. The finishing issue came up again. That's still hard for you to look at."

So why am I leaving? Esther wondered.

"This process will continue after you leave. More will happen. I think for you especially—you've always liked to take what we do with you—without anyone looking over your shoulder—to have for yourself to work over it in solitude, away from any audience at all, where you can be sure no one is going to take it away."

Esther found her head shaking; up and down, side to side, in agreement, in despair. She had another incomplete. It was time to go. She stood up and turned to look at this diminutive woman around whom her psyche had circled all these years. Dr. Colangela reached out her small hand to shake Esther's large, reluctant one. "I wish you the very best." Then sweetly, "Goodbye."

Esther went out of the office and stood at the threshold of the outer door for a minute. When she stepped outside a limpid heat surrounded her. Nothing looked familiar in the clear light of day.

———•◆•———

TESS ENSCONCED

Tess is ensconced at the kitchen table. She's looking over the bills for the gourmet food shop, Questa è la Vita, that she's finally opened after years of planning. Dreaming about the shop had been a long-held pleasure while she planned and created it, but for the past few years, it wasn't in front of her, it wasn't brand new, and she wasn't working out the kinks she's faced with the day to day. She's been doing most of it herself, but she thinks she has to take the next step. Her husband, Max, is sick of backing her up. So she has lined up some interviews for a new manager tomorrow. There's a strong cup of coffee in front of her, very hot with foamed milk and two lumps of brown sugar. The lamp on the table is lit.

The kitchen table is still the nucleus of her world, the hub around which the rest turns. It's one of the places from which she feels as if the world belongs to her, her mother's kitchen table. Occasionally she feels this at Questa è la Vita too, on long afternoons when her customers drop in and chat, and there is no crisis with the staff, and none of the kids who deliver the food to her customers is in serious trouble at school, no one she knows has been mugged recently or, more importantly, diagnosed with breast cancer, and there are no floods in the basement of the store. The afternoon rolls gently away under her feet. At these rare moments she sits at the center of a world that she knows and understands. She's learned a thing or two, she allows herself to think briefly before saying a quick secret prayer of thanks. She doesn't even know if she believes in prayer, but those words are still right. Gratitude and praise. It is even better if it's really lousy weather outside. A damp penetrating cold or horrible winds and rain.

Max is at the shop now. Their son, Paul, isn't home from school yet. It's a cold and rainy November evening outside. Inside it's a refuge from all that lays in wait outside. You are one of the blessed who has a place to go inside that belongs to you.

Paul is on the subway on his way home from school. Ed had to go to his Hebrew class after school, so he couldn't take the train home with Paul. And Paul really needed to talk to him. Amelia might be breaking up with him. He wasn't sure. Zoe said that Amelia told her some real nasty things about him in art class. Amelia said that wasn't true. She claims that his friends never liked her, and they were just trying to break them up. He wanted to believe her, but he had heard things like this before. Like at that party, and he went to the bathroom. Later Zoe told him Amelia had said that sometimes he used a fake laugh. He hated both Zoe and Amelia right now.

Max is waiting on an older woman customer, Mrs. B., someone he always goes out of his way to be especially kind to. She looks like his Tanta Yetta.

"I have a perfect dish for you tonight. You're going to be in heaven. You'll finally marry me for sure."

"You think this is a soup I should enjoy?" She looks away with a shrug that says, I'm not so easy.

"Would I allow you, my own special Mrs. Yoouuuu, to eat something that wasn't delectable? It's as good a cabbage soup as your own Mamale made. Some boiled beef, tomato, a bissel onion, a little sugar. I'm not giving away all my secrets." He kisses her hand across the counter.

Part of their deal is that she gets to act suspicious of whatever he chooses for her, and he has to cajole her.

"You think I don't know what goes into a good cabbage soup?" she demands. "I'm just tired. My arthritis. All right put it," she gestures to the paper containers.

Max is vulnerable to any older woman who reminds him of the strong and lively set of women his mother and her sisters had been. Now only Tanta Yetta is left. If they yelled at him, he simply caved in. As far as he was concerned there wasn't any other possibility. He hadn't even tried to defend himself. He had sealed the pact too long ago. This is their deal. He is someone who owes her, and she has every right to be suspicious of him even though she is here because of his flirtation and help. Tonight, he thought, get it over with. It always comes out the same in the end anyway. But he just isn't in the mood for this today.

In fact, he wishes he had reneged on his promise to Tess to cover at the shop today. Someone told him that his proposal is in trouble. That it looked like the dean wasn't going to give it his crucial vote of approval. But he had begged off a couple of times with Tess recently, and he knew there would have been a scene if he had called and asked her to let him off the hook again. Maybe one of the kids has some grass he can smoke in the back before he goes home. He's so tired with disappointment today.

When Paul puts his key in the door he's hoping he'll have the apartment all to himself. He just wants to go to his room and watch the comedy channel. He doesn't want to talk to anyone and think about school or Amelia or anything. He just wants to veg. He wants to make a sandwich and veg.

When he opens the door he can hear his mother is listening to opera again.

"Hi buddy. I'm in the kitchen," she calls when she hears the door open and close.

Shit, Paul thinks.

"Okay." Is she in there guarding the predinner foods? He goes to his room to dump his backpack filled with those pieces of concrete they call textbooks and to take off his shoes.

"Pauuull," she says. "Do you want a cup of tea?"

"I'll be there in a minute." Jeeez can't she leave me alone for a minute? He can hear her coming toward his door. He wishes he had the nerve to lock it in her face.

"Paul, I just wanted to ask you . . ."

"Mom, don't come in. I'm undressing." He can see that the day wasn't going to be getting better.

When he goes to the kitchen a little later he tries to pretend that he is feeling cheerful, so she won't start talking to him, hinting around about when she was a teenager. He couldn't take that today.

Tess allows some quiet to pass. She knows that in two minutes he'll head out of the kitchen and will put himself off limits.

She takes a deep breath, "Grandma called twice this afternoon. She wanted to know if you had gotten her card. You promised you'd call today. Please?"

Paul only wants to make his sandwich. He slaps the wrapped cold cuts onto the wooden cutting board next to the jar of homemade mayonnaise and the tomato he'll slice in a minute.

"Would you mind making it after you call Grandma? She's called every day this week. I can't take it anymore." Tess goes into a high pitch pretending to be her mother, "That's all right. The other ones didn't call either. I know they're busy. I just wanted to make sure he got it. He's a good boy." Paul forces out a smile to please his mother. She used to be able to crack him up so easily doing exaggerated imitations of any and all relatives.

He's trying to peel back the ham from the pile. The slices of ham are sticking together.

"What kind of ham did you get? Why doesn't this damn ham come off the pile?"

"You know you might want to make a half a sandwich. I'm making grandma's meatballs tonight."

"Mom, I'm hungry now."

"That's because it's sliced so thin. It tastes better when they are sliced thin."

"Are you trying to sabotage my sandwich? What kind of an insane person sabotages another person's sandwich? How about answering that one Evil Demon Woman?"

Because he has called her Evil Demon Woman Tess knows he's trying to be nice. She beams at him. "But you have to call Grandma."

"Could you turn the screaming down Mom." He gestures toward the stereo in the living room and the aria coming from it. "I'm kind of tired."

"What time did you get to bed?"

"Mom, please. Please." Tess picks up her pile of bills from the kitchen table and passes through the living room to click the music off with the remote. Then she picks up the portable phone and goes into her bedroom.

"Where's the milk cap Mom? Oh shit!"

Tess hears something spilling. "This is all your fault!" Paul yells. She rises from her bed and goes to lock her bedroom door.

———•◆•———

SEEDING MEMORY

"Look!" Leah said in a low voice to Tess, pointing ahead of them, "it's the crazy flower lady."

"Where? Are you sure?"

Leah pointed to homeless woman up ahead of them—everyone called her the Crazy Flower Lady—when she reappeared each year in the neighborhood, as the cold spring rains drove winter down into the cracks of the wet pavement.

In the warm weather she wandered up and down a certain stretch of Broadway, a spray of gray braids, the color of pussy willows, spread out from the crown of her head, a star of hair guiding her travels. Her long arms held out arrangements of flowers for sale that looked as if they were made of things gathered from neglected meadows as they turned back into woods. Bony branches, loose grasses, dangling tendrils mixed with daffodils, tulips—other densely leafed stems. "Five dollars, just five dollars," she'd hold out her weird, beautiful concoctions.

Women like Leah and Tess bought these bouquets, pleased with themselves that they were willing to approach her, to breathe in her dusty smell, to brave contact with the untamed. The flowers made them courageous. That, and the fact that her wild presence horrified them. She was so dirty—her crazy hair so startlingly done up—she drew the women to her. Stunning them into closeness with her.

Tonight, though, all of the Flower Lady's resplendent brown glow had gone. Instead, she was at her ashy worst; this is the way she looked when she first appeared every March. Her hair in this season, instead of being an array of points, was matted and filthy. Her clothes were dirty and she was encased in a filthy blanket, dusted with withered, musty leaves: a creature that had emerged from hibernation. Leah and Tess kept a careful distance away from her as she dragged a cart behind her that held rusty shovels and other tools sticking out at all angles.

"Where do you think she goes in the winter?" Tess asked.

"I don't know." Leah pointed behind them to the park. "Maybe down there in the old train tunnels."

"You think she lives there in the winter?" Tess asked.

"I guess. I know she refuses to use the shelter on 114th Street."

"How do you always know these things?"

"I once stopped by 114th Street to ask one of the administrators if he could get her into their facility. He said he had tried repeatedly."

Tess knew that the Crazy Flower Lady came and went, but she didn't remember exactly when. This was the kind of information Leah seemed always to know with certainty. A self-appointed observer of the neighborhood, she always seemed to know when a new wine store was coming in, where the old shoe repair shop had been, as well as details of the new police policy on street peddlers.

Before Leah spotted the Flower Lady, she and Tess had been walking on one side of the triangle of Straus Park, the shade of danger giving it dark appeal as they went along the edge. They were on their way home from a Friends of Riverside Park meeting where Leah and Tess had just presented their plans for the plot of ground in the park that had been theirs to cultivate for the last few years. The moon was low on the horizon. Spring threatened its arrival with a swirl of dust up from the sidewalk, then flashes of crisp air. Their conversation had just shifted from whether they should plant purple irises behind the hyacinths in their garden plot that ran along the promenade in Riverside Park, to why Leah's daughter, Zoe, seemed to be, in her thirteenth year, always furious at her mother.

"She claims that her friends are allowed to stay out until midnight. She's too young. I can't stand it. Having Sam was too much for her. She's never going to forgive me." Leah had had a baby the year before, when Zoe was twelve.

"Sam is just her excuse. Don't you remember how we felt about our mothers at this age—how utterly stupid they seemed to us?" Tess said.

"But we aren't our mothers. Aren't we different?"

"C'mon. You know how it is. Yes, and God I hope not," Tess said lightly, sensibly. It was not her son Paul being discussed just then. She could be reasonable, even detached. Leah and Tess had been friends since high school. They'd sat at each other's Formica kitchen tables, they'd sat on the chenille bedspreads of their childhood bedrooms; they had seen each other through high school heartbreaks and, later on, abortions.

"Our mothers lived on another planet. I remember when Richie broke up with me, and I was weeping in my bedroom, and my mother said to me, 'Don't give him the satisfaction.' All she ever worried about was how things would look to someone peering through the window. Even in the privacy of my bedroom her measure was that an outsider seeing me crying would think that someone had gotten the better of her family. Now Zoe is always saying things like, 'Do you have to laugh that way? You sound like a donkey. And your teeth look so big when you throw your head back like that.' I promised myself that the one thing I would make sure a daughter of mine would know was that I would always listen if she wanted to talk. But the only thing she wants to say to me is, 'Leave me alone!'" Leah's elegant face was tensed. Her face had beauty that yearned for quiet and calm, the expression she had when she was walking Pazzo, taking photographs, rocking Sammy, all of its quiet planes at rest. When she worried, the tension crawled along the wide cheekbones into the crevices around her slender nose, the mouth tightening.

The subject of her recent work had been domesticity on the street, particularly her neighborhood, 106th–116th, Amsterdam to deep inside Riverside Park. Someone reaching down to pick up a piece of paper from the sidewalk as if it were on the floor of her living room, the Cuban magazine shop owner sitting in a folding chair reading a newspaper, smoking a cigarette, using the standing ashtray at his side. More and more her photographs had come to be of homeless men and women against the backdrop of the plenty she and her friends took for granted. As Leah took these photographs, the complaining she and her friends engaged in about the frantic pace that attended their abundance became a din in her ears.

After Sam had been born, Leah had stopped taking photographs, concentrating instead on the actual people instead of the images of them she had been freezing. Last autumn the Flower Lady had become the particular object of her focus.

In the fall Leah watched as everything around the Flower Lady slowly disintegrated. First there were fewer flower arrangements offered. For a while she sold damaged vegetables she'd lifted unchallenged from the bins on the sidewalks of Broadway markets. "Get the freshest corn you'll ever eat. Get it right here and now." Her appearances grew less frequent, her presence dimmer. Then she'd disappear as if she had fallen off the edge of the year.

When everyone living on the West Side hurried out of the cold into their warm apartments, a large silence was left on Broadway where the woman's crazy presence had been all through the spring and summer.

Then early each spring, as she had done tonight, she seemed to rise again out of some dark winter hole, looking crazier and more disheveled than ever.

"Where do you think she learned to arrange flowers like that?" Tess asked the dark air.

"She told me once that she learned it on her island," Leah whispered. "She calls herself Alba, which means dawn. I'm the sun rising,' she told me."

"You talked to her?" Tess asked. "What else did she say?"

"I asked her where she got her flowers. She said that the flower stores and restaurants saved stuff for her. I guess she *could* get some stuff like that."

Everyone in the neighborhood knew that the Flower Lady stole some of the flowers she used from the plots that Leah, Tess, and their fellow committee members so carefully planned, tended, and raised. She'll probably steal the new irises we're going to grow this year, Leah was thinking, when the Flower Lady, walking in front of the two women, whipped her long head around and stared at them for a moment as if she had picked up Leah's thoughts.

"You leave me alone," she screamed. "I don't bother you."

Her eyes seemed to be looking in different directions, and out of her mouth sounds were coming that were not quite human, a moaning, almost neighing sound, somewhere between a fury and a whimper, "Where is she? What you do with her? I want to know! Where is my girl?" She started to rush at them.

The two women linked arms and darted across the street, their eyes wide with dread and awe, enjoying the thrill of it. The string of yellow lights turning red up Broadway brought them back into their reality as they hurried into the Westside Market. When they emerged, the Flower Lady was nowhere in sight, and the two women walked quickly up Broadway to get home before they could run into her again.

When Leah walked into her apartment, her daughter, Zoe, met her at the door holding out Sam in front of her, saying, "Your baby's been looking for you. You know my botany project is due tomorrow. I haven't even started my myth reading."

My first baby, or my last? Leah wondered, though she could see that the dirty smears on Sam's fat cheeks confirmed Zoe's pronouncement. Last year when Leah told Zoe that she was pregnant again, Zoe had at first been ecstatic, but then slowly, quietly moved away from Leah. As Sam turned from a newborn into an infant, sitting up and looking around, demanding more and more of Leah, Zoe had moved out of her mother's orbit, finally wrapping herself in her own moons.

Leah sat down with Sam in her arms, watching Zoe stalk out of the room back to her interrupted homework. Aaron, Leah's husband, came out of their bedroom. "Hi babe." He bent down to kiss Leah. He looked sleepy, relieved about something.

"Couldn't you have picked Sam up?" Leah asked. "Zoe's having a fit."

"I was just going to get him and then the phone rang. It was just a couple of minutes ago—it was my mother, convinced she was having another heart attack. I had to ask Zoe to get the baby."

Aaron was upset. Leah always assumed he had handled whatever related to the family badly. "Look, I'm going to watch television. This is one too many angry women for me tonight." Aaron went off to their bedroom. Zoe was angry that her mother hadn't stayed home to help her with her botany project, and Sam was whimpering. Now Aaron was angry.

Later, after Zoe's homework was done and Sam had had his eleven o'clock feeding, Leah went to join Aaron in their bedroom. She had decided to ignore the earlier tension, hoping he would too.

"Arele, you know that lady who sells flower arrangements on Broadway sometimes, with the flowers she picks from the park?'

"Maybe." He twisted toward her.

"You know, the one with this crazy hairdo. She's always out there in the summer? With these incredible flower arrangements—as if she'd been trained by some Japanese wildflower specialist; they have vines hanging and sprigs of purple thingies arranged with delicate tree branches?"

"Is she one of the homeless?" He had one arm propping his sleepy head. Is she going to take up another homeless person? Aaron was wondering, touched and irritated—Why?

"Yeah, sure. She must be." Leah lay down against her soft cotton sheets, into her firm pillows. He hasn't noticed her? she wondered, pulling up the thick comforter, blanketing their bodies with designs of muted greens and large soft-petaled red and pink flowers—the pleasure and guilt of having rising toward her with the hem of the comforter—thinking about the woman curling up in piles of decaying leaves wrapped in her dirty white comforter. And Leah wondered—Where?

One afternoon in the late fall, Leah had followed the woman's scent up Broadway, past Bank Street Bookstore, University

Housewares, past all the markers of the normal comings and goings of the neighborhood. Leah, intrigued by her as always, decided that day to try to find out where she was going when she left the perimeters Leah knew. She had followed the woman into the twilight of Riverside Park. But once they were on the promenade the woman had headed down toward a tunnel in a part of the park where Leah never permitted anyone in her family to go. That part of the park didn't belong to people like Leah and her children. It didn't belong to the Parks Department or even to the city. It belonged to the homeless, the way the homeless should have belonged to another time. When Leah had seen where the woman was headed, she had turned back and retreated to her apartment.

The next weeks after Leah and Tess had first seen the Flower Lady on Broadway brought waves of cold rain, relieved only by wet snow and mean, bullying winds, pushing people around who were used to only being pushed around by one another. The rain finally warmed to the merely cold, readying the trees, but people still hurried through the streets to get where they were going, wearing down jackets, Arctic fleece, scarves, and hats. Spring just wasn't going to come this year. On one of those wet days late in March, Zoe came to her mother and said, "It's come."

"The stuff we ordered from Crew?"

"No, you know, the thing, blood . . ." She stood in the doorway, waiting for her mother to understand.

Leah put down the laundry she was about to fold and turned to look at her daughter. Her straight, light brown hair curtained the sober brown eyes peering out, where she waited, under the cover of her hair for a response. Leah stared at her standing there, framed in the doorway, her long legs balancing a delicate torso, her neck bent, her eyes looking just past her mother to where the light came in her mother's bedroom window, then noncommittally at her mother's shoulder. Zoe had on her usual jeans, a sweater the color of jade—in twilight between green and greener—that lights her way. It was as if Leah hadn't seen her for months, as though she had gone away and come home from a trip, grown taller, more poised. Now she seemed to stand waiting to step out onto a dance floor alone, with people in a large circle waiting expectantly for that single step to give them back some piece of memory. "Zouiska," Leah says, "my Zoo . . ." Zoe had been called Ziz, when she had been little, sometimes Zizzy, then Zizster, which became Zooishness when Zoe had been two.

"Mom," Zoe warned, peering out from behind her hair.

Leah sat down on the bed looking up at Zoe. She felt the mattress give in to her weight, her body, the way her daughter wouldn't. "Zoe," she pleaded, "let me . . ."

"We have to go and get stuff. You know those things."

"Okay, sure. You want me to help you choose?"

"Not choose, just buy. Okay?"

Leah went to get Sam. "I'll be ready in a couple of minutes."

Leah caught up with her by the elevator after she'd woken Sam from his nap, wrapped him up in layers, and tucked him into a snugly. Sam had whimpered briefly in his sleep while being moved around, but then went back into a deep slumber against his mother. As a baby Zoe had screamed furiously when Leah had done something like that to her. That fury had turned to a keen alertness once she had become mobile and could do things for herself, and then lately that awareness had turned on her mother's inadequacies. Sam just waited for things to turn out right for him. Leah reached out her hand, put her arm around Zoe's shoulders, and started to twirl the soft auburn strands at the girl's neck.

"Mom please, don't do that," she said, in very dignified tones. "Don't baby me."

"Where did you want to do this errand?" Leah asked dropping her arms immediately.

"Don't you *know* where to go?"

Out on Broadway the wind was finally blowing away the rain, and the sun slipped in and out between the blue-black, fast-moving clouds. The streets, still wet, glistened with wet and sun. Sam stirred against Leah.

"Have you thought about what you'd like to use?" Leah asked.

Zoe looked up at her mother with gratitude. "Yeah, I think I know, but I wanted to ask you one thing." Her mother had finally stumbled onto the right tone. What did I just do? Leah asked herself.

When they emerged from the drugstore, there was something happening on the corner. Although people hadn't actually stopped, they seemed to be slowing down as they walked. Zoe let her mother hold her hand briefly as they left the drug store. Leah could see that the Flower Lady was making a kind of ritual dance. She moved in a large circle, one arm held out at her side, a purple scarf rippling like a flag alongside her.

"You'll see, you'll see, I'm right. Just wait." She seemed even crazier, but more beautiful. She looked taller, a large wild goddess, as she stretched her arms out into the circle she made. Leah lately had begun to use her radar to make sure to avoid her. Today her hair was arranged, a silver crown. She had on only one layer of loose flowing clothing that floated behind her, trailing her dance. There were no flowers, no vegetables, no cart. Just her, possessed of pleasure.

"Mom, look at her."

"She's beautiful today."

"Mom!" Zoe rolled her eyes and laughed at her insane mother and then leaned over to kiss her brother. "Hi, Sammy rabbit."

In April, days of rain, drizzle, mist captured Manhattan—gently wiping away the last of dingy winter. The piles of dirt and debris that had been hidden and preserved by the snow began to be readied by the rain for the brooms that would come to sweep them away in the next days.

One Saturday filled with something between a fog and a mist, when most people were inside, Tess and Leah were scheduled to be part of the Riverside Park cleanup. They knew only a few members would show up, but they were glad they'd put themselves among the few. The mist seemed to have risen from under them as much as it came down around them. Walking through this primal matrix connected them to everything this moist tissue touched: cars, buildings, lampposts. The two women descended into Riverside Park to wait in the long ribbon of park for the others to arrive. Lying at the edge of the hard blocks of buildings in which they lived, the park was an offering of contrast. The trees were preparing to canopy into the color of new limes. The women sat silently waiting for the others to arrive. The mist held them both together and apart.

From down below in the park two women rose up toward Leah and Tess—the Crazy Flower Lady and a slender-ankled girl. Neither Leah nor Tess had ever seen the Flower Lady with anyone else. As the Flower Lady and her companion came closer, it was apparent that there was some resemblance, more a memory of what the Crazy Flower Lady could have looked like in an ancient past. The girl's long neck stretched out. Whereas the Flower Lady's hair was carefully arranged in that snakelike hairdo, the girl's hair was boisterous—an extreme mass of brown curls, brushed with gold. One or two flowers were stuck into her mass of straw curls. Her large, dark eyes disguised whatever she thought as she walked at the woman's side. Who was she, and where had she come from? They passed Leah and Tess's bench wrapped in their own mists.

By early June, the flowers in Leah and Tess's plot were emerging. It looked as though the garden they envisioned in the cold light of winter was going to surprise them. Roses, iris, hyacinths, crocus, violets, narcissus. What they had worked out so carefully in their heads and on paper, over many cups of tea in January, came to life on its own terms: plants growing taller than expected or in different shades of color—what had been conceived as long, intense stalks of purple came up in subtle shades of pale blue.

   Leah noticed that the Flower Lady and the young woman Leah now accepted as *the Daughter* had been digging in the meridian at 110th Street and Broadway. No one seemed to notice they were even there. They looked like two farmwomen, at first bent over with hoes, digging up the soil, then weeding the small neat rows they had hatched out of the land, caught between the two streams of constant traffic. For them what flowed by might as well have been two streams. One of them might unbend, one hand rubbing the back of a hip, looking off to the fruit stands across the street, or into the farmer's market stands as if they were looking out across fields of wheat. Though they weren't offering bouquets yet, the neighborhood seemed marked by their presence.

Between Leah and Zoe things had gotten worse.

One day Leah resolved to leave her daughter alone. She knew Zoe needed more independence. But this attempt at neutrality seemed to incite even greater hostility. "Don't you even care whether I make the team?" she stormed, when Leah had carefully refrained from asking how the tryouts went. The next couple of days she asked solicitous questions about teachers, coaches, girlfriends.

"Mom, why do you even care about this stuff? This is my life, not yours. You're always at me." Leah felt as if she were constantly fiddling with a dial trying to tune into some radio station that was out of her range. She turned more and more to Sam who accepted her as if she belonged to him. This guilty pleasure led Leah to the certainty that she'd better do something about Zoe.

"Why would you force this on her?" Aaron's pale, handsome features were lining up in disbelief. He was trying to contain feelings that bordered on irritation. "You're just going to drive her away from you. You're repeating your own mother's mistakes."

"Don't say that. I came to you because I'm worried. Whenever I open up to you and tell you how nervous I am, you make sure to explain to me how I'm screwing up. Can't you just support me in this?"

"I thought you wanted my opinion." He sat down in a chair at the dining room table. "What do you want me to say? I think it's a bad idea."

"But she knows she's not allowed to be here with a boy when you and I aren't home. I've found her in her room with Laz twice in the last two weeks. I couldn't bring myself to tell you about the last time. I found them here alone. The door was closed. They didn't even come out immediately after I heard them and yelled to Zoe that I was home."

"What do you expect from them? They're teenagers."

"Zoe's too young for this. And she won't even talk to me about what they were doing in there. If I even go near her she gets up and then just has to leave the room. Sometimes I think I smell cigarette smoke in her hair."

Aaron knew that if a hint of a problem arose, Leah thought immediate action was called for. It didn't matter if it were the super not treating one of the doormen right or a homeless man living in a cardboard box in the snow, Leah felt it was up to her to do something. But usually with her children she was sensible and down to earth. Slower to react. Before Sam, she had had the confidence to wait and see how things unfolded, to let Zoe find her own way of slipping her mother the necessary information.

Aaron also knew that the closeness Zoe and Leah had known had pressed on Zoe. Sam's birth gave Zoe the excuse she needed to break away.

He leaned across the table, put his hand over Leah's. "We knew it wasn't going to be easy on her when you got pregnant. Why are you so surprised?"

"It's one thing to be reasonable abstractly. But when she looks at me with such hatred when I snuggle her brother, I don't know . . ."

"But to make her go to *therapy*. I just don't think you can push that on a kid. What did she say?"

"She said she knew all about that stuff from her friends. And she knew it didn't help any of them. That it was stupid. Were you and I getting a divorce? I promised her that no we weren't, and it wasn't stupid, and I asked her to do it as a special favor to me— just once. I would buy her whatever the next piece of equipment she'd asked me for a couple of weeks ago."

Aaron put his hands up to his eyes and pressed his fingers hard into his eyes, squeezed shut against this wrong his wife's earnestness was pressing on his family. He looked up at her shaking his head.

"What? What!" Leah needed the right response from him.

"Leah. How could that possibly be a good idea?"

"I know. I know. What should I do?"

Leah's old therapist was on a tour of China and didn't get back until late July, by which time baby Sam, garden plots, the Flower Lady's meridian plantings, and Zoe's disgust had all grown. Corn, as tall as the Flower Lady, dusty from the traffic, was growing in the middle of the island. The two of them set up shop every day just in front of their garden. There were two folding chairs, one with an awning shade, a small table where the Flower Lady worked on her flower arrangements when she wasn't in her garden. The purple scarf was a tablecloth draped over the table now. The girl, hair in neat cornrows, assisted her. She offered a branch or stem for approval. But the Flower Lady shook her head, "Longer, I need a longer one." Leah found excuses to pass their way. She stalled, making small talk so she could eavesdrop on their talk to one another. The Flower Lady was stern. Took no back talk.

"Did you speak to the minister man like I said?"

"Yes, Ma'am." The girl bent her head, the neat lines of braids lined up, and looked down nervously at the rips in her sneakers. "I asked the man at the church. He said we could pick the flowers up tonight after services."

"Did you ask him the time?"

"He said right after vespers. I told you."

"Don't you 'I told you' me, girl! You hear me."

"Yes, Ma'am. I'm sorry, Ma'am. Right at seven thirty we're to come by."

"Okay then. Come and help me with this one." The girl's eyes darted to the Flower Lady's face briefly before they zoomed out into traffic where the cars flowed by.

When the day came for Leah and Zoe to meet at the therapist's office, Sam had had a fever for several nights running and had been up crying much of the night before. Leah was exhausted. The babysitter was late. She was going to meet Zoe in front of Barnes and Noble at Eighty-Second Street. Zoe was coming from her dance classes at the Lucy Moses School. The idea was for them to walk quietly over to the therapist's office on West End Avenue. Leah had been planning her remarks to Zoe. For once she would be calm and friendly, whatever Zoe said or did. But now she wasn't sure she'd even get to Barnes and Noble by the time they should have been entering the therapist's office. Instead, Leah was walking in the street sliding along the edge of the parked cars, looking over her shoulder every few steps for a yellow cab. All of them had off duty lights on. It was time for the shifts to turn over. A gypsy cab screeched to the curb dropping off a passenger, and Leah raced in gratefully behind the passenger's exit. Loud reggae was blasting from the speakers in back as they bucked their way down Broadway. But at Ninety-Ninth Street, traffic started to crawl. Leah kept counting her money, deciding to get out of the cab, then deciding to give it another minute. It was probably just a triple-parked car. "Could you *please* turn down the music?" She found herself saying more shrilly than she meant to.

"You don't like good music?" He shook his head.

She stuffed a wad of bills at the driver, so there wouldn't be a dispute about the fare and leapt out of the cab. When she got to Ninety-Seventh Street she saw that the street was cordoned off from Foot Locker to the meridian. All the traffic was being diverted to turn west. She started out into the street to get by the yellow plastic ribbons.

"Hey Lady. You can't," one large cop said to her. His partner looked off over her head.

"What? Why not?" Leah looked at her watch. It was four nineteen.

"Get back, I said." The cop didn't look at her directly. He gestured for her to get out of the way, a dismissive wave of his hand.

I hate this city, Leah thought.

She started again into the street. Two women who looked Caribbean were standing there, each with a carriage in front of her. They were shaking their heads slowly, mouths pulled back looking beyond the ribbons to a car smashed into the window of the store. The red neon border that framed each window was twisted and broken.

"What happened? How did that car get on the sidewalk?" Leah asked one of them.

"Jumped the curb, nobody knows . . . a baby carriage got pushed into the window when it came up on the sidewalk. The babysitter was just taken by the ambulance. They're saying the baby died."

Leah looked at the large, brass, leaf earrings on either side of the one woman's face. Looked at the woman's friend's lips pressed tightly together, then down at the two babies who were in their charge. One was a pale little boy, the other a tiny Chinese baby girl. They were slapping at one another. Leah turned to walk away. Then walked back. "Thanks for explaining."

They looked back at her and nodded. "We're hoping it's not people we know from the park."

"Oh God, I hope not." Leah turned shocked that it could be the baby of anyone who someone knew, that it could be a known baby and walked down Ninety-Seventh Street toward West End Avenue. It was four thirty now. She was going to be very late.

When she arrived at Barnes and Noble Zoe looked both furious and terrified. "This is so lame. Where have you been, Mom? You're totally late."

Leah walked over and put her arms around her daughter, put her head down on her daughter's bird's wing of a shoulder, and started to cry. "A baby died," she wept into her daughter's hair.

"What? What! Sam!"

"No, no," Leah's breath was barely coming out. "No a baby. Not our Sammy. On my way downtown. A baby was killed in front of Foot Locker."

Zoe jerked her head forward in small staccato tugs and then swung her head back, and that released her fury. She began to swing at her mother's body, making wild angry contact, pounding on her mother. "How could you? I thought you meant ours!" She leaned into her mother sobbing. And stayed there.

Leah enclosed her, absorbing the convulsing relief. Zoe's hair smelled of Pantene conditioner. Underneath that smell, her own hair oils were subtly there. This smell was incising itself into Leah's brain as that combination of sorrow and love that, for Leah, Zoe's connection to her brother would mean from now on.

They walked up West End Avenue. Leah's face loosed from the tension she'd lived with for months. She looked exhausted, undone, as if she'd worked in a field for hours that day.

"I can't walk by the accident, Mom," Zoe said turning them toward West End Avenue, where Leah stopped and called her therapist to say, "I'll call and explain tonight. Right now we can't." Zoe didn't ask who her mother was phoning or what had happened about the therapy. But she walked at her mother's side up West End Avenue as if she belonged there.

When they got to 110th and Broadway, the Flower Lady and the girl had their small table set up in front of the vitamin shop selling their products. The girl held out a wreath of branches twisted into a circle, small spiraling tendrils escaping the circle connecting the wreath to the air around it. Small ears of corn were fixed to the wreath. "Mom?" Zoe asked.

On the walk uptown it was the silence that emerged between them that had the quality of resolution. The quiet between her and her daughter held them together, so she simply nodded her head and handed over her wallet. Zoe hung the wreath on her bedroom door, which Leah tried to keep in focus, when she closed that door to stop herself from looking in at what lay beyond.

For Halloween that year Zoe asked to go to a party with Laz. Could she stay out until eleven thirty? Leah said, "Let me talk to Dad," which Zoe knew meant yes. Dad thought life was like Sunnyside in the fifties—easygoing, no real danger. Not for him, not for his. Any teenage girl was able to see that this just meant Mom needed time to breathe through the idea.

Zoe bought new clothes, was allowed to put a rinse in her hair, making it glow a shade of hot copper. Leah was so involved in keeping herself in check she only realized at the last minute that she'd forgotten to buy the candy for the children who would be arriving at her door soon and ran out to Westside Market late that afternoon. A green storm was coming up from the river, a hint of forgotten summer held in abeyance until the release today.

Leah saw the Flower Lady standing in the dry cornstalks on the meridian. She was ripping out the old cornstalks left dying there.

The girl wasn't with her. Leah realized reluctantly that she had to pass her to buy the candy. She heard those strange sounds escaping from the woman in small bursts. The smell of old stalks and dusty soil came up with the plants as they were yanked out of the wet surface. The Flower Lady turned and looked directly at Leah from behind the benches. "She'll be back, don't you worry. They *got* to give her back to me. She's *my* daughter!"

———•———

OCCASIONALLY

David sits in his chair, which sometimes he calls his yacht. "I'm going to read on my yacht." It's big, a beaten up old leather thing he inherited from his grandmother. He's had it since college. His mother had it reupholstered once for him for his twenty-fifth birthday—by now *that* leather too has been worn into a thing of the past. The chair knows his body; his body knows the chair. He has just put down volume 4, part 3 of a first edition of Needham's *Science and Civilization in China*, which Sage has given him for Christmas. She has found eleven volumes by now, a few at a time. She's building the set for him. David intends to spend years reading them.

Sage is in her chair, a smaller, simpler chair. She gets the ottoman.

A few days after Christmas, it's only 7:46 at night, but it has the dark quiet of late night. It snowed that afternoon. A wind sweeps the snow around outside. Now the sweetest hour has arrived, the one to be held onto and held off at the same time. Sage is wearing a mossy green velvet bathrobe, one she has owned for so many years. The garment always makes her feel she's still at her peak. David is wearing long underwear.

They are drinking a bottle of Italian red, one they discovered on a recent trip to Italy, a Piemontese—Dolcetto di Dogliani. Its rich taste is enhanced by its dark red color. They are nibbling on calamata olives, cheddar cheese that has been out of the fridge for hours, and roasted almonds.

Ella's voice swells and abducts the air, "I'll sing to him, each spring to him." The fact that it is utterly not spring inhabits the room.

Richard's death is not here; the bank's complicated negotiations around the recent real estate deal never began. For the moment, the light in their living room glows from the many tall candles that sit in front of a large old gilded mirror that Sage found on the street, so there are twice as many flickering flames radiating into Ella's song, the wine they are drinking, the fact that they get to sit here together, apart from everything not in this room.

"I used to wake up in the middle of the night, and I'd hear my parents' whispering on the other side of the wall. I never made out the words," Sage puts down her glass of wine, "but the wash of their voices was the most consoling sound."

———•———

PERFECT HATRED

Sometimes, for what seemed like no apparent reason, Tess took a complete and intense dislike to someone the moment she saw them. Another woman, her age, moving into her line of sight wearing a blue business suit might look at herself in a mirror approvingly when Tess thought that the suit was so straight it should be made of metal. Or a younger woman wearing a tight black dress and sunglasses might arrive at a dinner party contemptuous of everything that wasn't her. These episodes brought up a surge of hatred in Tess that surprised and satisfied her each time it happened.

Tess watched these strangers surreptitiously so that she could position her virtue above theirs. Restaurants and hotel lobbies were among the best locations for these occasions.

Tess and Max were at Doc's, a small restaurant near Lake Waramaug in Connecticut. Surrounded by windows, the dining room felt like a sun porch. White cloths covered plain wooden tables. The only other decoration was a mix of odd chairs in various styles and shapes, some left in their original brown wood color, others painted a shade of green, evoking old schoolhouses and apples. This mix of plainness and design made you feel you were in a place of sophistication and unpretentiousness measured in equal parts. There was an air of modest ceremony to the room, congenial to appetite.

The room, though, was a minor pleasure compared to the taste of the food. It was a combination of Old World peasant food—vegetables, pastas, beans with the soft matrix of their juices combined, the gush, Tess liked to call it—and hip America at its most vital—lively touches of unusual combinations of herbs and legumes, as if they had been grown from seed that morning. Each bite brought these worlds together, deep, rich, and ancient, fresh, new, and young, a fine response to hunger.

There's a simple purity here in the white and green room. Food and drink along with the leisurely taking of measure and rank.

Doc's was quiet, only three tables with guests. The waitress, a young, chaste-looking woman with sandy hair wearing jeans and a white linen shirt pointed to a couple of tables. Most were still empty. They could have whichever they wanted. Tess hesitated. Max quickly chose the one nearest the kitchen. There were others by windows and this one was right across from the entrance. Tess resisted her impulse to overrule his choice.

They settled in, smug in their contentment. Above and behind Tess's head was a shelf that held wineglasses, bread and knives, stuff prepared for the night's service. Tess could see now that Max's choice of table was better than the one she would have made. The floor tilted slightly up at this end of the room, and there was space around the table—it was in the clear. The room spread out in front of them. They would watch it fill.

"Can I open that wine for you?" The waitress arrived and handed them menus. She reached behind Tess's head to the shelf, and grabbing a corkscrew, opened the bottle efficiently, pouring for Max first.

Max lifted his glass to the waitress, toasting her service. Tess could see that Max had won her with that gesture. The waitress moved off skillfully to the door to greet other customers.

Tess and Max had driven up from New York that night for an extended weekend of rest and reading. Their son, Paul, was on a school trip. They were free of all work and duty; even the renovations on the small food and wine shop, Questa è la Vita, that they owned, and Tess ran, were behind them. Tess had been a school-teacher for many years. "I'm sick of taking care of other people's children," she had said when they decided to start up the business. It had taken five solid years of hard work, catering to the needs of her Upper West Side neighbors. Sometimes it felt more like a set-tlement house for the overworked middle class. Everyone pulled up the small stools strewn around the store, sat drinking their cof-fee, talking. Occasionally Tess wished they would clear the aisles but that she knew that was what made her business work. She chatted with the children, recommended the right prepared pasta for a rainy Friday night, and mentioned a great movie to go with it—fennel and orange salad going with chicken cutlets with extra Reggiano Parmigiano sprinkled over the chicken at the end. "After the kids go to sleep, watch *I Am Love*," she'd whisper to a mother. "Make sure they are really asleep though." All of the food was, if not a family recipe, one inspired by the food she grew up cooking, eating, and licking off of her fingers.

Max helped out at the store on weekends. He often knew just which food would please some of the customers, sometimes bet-ter than Tess. Say the cold seafood salad for Mr. Rovit when he needed to be cheered up on Friday nights with something a little special but never pretentious. It was worth the little extra without being silly.

Tess was customer queen. She stood behind the counter, wait-ing for a moment when she could find a way to say something kind. She assured them that she was worse than they and that they were in this together. Young mothers coming in with small children on a rainy day provided Tess's opportunity. She knew they would begin by explaining their need for relief from these long days. Tess saw these moments as her opening. "When Paul was little I used to give him four baths on a rainy day. And I didn't care if he watched TV from six in the morning until he went to sleep, as long as we both survived." She had no shame. She lied, concocted details to suit whoever stood in front of her. It was her world. She invented and owned it.

It even looked like Questa è la Vita was finally going to make some actual money. But they were tired. It had taken a great deal out of both of them these last years. But this weekend they had a room with a fireplace at an old inn on a river, and it would be only about eating other's people's cooking, drinking good wine, and not talking business. She was going to pretend to be a regular person.

At the door of Doc's, two older gay men were making their entrance. The young waitress turned to them, gesturing with her hand: the room was theirs. The slim one wearing the cravat was boyish looking, even though his translucent skin was finely lined. One could see he had looked the same since he was seventeen: blond with brilliant blue eyes; his eyes had been his passport out of a box he had left behind. He fingered the silk at his neck as he looked around the room to see where they would sit. Then he strode across the dining room, settling in reluctantly at the table Tess would have chosen for him, just across from Tess and Max, by a window. His companion followed him.

The other man, who was older, had what had once been a large, handsome head. Now his loose flesh had betrayed his beauty. His shaming body was carefully draped in fine wools, cotton, and silk. He had the look of a deposed king who was sorry for all the trouble he'd caused, was filled with resignation. Tess liked him immediately.

The Boy had settled on a table as if he were granting a privilege, but it was a remark Tess heard the Boy address to his companion that made her feel a distinct dislike of him. "Whatever you do please don't tell the Monty story again." When he looked around to check the room, his eyes scanned past Tess and Max. Probably the Boy would have been Tess's object of disgust for the night if the *other one* hadn't arrived a little later.

Doc's was filling rapidly. In between sizing up the Boy and the Old King, she and Max had been anticipating the drinking of their wine and conferring about what they would eat, a ritual they enjoyed as they watched the pageant. Looking over the possibilities in the menu, Tess could feel her appetite take shape.

A middle-aged couple stepped into the light. He was long, neat, and bald. But it was the woman who caught Tess's attention. The woman, probably Tess's age, had on black crepe pants and a white silk shirt, with a gold necklace, two arrows joining together in a point. On her arm were noisy gold bracelets.

Her hair was chemically red, a rich bronze color that had no relation to actual hair. This hair was carefully coifed into a large bronzed helmet of curls, curls lacquered for battle. She had the sculpted head of a Greek warrior. Her lips opened over her white teeth, which were set wide, and she had the relaxed look of someone who anticipates with easy assurance that her appetites will be satisfied. Even her walk annoyed Tess. The woman moved with a confidence so complete it could only come from arrogance. No one was worth that much.

"Thinks she's all that," Tess muttered, quoting Sharif, their delivery boy from the store. Tess's story object had just arrived.

The woman sashayed across the room headed toward Boy and the King sitting at the table across from Tess and Max's. Baldy followed demurely. Normally, friendship with a gay couple would have made Tess more kindly inclined. The woman lifted her hand beneficently over the two men they were joining for dinner, "John, can you forgive us?" Conferring her presence upon them, she insisted on mercy.

Max watched Tess. A story was being conceived, about the table, but especially about the woman. Max could see that Tess was making a swift character analysis of the woman's presence, but he'd have to wait until they were back at the inn to hear the full narrative.

Tess and Max always chose what they ate carefully and with pleasure. With one dish from each course, they'd be able to taste everything. Max suggested they begin with mixed green salad with goat cheese, red onions, pecans, and a citrus dressing. Tess was wondering if the pecans would go well with the greens and the goat cheese. But Max had suggested it, and Tess felt she had used up her large capacity for bossiness for the night, back at the inn. She was being more than usually cooperative to make up for what she had done earlier.

"Yes, we'll have that to start," Tess agreed conscientiously. Max raised a hand to signal the waitress they were ready.

"How do you manage this menu?" Tess asked the waitress when she came over. She wanted to establish that they were the right kind of people, fans. "It's always splendid."

"Oh you know, we keep slaves in the kitchen chained to the stove," the waitress said cheerfully. "He *is* good, isn't he?" the waitress smiled and continued. She meant the chef. "He plans the menu every week, and we get fresh deliveries every day."

"How about we have the polenta with Gorgonzola after that?" Max leaned across the table smiling at Tess.

At this dish too she hesitated. The polenta would be fried, which meant fat, but again she yielded; she was determined not to always have her way. Max guessed that Tess was still atoning.

The inn had been dark when they arrived earlier in the evening. It was Wednesday, and it was clear they were the only guests. The innkeeper, Lucas, had shown them to a room with a king-sized brass bed and a fireplace. But the brass of the bedstead was fake, and the spread had many white ruffles. Tess had noticed that the rooms weren't locked, so as soon as Lucas and Max descended to register them she had slipped around the dim hallways peering into the other rooms. She found a small, quiet blue room with a fireplace and two chairs sitting in front of it.

When Max came back upstairs she began to hurry him around the rooms, "Wait till you see. Look here."

Max didn't like this particularity of Tess's. They had to buy the red plaid pillowcases. No, he couldn't have the white phone; it would look silly on his antique desk. That Valentine's card would never do for his mother. She would think Max didn't love her. He found this trait of Tess's wearisome. But he knew it would eat at her all weekend if they were in the wrong room.

"Which one, Tess? Decide." They could hear Lucas ascending the stairs.

His thin, mournful face appeared at the top of the stairs.

"Would it be a problem for us to stay in this room instead? I've looked around a bit." Tess indicated the smaller blue room, smiling apologetically.

Max joined in, helping her with his best courtly manner, the

Old World behind his Bronx upbringing, "Would it be terribly inconvenient?"

The young man's shoulders sank just a little, "Well, we were supposed to have someone coming for that room in two days."

"Could we have it till then?" Tess pressed.

"It costs more than the other one," Lucas said sadly, "more than what I told you on the telephone."

"Oh, that's not a problem," Max and Tess stepped on each other's words, hoping to make up for Tess' transgression.

Max wished she didn't care so much about these kinds of things. It meant life could disappoint her so easily. Why can't she relax and enjoy herself? he thought, as they sipped their wine.

The salad arrived, with lots of pecans. The greens were baby new, not a blemish on a single curled leaf. The dressing was tangy but delicate. The pecans crunched against the virgin greens. The wine was warming into its full taste. Tess took a long slow sip of wine.

The Greek rose now to make her way to the Ladies Room. Head held high, she stopped to check herself in the mirror by the door. Her necklace was slightly askew. She centered the arrows to point directly at her sternum. But as soon as she turned away from the mirror the arrows shifted back to the left. Max watched Tess watching her.

"Don't you think we have to try the lamb sausage?" He pulled her attention back to their table. The menu said it was prepared with garlic, white beans with rosemary, plum tomatoes, and mushrooms. "Isn't Vincent's on Arthur Avenue the only place in New York that makes lamb sausage?" Max said.

"I always thought so." Tess said, picturing the window of Vincent's Meat Shop, the glare of the glass so transparently displaying the slaughtered animals hanging by their hind legs, their heads dangling just above the white enamel pans, the black fur cuffs around the white legs of those creatures reminding her again where lamb sausage comes from. She pushed the window out of her head.

The waitress arrived with their polenta now.

"This place is too much. Make sure you tell the kitchen we think the food is spectacular." Tess was at her most expansive.

Max was laughing as she turned back to him. "I know you're dying to get into that kitchen, but I want to go back to the inn to read my *New Yorker*. So just don't belly up to the stove, like you did that time in Queens." The Greek returned to her table without episode. Even Tess seemed to be too involved with the pleasures of eating and drinking to notice her.

Close to standing room only now. One table cleared and three new people entered. This time, an older woman with two young men. The sons? Tess liked her immediately. She was Goodwoman, tall, worn, filled with reality and exhaustion. Her hair was gray, a good cut, but only her fingers had combed it recently. There were circles under her eyes; her lipstick had been recently applied. In the car, after they parked, Tess thought, certain of her judgment. She wore a coat the color of dusk, and a terra cotta–colored shawl almost falling off her shoulder unnoticed. She had an air of authentic grace and dignity. Both ample and contained, she was the real thing.

A young woman sitting with friends got up from her table as soon as she saw Goodwoman and went over to her. There was admiration, a furrowed brow conveying condolence, "How's . . . ?" There was a hesitating fascination with sorrow.

Although clearly tired, Goodwoman seemed tolerantly grateful for the young woman's concern. "Well he's . . . we think." Her sturdy sons stood there, in their good knit sweaters, sober disciples, staring into space. One was holding a bottle of wine; neither said a word. The young woman's friends also stopped talking and looked on, gravely observing their friend with Goodwoman.

"Is she a niece?" Max asked. He wondered where this older woman would fit into Tess' narrative of the evening.

"Can't be. The boys would be cousins. They're not saying a word to the young woman. Don't even know who she is."

Even the Helmet was looking at Goodwoman and the young

woman. Tess wondered what the Greek could be making of this scene.

The young woman was aware only of Goodwoman, whom she admired and wanted to have a piece of, even if it was a piece of sadness. Goodwoman took this young woman's need of her into her emotional housing with a largeness of spirit.

"I wonder why the sons and the young woman don't know each other."

"Who could she be?" Max thought she might run the secondhand bookstore. Tess thought she might be a psychotherapist.

Tess could hear the Greek Helmet's escort, Baldy, saying, his head turned toward Boy, "If you like movies, you have to admire this one." The King looked nervously around the table, ready to agree with whatever was being said. Max looked across the table. "So which is it?" They were always tuned in like this, no transitions needed. He leaned across the table conspiratorially, "It's probably *The Piano*," he said shaking his head.

"Yes, of course," Tess laughed. She wanted to hate whatever they thought was good.

There were no other clues. The King had found a small opening and was talking about Italy now and where they had to eat when they were in Rome. His jowls shook happily as he spoke. "There's a small gem in Campo di Fiori that you really shouldn't miss."

"Oh yes," the Greek said. "I've eaten there but once you've eaten at the Hassler-Medici in Rome, everything else pales." The King sank back in his chair.

Tess and Max had drunk a couple of glasses of wine by now. The polenta had come and gone; the lamb outdid the other dishes. The spice of the sausage against the beans cooked tenderly, but not into softness, was done just right, held together in a light sauce of tomatoes, garlic, and herbs. They ate to savor, trying not to make themselves unpleasantly overstuffed.

They had a room at the inn, food, and wine. Satisfaction filled them. For the moment, a balance held, and they were neither hungry nor stuffed; the beasts were in the dark; they were in the light.

"This is a feast. You guys are really amazing." Tess begged the waitress to take their compliments seriously, when she passed their table again.

Invoking other pleasures, they were remembering other great vacations by now. "The one on Martha's Vineyard when we borrowed Leah's house."

"That log porch in the Adirondacks."

"That room without the bath in Rome—remember?" They were back to their origins now.

Max's coffee came. The waitress asked if he wanted sugar. "I've got it," Tess said smiling at her. She reached up to the shelf behind her head and got the small bowl with the Equal Max wanted.

"What a great table," the waitress said. Max could see that Tess was really happy now, as if she had been given a prize. Acknowledgment from a waitress was the kind of thing that made Tess' day.

Although she wished she could find a way to smile discreetly at the King, she tried to keep her attention from being drawn back to the Greek Helmet. Why ruin the mood? Just then an older man got up from a corner table. The Greek started waving to him. "There's Doctor Stan," she said in a stagy voice to her table.

Another scene unfolding; Tess looked away, the soul of discretion. Something like a sensation, almost a taste, slipped in Tess' viscous membranes: the Greek was making an attempt to imitate Goodwoman. She thought she could attain that status? Is that what she had made of that scene?

The Helmet started calling out her acquaintance's name. "Oh Doctor Stan," she said, "yoo hoo." He was paying the bill. He didn't hear her. Everyone at her table had to stop talking and wait for this greeting to be acknowledged.

The table waited quietly, looking down at their napkins. The Boy was turned toward Doctor Stan. She called out to him again, "Doctor Stanley!" Still Doctor Stan didn't seem to hear her.

She leaned across the table and snapped her fingers, bracelets jingling, necklace dangling. "Doctor!"

"Oh hi," he said, finally, a distracted and dutiful greeting. He was fumbling to get his wallet out. He seemed to feel little of the Greek's enthusiasm for this encounter. But she had exposed herself, now she had to carry on—there was no way to retreat now. Tess' heart beat a little faster.

The woman leaned slightly across the table and stretched out her hand for Dr. Stan to take. "How are you?"

"I'm fine." He looked back down to make sure he had left the right amount of money on his table. Her hand didn't seem to exist. He made a small step backward, a graceful retreat, opening the air between them. Her chest leaned further across the table; her necklace banged into a wineglass, knocking it over, spilling wine on her shirt, a deep stain spreading across the white cloth.

The King immediately began mopping up the wine. The others at the Greek's table looked away, while she mopped at the red stain on her shirt, "It's great to see you," she said uncertainly.

Tess leaned back and breathed in. The feat had been accomplished. Doc's was hers.

A twinge of pity for the Greek twisted in Tess, surprising her. She wondered why she needed these clandestine assertions of her worth among people she didn't even know. This predilection was as mysterious as it was uneasy. She felt sorry for the bald man, sad at her own grim satisfaction.

Max counted the money out onto the table, leaving an excessively liberal offering. Tess checked the tip to make sure it was enough. "She has to protect the world from *me*," Max always laughed when he told their friends that she checked every tip. They stood up. The two of them saluted the staff as they walked by the kitchen.

Tess, waving goodbye to the waitress, bumped into someone coming into the restaurant. She turned to make her apologies, but the person had slipped past her, and Tess found herself looking into the mirror instead. Longing lay in her sagging jowls.

The biting cold air cleansed them as they walked to their car. The stars flashed their messages. The universe is infinite. It will continue. Even *you* will for a while. In the city there was no sky to soothe her.

Where did this Sculpted Head live? Was the Bald One some-one Greek Helmet was dating, trying to impress? Had he liked her hair? Her imperious airs?

Max was singing, "In a small hotel, by a wishing well," con-tent to wait for Tess to put the finishing touches on tonight's tale. Max had come to understand in his life with Tess that ordinary women write their stories on the breezes of backyard fences, on the currents of telephones, in murmurs in dimly lit bedrooms, daring only to tell public stories with incisive subtlety in private, but rarely the opposite. When they climbed into bed and Tess told Max her night stories the world was shaped by what came out of her mouth. He drove along slowly down the dark roads. No real menace nearby, only dogs and stars.

————•◆•————

LOVE AT THE DOOR

Aaron's words drift down the hall and into the kitchen toward his wife, Leah. "Joel called me at work today. Wait until you hear this."

Leah is sorting through the mail trying to decide where to put the American Express bill until later. "What?" she says.

She hears his sneakers squeaking against their floorboards in the hallway. He's coming closer. That exact weight of that footstep on creaking floorboards has been a part of her life with Aaron all of their time together. She knows that he's turned into the bathroom for a minute. She stuffs the bill behind the cookbooks on the shelf nearest to her. "You want red or white?" she calls to the footsteps.

"Sam Adams," he says appearing in the doorway. "Joel says Mom is having an affair with his doorman."

She looks around the fridge door. They both begin to laugh in surprise.

"It's been going on for a month, Joel says. Ever since she came to stay with them while Dad's in the hospital. He's Muslim. You know that sweet guy? He's married, has grown children and grandchildren."

"I'm thrilled. Freaked. How did Joel find out?"

Aaron takes the cold bottle from her outstretched hand. "Where are Zoe and Sam? Wait until you hear."

———•◆•———

TIDAL

M ax, the husband, opened. Tess, the wife, closed. Max spilled, dropped, stirred. Tess wiped, picked up, quieted. He flung, scattered, cast off. She caught, held, fastened. He set sail; she harbored.

Max got up early, opened cupboards, drawers, left them where they landed. He made the toast, dropping the crumbs, made the coffee, spilling coffee grinds in several places. He got their son, Paul, up and out of the house in the morning, brought Tess a cup of coffee in bed. He started the day going.

She closed the cupboards, the drawers, wiped up the crumbs and coffee grinds. She stayed up late, turned off all the lights, made sure Paul was in the vicinity of his bed, pulled the blankets up around Max's shoulders. She brought the day home.

He stirred things up, told jokes, laughed at his jokes, made them all laugh, made them despair when he didn't know enough to stop. He tended toward the hysterical.

She calmed things down, negotiated the rough seas, found the lost, mended the broken, kept the faith. She tended toward the melancholic.

Now it had become clear that Paul was turning out to be just like his father: a joker, chaos maker, a large anarchic male. A pisser. A beauty.

Today, Tess is wandering around her house, in her nightgown, kneeing drawers shut, snapping lights off, picking up scattered newspapers to put in a basket used only by her. Ordinarily, she picked up the house without thinking about it, but lately, now that there are two large Y-chromosome types, she's feeling outflanked. She's aware.

She hears a gushing noise, a flooding of liquid, a hosing sound, through the open bathroom door. When she goes into the bathroom to drape a towel back on a rack, she finds the toilet seat up, a bowl of golden pee, clear, luminous, an energetic ring of bubbles around the edge. It has the look of celebration about it. What's in this stuff, she thinks, that makes it sparkle like that?

A pungent, urgent smell rises from inside the white porcelain. Doesn't it occur to him that someone is going to come behind him? And her. What is she doing standing there, staring at her son's piss?

Tess, buoyed on the currents of memory, remembers an arc of clear pee rising from her newborn son's body splashing into her startled eyes. The little animal that she had pulled from her body only days before, which she had left naked so the breeze fluttering the curtains could visit his almost untouched skin, had peed in her face.

She'd jumped back, picked him up in the air above her. "He peed on me," she'd squealed to Max, whose pleasure almost matched her own. Their son had peed on his mother.

Now she is standing there looking into the toilet bowl at urine that she has no cause, no right to see. All the air that they had shared has disappeared.

"Paul, come and flush the goddamn toilet after yourself." He can't hear. His door is closed. The piece of paper taped to the door commands in crude letters, *Knock before entering*! She stands there knocking politely.

"Whaaaat?"

"Can I come in?"

"What do you want, evil demon woman?"

She's torn. She likes it when he teases her—calls her evil demon woman—assuming her love, assuming he could call her whatever he wants to because she belongs to him. But she hates when he and his father tease her to deflect their sins. When it comes to the messes they make, they get to be funny; she gets to clean up.

"I want you to flush the toilet!" She opens the door. Paul is lying on his bed talking on the phone. He glares at her.

"Mom! Are you on crack? I'm on the phone. Give me a minute."

She turns and slams the door. She goes back through the apartment picking up dirtied plates and glasses along the way, wrinkled napkins, single shoes. She drops things off in closets, hampers, sinks before she gets down to business in the kitchen, wiping down the table, throwing out garbage, emptying the dishwasher. She's muttering to herself when Max finds her there, in from his morning walk.

"What's up?" He wraps his large sweaty body around hers.

"Private conversation." She slides away from him. She doesn't want his clammy skin against her. Isn't he aware of what someone else's sweat feels like when you're not sweating with them?

Then, making reparation, she asks, "What is in pee? Is there sodium?" She says "sodium" to sound objective, scientific.

"Why'd you want to know that?" Max asks.

"I don't know. It looks salty to me. Are there hormones in it?" She doesn't say what she thinks: that when she's at the ocean and pees in the water she has the feeling that these two liquids—the world's vast salty waters and her own liquid supplies—belong together, that these substances, from the same primal pool, are being recombined, reunited, coupled. Where did she get this?

"Maaaa," Paul is shouting from the other room, then his large bones thunder into the kitchen.

"Ma, come on, we have to go buy my sneakers. Ed's on his way over, and we have to meet Emily in an hour." Paul's face is close to his mother's. "You're not even dressed." He's appalled.

"What are you talking about?" Tess asks.

"My sneakers. You know I need them for my bike trip. I'm leaving tomorrow."

"I know. I've been trying to get you to go shopping with me all week." Max looks at Tess, raises his eyebrows, shrugs, and retreats to his shower. This one is yours, he's saying. Why is that? she'd like to know.

Tess will oversee the labeling, rolling, packing, making certain that it's done by midnight. She'll mark Paul's flashlight with an indelible marker, see to it that the requisite pairs of socks, shorts, T-shirts are rolled, fastened by rubber bands, packed watertight.

"Well, we have to go. *Right now*," Paul says.

"What do you mean, we "have to"? All week you said, 'Stop bothering me, Ma. Don't make such a thing about it.' We had a date for noon today. 'I promise Ma.' Remember?" Tess reminds them both.

"Emily told Ed she can only come over at noon. I haven't seen her in two weeks. She has to babysit her sister at one thirty. And I'm leaving tomorrow."

Tess knows that Emily is a dream in her son's liquid nights. She knows that Paul is completely desperate at this minute. His mother is being so annoying. He's willing to go and get the sneakers, isn't he? But he *has* to see Emily. Tess remembers the pull toward the one who will never belong to you.

She breathes deep, and her shoulders sink; with a slight pull of her head down and away, she surrenders.

"All right, I'll get dressed. We'll go to Foot Locker first." Tess caves easily, often, with frustration. She remembers too well. She identifies too easily. She ends in a fury.

Paul looks down into her surrender, understanding for just a moment what he's asked, what he's been given. "I like this, Mommy," he says in a pretend child's voice, the resonance of maleness submerged momentarily; he's beseeching mercy from another time.

"I'll be dressed in five minutes," Tess says.

"Ed's downstairs waiting for me. Just give me the money, and I'll buy them myself."

"I don't have the money. I have to go to the bank, and I want to see what you're picking out." Tess is not handing over her cards. Keys go missing. There have been several pairs of sneakers that didn't fit or were so ugly that even Paul had realized it after wearing them a couple of days.

"You and Ed ride your bikes down to Foot Locker. I'll get dressed, go to the bank. I'll meet you there."

Tess had been looking forward to the walk in the sun down Broadway with Paul. Her son was a great, if reluctant, companion. Details on the street triggered meandering talk. It was a way to get to know him again when he wasn't looking.

The last time they had walked together, rain glistening against the black macadam set him off. "We're working on fluid dynamics in physics. Mr. Rothenberg is teaching us to calculate the surface velocity of water. "I'd like to be the one to come up with the equation for water as it flows over a rock," he had said. "Man should be more like water, flowing in harmony with the natural world. Not just using it." This from the guy who spends hours playing Sudden Death on his computer, who dances to techno music in dark, smoke-filled clubs or wants more than anything to surf, skim, slide on fiberglass-laminated, computer-designed boards of varying dimensions over surfaces of differing densities.

That kind of walk would not be taken today.

When Tess gets downstairs, Thomas, the doorman, says, "Paulie said to tell you that he decided to go to Sports Works instead. His friend told him they have *really cool* sneakers there."

Tess's face freezes and then sags. Then she shakes her head. "Driving you nuts huh?" Thomas laughs. "I know. I know."

Tess runs to the bank, grabs a cab, tapping her fingers the whole lurching ride down Broadway. She slams the door of the cab just in time to see Ed and Paul as they're coming out of the store. Were they even going to wait for her?

"They don't have any that fit me. We're going to have to go back uptown to Manhattan Sports. They have just the kind I want. Emily will be over in a half-hour. She only has an hour, Ma." His eyes are wide, "Okay?"

Ed, his friend, looks away, embarrassed for Paul that he has to put up with his mother following him around. Paul holds out his hand. "Can I have some filthy lucre?"

Tess hesitates.

"What's the problem, Ma?"

Where to begin? "Nothing. Nothing." She takes out the money and hands it over. He bends over her, reaches out a hand large enough to crush what had been his original body, and touches her face gently. Then he bends down and kisses her cheek, "Bye, short stuff."

Only recently he has risen past her. First, he was only an inch or two shorter, then a short while later he was even with her, and when she looked next, like a fountain just being turned on, he quietly rose up past her. One day he had looked down and said, astonished, "I have a little Mommy. You're so little." For a couple of months he said this to her often. They'd bump shoulders in the kitchen laughing at this turn of events. She would reach up and tousle his hair just to claim she still had rights to him. But it had become a commonplace to him, and he'd stopped saying it.

For Tess, the fact that she has to look up into his face is still a raging, weeping surprise. He's a large male person. Messy, chaotic, half civilized. He doesn't pick up his dirty underwear; he doesn't clean up his dishes. He doesn't think about how he affects the people around him. I've allowed him to become a guy.

Is *that* the problem? Tess asks herself, as she walks home, buying the odds and ends she had pictured the two of them shopping for together—socks, deodorant, another keychain.

When she gets to the lobby of her building, Thomas is laughing. "They just left. Paul said to tell you he's real sorry but he had to walk Emily home. He'll call you in a while."

Tess sits down on the bench in the lobby. Her head is down; her belly sags. "How old is he?" Thomas asks. Then before she can answer him, "Fourteen, fifteen? Right?"

Tess looks up at Thomas. He knows something. His tone, his expression: the look of the adult rendered helpless. Thomas, too, had been left adrift on open waters. She sees on his face a smile, a memory. "I remember. Drive you crazy," Thomas says. He looks off into his own children's past. "Teenagers, phew. I went through it with mine, five of them." He shakes the memory off. "Just remember, you love him. Right?" Outside on Riverside Drive Tess can hear the traffic flowing past her building. Down beyond the park, the Hudson River moves steadily out to sea.

She gets in the elevator, presses the button for her floor. All that stuff, when her body fluids flooded to his hunger, his sobs, his rolling waves, when his body products had been hers to tend to, to wash, to wipe away. Before that, his father's secretions and her own juices had slid together into this—him.

Now his fluids are rising, lapping through his veins, washing over him—floating him away from her out to his own seas. Only the violation of custom has left behind a bowl of golden yellow pee.

Tess has arrived at her floor. She unlocks the door to her apartment, "Max," she calls, as she goes in, leaving the door wide open behind her.

———•·———

GESTURES

"I think he's having an affair," she says and then glances quickly up at the door of the restaurant, which is opening. Outside there's slanting rain, umbrellas and people hunched under them. People just want to get home.

"What makes you think that?" The other tilts her head a bit and leans over the tiny table filled with water glasses, wine glasses, and small plates. She is glad the hum of the place is high and holds them in place.

"He's always got somewhere to go. Whenever I try to make plans with him, he's got something he has to do."

"That doesn't sound so suspicious. Anything else? That just sounds like any husband to me." She is not sure what to say.

"I don't know. We hardly sleep with each other. Other stuff. Just instinct I guess."

"Do you trust your instincts?" This isn't the first of these conversations. Everyone knows the husband has affairs. First, they guessed, then they assumed, then they knew. Eventually they talked about it openly.

"Maybe you should. This isn't the first time you've said something like this." She opens her eyes, looking sincere and helpful. She holds up her wine glass to show the waiter she wants another Russian River. "Remember a few years ago when you were worried."

"But I was wrong about that. It turned out to be nothing. He was just worried about a big job that wasn't going well back then. I just panic."

"Well, good. Then it's probably exactly the same now. Do you want some more wine?"

She nods. "I'm probably just being paranoid."

"Yeah," she agrees.

They both gesture to the waiter to make sure he sees they both need more wine.

———•◆•———

SNOW STRUCK

Leah knew a box. The box was how she knew the person. She never actually met the man in the box face to face, but she had spoken to him on a couple of occasions, and she saw the box whenever she went to walk her dog in the park. That was how she had come to know the box. It and the man who inhabited it lived in the small piece of park right across from her apartment building, where she walked their dog, Pazzo. Pazzo and Leah walked there several times a day sometimes, although Leah often took Pazzo down to Riverside, the larger park nearby, for long runs along the lower promenade. There, Pazzo would meet his friends and enemies. Leah would meet the handsome young men who walked dogs for a living. They would talk to her each time as friendly as could be, as if she was someone whom they had never seen before. And she would meet other middle-aged women who knew what it meant to lose your youth and beauty and gain your sanity. It was a worthy trade, though they would have liked to push those young men's faces into something, shit or snow, depending.

Lately, though, Leah found herself depriving Pazzo of some of her long runs, or asking one of the other family members to take her. Once, she left a sandwich by the box and said, "I'm leaving a sandwich here." He hadn't answered. It was a very cold winter. It

was even a white Christmas that year, which never happened in
New York City.

She caught a glimpse of the box man's back one day; as she came
out of her building, he was fixing a small sheet of plastic over his
baby stroller. But by the time she walked up the small steps to the
area where the statue and the box were, he was back inside his
home. The wind that day came up off the river with icy whips,
beating whatever was in its path, angry at whatever dared to be
in its way.

    When she went home she had decided to take her husband's,
Aaron's, old sleeping bag to give to the man. She would have given
him hers, but her daughter had given it to her on her last birthday.
Leah's was a muted green; she had never seen a sleeping bag like
it. Aaron would just go and buy another. He loved buying things.
He didn't like it, though, when she took his things without asking.
She had to act immediately. The temperature was threatening to
drop well below freezing. She'd deal with Aaron later.

    Leah went back to the box. It was lying near the statue where
it always was. It was long and slender—the size of an elongated
trunk. There was something like a piece of fabric covering one
end, the entrance to his home. "I'm leaving a sleeping bag here,"
she said into air. The box didn't say anything back. She said, "I
thought you might be getting cold." She placed the sleeping bag on
the box and walked away. She wished the zipper weren't broken.

She went home and put Aaron's closet back in order, so he
wouldn't ask what she had been doing in there again. When she
had put his Columbia Hot sweatshirt in their kid's school fair he
had been really annoyed. "Just ask me!" he had said adamantly
when he found out.

    The next day another woman who sometimes walked her dog
there too said, "Oh hi. Guess what? Someone left him a sleeping
bag. He's so happy."

    "Really? How do you know?"

    "He told me."

    "What did he say?"

"What? You don't believe me? You think there's no one kind anymore?"

"No, no. I just wondered. I didn't think he talked to people like us."

She waited for a couple of days to tell Aaron. One day just after he woke up from a nap, she lay down next to him. She said, "Arele, my Arele." She used the love name. "I did something."

"What have you been up to?" He was still sleepy. His muscles were still given over to loosening sleep. Leah looked soft and lovely in the afternoon glow coming in their bedroom window.

"I gave your old sleeping bag away."

"Oh you," Aaron said. "You love to take my things."

"To the box guy. The one I've been telling you about, when I walk Pazzo."

"Oh."

"That's all you're going to say?"

"What do you want to me to say? You want me to be mad?"

"I didn't ask you."

Aaron was a little hurt that she would think that about him.

A few weeks later, after the holidays were over, the blizzard came. It snowed light powder, slowly covering the cars. Then the wind blew that first snow off onto the streets. More snow came, slowly covering the streets and windowsills. The weathermen were excited. "This is going to be *quite* the snow storm," they announced breezily to the anchors that had been momentarily displaced.

Mothers all over the city said, "This is the way snow used to be." They were trying to say, This is how we meant for life to be for you the day you were born. This is how life *should be*. The whole city took on the feeling of exception, revelry, celebration. Schools closed. Fathers stayed home, getting underfoot. Children slid down the hills screaming. They came home with burning red cheeks. When they took off their fleece-lined jackets, their ultra light waterproof boots, their Gortex mittens, and piled dirty wet hills of synthetic materials on the floor just inside the front doors of their apartments, the mothers, looking at their children's shining faces, swallowed their motherly fury and said, instead, in voices they had rehearsed in the first weeks of their children's lives, "Who's for hot chocolate?"

Leah went to see the box.

When she got there, some sanitation men were talking to the box. The woman who had actually seen the box man had just arrived too. They were both worried that the men would take him by force and leave his stuff there. They knew that was why he wouldn't want to leave.

"Don't take his stuff," Leah said to the three guys standing there. "Please."

"Lady, we're not going to take the guy's stuff," one of the men said, separating himself from the others. "We just want him to get in out of the cold." The young man looked like Leah's cousin Tommy, that same one-sided grin Tommy used to have.

"No, I mean, he isn't going to want to go, because of his stuff. He'll lose everything," the other woman said.

"Look, what do you want us to do? Leave him here?" the guy asked.

"I don't know," Leah said. The other woman nodded. They could agree on hesitation.

The three of them stood there in the snow. A father and daughter were cross-country skiing down Riverside Drive beyond them. The powdery snow was whirling overhead, filling the sky for some immeasurable distance. It seemed to pile higher as the three of them stood watching it. It was well over eighteen inches by then. Eerie, it had the kind of quiet beauty that has never been disturbed by beeps and buzzes from cellular phones, wristwatches, computers, and car keys. It didn't belong to New York City, not in this century; nothing this beautiful was left from the earth's original natural state here.

The sanitation worker and the two women folded their arms and stood there feeling foolish. "Com'on," one of the sanitation men called to the young handsome guy standing with the women, "we're going."

"Well," the young sanitation guy said, raising his eyebrows with a small supplicating smile, "I guess I gotta go. You know you should call 911, and they'll take him whether he wants to go or not." Now that he was leaving and the decision was no longer his, it was an easy thing to say. He waved to the women and climbed into his truck.

The women stood there. Since they had no truck to climb into they were left with their confusion. "Do you think we should?" The woman who had seen the box man asked Leah quietly so that the box man wouldn't hear them.

"I don't know." She started hesitantly toward the box; she turned to look at the other woman, who had stopped somewhat behind Leah. Leah was the leader of this expedition. The box was almost completely covered with snow.

"How are you?" Leah asked the box.

"I'm okay," a voice with a sober but clear timbre answered.

"I think I'd better call the police to take you to a shelter tonight."

"Please don't, lady. I'm okay."

"I'm worried because of the snow."

"No. I'm all right."

"Would you like some money?"

"Uh-okay," the box said.

Leah fumbled taking off her glove, reaching under her jacket, and found ten dollars. She was glad she had more than a couple of bucks on her. A hand came out through the opening at the end of the box. It was covered with a red wool mitten, a dirty beige padded sleeve. Leah put the money into the red fingers.

Then she retreated to talk to the other woman again where he wouldn't be able to hear her. "I'm calling someone."

"Yeah, I think it's a good idea." The woman seemed relieved that a decision had been made. "I'm Rose," she said. "I love our neighborhood so much. It's the perfect place to live, but that we have people without homes here is the opposite of everything that's good now. We used to live with the SRO's next door to us. They were just there. It wasn't benevolent, but it hadn't been as ghastly as this. Instead this is what we've created?"

"Leah." Their gloves touched.

Leah called 911 when she went home and told them about the box man. They would come they said.

Later she asked Nick, her super, if an emergency vehicle had come to pick up the guy in the box. "Oh yeah," he said, "they came askin'. I told them where he was. They went over there a while ago."

There were two young boys sledding near him, when Leah worked up her nerve to go back over there, insisting that Aaron come with her this time. "How could the ambulance people have come? There are no foot steps." The box man's things were still there, piled in his baby stroller. "I wonder if they made him leave his things." She walked over to the box and leaned down to see if she could tell if anyone were there.

"Hello."

"Hello," the voice in the box said.

"Are you okay?"

"I'm okay."

"You'll freeze tonight."

"No, I'll be all right."

"Do you want some soup? Something hot?"

"No. No. I'm fine."

"How about a little later?"

"Okay." The air held his voice aloof in the cold. Then, "Uh, thanks lady."

Leah and Aaron walked back to their apartment. They didn't say much.

Leah asked Aaron to go back with her around ten that night to bring some soup. He was deep into an article in the *Economist* about Central Asia and the pipelines. He shook himself loose, "What?"

"Nothing."

The snow had made a white roof on the box. "Here's some soup," Leah said. The box didn't say anything. She placed the thermos in the snow right near the fabric flap of the box.

In the morning the box was pretty blown apart. There was no one in there. The baby stroller was turned over on its side. The box man's things were buried under the snow. The wind in the night had blown away any sign of footsteps. There was a snow dune just in front of where the entrance to the box had been. The soup might be still be where Leah had left it, there, under the snow.

———•·•———

SOMETHING ESSENTIAL

Paul has a cold; he's tired; he's happy.

Tess has been timing her son Paul as he takes the SAT II practice test on and off all day. After she got him out of bed at noon—insisting, "This is why you stayed home." She made him pancakes for breakfast before he began the three-and-a-half-hour practice test. There's a box of Kleenex on the table from which he pulls a sheet, tearing it to bits, which he rolls around in his hand and then tosses to one side. Next he'll pick up the large strainer and twirl it around. Tess has taken the phone off the hook, has settled several cups of tea in between the tiny rolled up bits of Kleenex, whisked them away when they were drained or cold. He's taking a break.

Tess goes toward the bathroom door where Paul is putting in his contacts to ask him to help her undo the nuts in the dishwasher because a glass has broken. The week before they had had a motor replaced precisely because some broken glass and olive pits fell in through the filtering mechanism and messed with the motor. She needs his help: this is not her area. Paul is proud of his ability to build, to fix, to understand how things are made, how things work. He's in charge of the tech crew at his high school. All the dangerous tools he's ever dreamed of.

"Mom, I'm busy. Can't you see that? Damn." The new throw away contacts he's trying to put into his eyes haven't been going in too easily. He's only been using them for the past couple of weeks.

Because the pollen level is very high his eyes are extremely sensitive these days, so he has had to take them out a couple of times in the past week and put new ones in. He's gone through four pair just this week. One contact fell down the sink drain. He turns and glares at her, "You just made me swallow one!"

"What?"

"When I answered you, I had one in my mouth, and I swallowed it."

Tess knows not to laugh. "Oh, sorry." Tess stands watching him as he readies another to hold just above his eyeball. Fascinating. How do you get them in there, she wonders. But whatever he does fascinates her. She has to look up now to talk to him. She's shocked and delighted by this. He's able, and he's her son.

"You don't have to do that," he says, his tone menacing, almost a growl. He's pulling his lid down over his eyeball, blinking, trying to settle them in.

"What am I doing?"

"You were staring at me!"

"Why is that a problem?"

"Would you like it if I stood there staring at you?"

"I'm just interested in how you put them in?" Tess goes to stand in the living room. "I'm not trying to do anything to you."

He comes out and stares down at her from his superior height. "That's so annoying."

"I was just watching you." Her voice is high, defensive, a little girl's pitch.

"Okay." She's trying to pitch it to a more normal tone. "I wasn't trying to annoy you."

"You should just say, 'I just wanted to watch you.'"

Tess looks at the curtains in the living room. They're filthy with city soot, she sees. I have to wash them. How I hate that job, she thinks, as she tries to catch her rising irritation, "Jeez you're so " she swallows hard not to say the word "sensitive," the word her mother had used when she was a teenager.

She looks down to collect herself where she finds her son's legs. They are tree trunks, sturdy, hard, immovable. She's distracted from her irritation. "You know, Paul, you have really strong legs."

"I know," he says cheerfully. "That's because of snowboarding.

Feel this." He shoves one leg forward, offers her the rock of his leg. "And because of this summer, the biking.

You know I really miss summer. You know as much as I love snowboarding but I miss the summer." He's sat down on the couch in the living room now. Stretched out his legs in front of him, companionable.

"You mean from the biking trip?" Tess sits across the way, not too near.

"No, I mean being with my friends in the Village when we have nothing to do And it's seven o'clock, and I'm hanging out with my friends, and we're just looking up at the sky." His dark eyes look off into this season bright with dark pleasure. They both involuntarily look out the window now, where the last of summer is being washed away by an October rain. One of Tess's favorite seasons. It's definitely not summer.

When Tess turns her eyes back to his, he's looking off into the rain dreamily. "Mom," he says softly, "there's something I want to talk to you about."

"Shoot," Tess tries to say this easily.

"There's this knife I saw the other day. It's so beautiful. It's called a Fox. I was thinking that I'd buy it with that money grandma gave me."

"I don't know. We'll have to talk to Dad about that one. Look, shouldn't you get to work on that practice SAT test? That's why you're staying home from school, remember?"

Paul gets up reluctantly. "Okay, but it's essential that I have it."

The night before he had come home at ten thirty, a school night, because he was working on a theatrical production. He's a junior in high school. He's preparing for achievement tests. He has to see his many friends every weekend. This production has taken over his life so that he spends longer and longer hours hammering, sawing, painting sets, and smoking cigarettes. In short his life is close to perfect. The night before he had come home with a full-blown cold that in the morning had only been a slight hoarseness.

"I've got a cold," he had said with pleasure in this temporarily deeper voice. Tess and Max had looked at his tired, happy face. Tess raised her eyebrows, passing the decision to Max.

Once the decision was being passed off, they all knew it meant

Paul would stay home the next day.

"How's that work going?" Max asked when he came home a little later and found his wife and son in his kitchen. He liked to play the roles the theater of their life required of him.

"It's okay, Dad, really. But don't talk to me now. I've got to prepare for the SAT II's. Please." He looks down at the bits of Kleenex balled up on the table. "But Dad I have to talk to you about something really important later." He looks up at his father, sober, almost somber. "Something essential."

———•◆•———

QUESTA È LA VITA (THIS IS THE LIFE)

Tess nestles into Max, her head on his shoulder. Home. Where Tess belongs. Max doesn't look up, reaches an arm around her, pulls her in tighter, neck bent, his eyes on the page in front of him.

Max and Tess are standing on the subway platform at Ninety-Sixth Street, waiting for the local train late on a cold fall night. The damp, sharpened to knifepoint down here, slits tiny vicious cracks between wrists and sleeves. They are on their way back from seeing a Russian movie, *Slave of Love*, a movie about moviemakers suspended at the outskirts of the Bolshevik revolution.

The female lead, wearing an immense hat and a long chiffon scarf as she drifts from the set through white French doors to the "real" outdoors, washes in circles in Tess's head as she stands on the freezing platform. The billowing beauty of the scenes fills her, while the movie's accumulating violence recedes, becoming a shadow of the radiantly made thing.

Now Tess sees an actor picking up a small girl, whirling her in the savagely bright sunshine.

Tess drifts in the freezing subway station, storing some scenes, already forgetting others. This new version of the movie will comfort her for years to come. She'll be startled when she sees in the future that Mikhalkov has made a different movie than the one in her head.

Tensing against the frigid air, she is pulled out of her dreaming. She shudders and tries to regain her refuge. What had she just been thinking? How could it be that someone like Nikita Mikhalkov is alive at the same time as she? In the nineteenth century, sure, there were a lot of guys like this one around. If she were a character in one of his movies she'd make a small eccentric gesture now that showed viewers she wants to be at home in bed leaning back against a small hill of pillows. Tess tries to imagine what such a gesture could be.

She pulls herself loose from Max and presses her neck back against her large down collar and thick wool scarf, trying to enact this picture of herself ensconced against pillows. Her head strains awkwardly against the thick roll her scarf and collar make, tensing her neck muscles. She bends her head forward and then rocks it back and forth, loosening the stiffness.

Max insulates himself easily from the physical reality of his surroundings—good or bad—wherever he is, always, in exactly the same way. He reads. He never descends into a subway station, goes to the bathroom, or arrives at a picnic without a book, a magazine, a newspaper. He doesn't just read; he swims onto the pages. He is one with the black forms on the white fields, lost in the ample comfort of the not here.

On long lines at airports, post offices, grocery stores where Tess is likely to snap at an irritating clerk, when the clerk says, eyes averted, chin lifted, "I explained to you already," the eyes darting back in the triumph of, "we're not authorized to be of any help what-so-ever," Max is invariably unaware. He never minds that someone cuts ahead of him on line. He's not really *on* the line. How could it matter?

At the moment, he leans against one of the vertical I beams, one foot stretched comfortably out in front of the other, a shoulder rounded against the hard edge of the upright, an external spine, insensible to the air rigid with cold that surrounds him. She rubs his icy fingers. He turns the ends of his mouth up, the memory of a smile.

What reading is for Max, the act of awareness is for Tess: it accompanies her wherever she goes. She's unable to shut down the apparatus that registers every shade, every pitch, and every nuanced vibration bordering her consciousness. No matter how little she desires this registration to be taking place, no matter how ferociously she tries to shut stimuli out, they creep into her, onto her nerve endings pulling her back from whatever activity she might be engaged in, engulfing her, overwhelming her. She's not a swimmer, but a drowner.

Now, for example, she is unable to shut out the cold that penetrates from the gray concrete underneath her feet, from the air around her. She cannot *not* feel it. She's keenly aware of high-pitched sounds and the way in which they are amplified in damp weather. The express train (not theirs) coming in now across the platform screeches, making Tess want to scream at the same high, grating pitch. This kind of damp makes Tess feel as if someone had raised the treble all over the city. Car horns pierce, buses didn't just roar, they raked across her brain. Tess was not a pleasant person to be around on a damp day. In damp weather, she really should be confined to bed.

The icy cold is settling in, even through the rich paisley of the shawl around her neck.

Still, the images from *Slave of Love* break the surface of her misery. She pulls the movie back to herself, to close out the cold. Her new creature ascends right next to now. Tess likes to savor certain scenes after she's seen a movie, turn them over and imagine what went into the decisions to make certain shots or scenes.

Max likes instead to let thoughts crawl around his unconscious and then, clearing his throat, preparing for his declaration at, say, a dinner party, a couple of months later, announce, "The scene in *Slave of Love* that tells us everything is when the movie director looks around to make sure no one is watching him before he reaches up to swing from the tree. Remember?" Max would look around at his audience expectantly.

Across the tracks, against the broken dirty tiles of the station, Tess imagines Max at the dinner party, imitating the director perfectly, glancing around quickly, surreptitiously, then tugging his shirt sleeves. He'd stretch his arms up to the imaginary tree branch, to remind everyone of this small private moment in the movie, the import of which Tess and everyone else will have missed. The scene that Tess is watching on the dirty tiles dissolves

from Max's raised arms to the arms of the restless movie director as he struggles to lift one leg then the other. Then the scene
dissolves back to Max as he hops in his chair at the dinner party,
enacting the movie director losing his grip and lurching to the
ground, one hand clutching a stitch in his side. This image incises
again into a precise point on the map of Tess's brain: a man alone
making a small idiosyncratic gesture, which in company would be
odd or silly, which in this movie pulsates softly.

Max would be right, Tess thinks, holding off the cold with
these scenes until she can climb onto her bed to consider the
movie together, and consider the images again in warmth and
comfort.

The fact that there should be such an artist in the twentieth
century who has a limpid view of human frailties! The pleasure of
the made thing buoys her, carries a small raft out to Tess to drift
on. A redemption that fills her with life's promises, a bite into an
icy sweet honeydew melon sitting on a summer lawn as she lay
reading, say, E. M. Forster.

She knows that when she can recommend *Slave of Love* to a
friend, it will make her week. That kind of information made it
worth all the crowding, all the noise, all the giving up of clear,
fresh streams one can find walking down the road in the country.
Let's watch *Slave of Love* again, she'll say to Max when *Slave of
Love* becomes rentable—which they will do late on a Saturday
night when the whole of the Upper West Side has been fed and
lubricated, so she and Max can go home to check on their teenage
son, Paul, and make dinner.

When is the damn train going to come, so the cold won't take
away this raised up feeling the movie has created in Tess? "Max,
I can't stand it."

"Hmmm." He's deep in the *New York Review of Books*, the lat-
est article about Isaiah Berlin and Anna Akhmatova.

"Max . . ." Tess rests her misery on Max, exactly the way she
had earlier rested her head on his shoulder. He is the column on
which her life rests. His wide, sturdy body doesn't always notice
she's leaning, but it never minds if she does.

"What, honey?" Max finally folds his paper and turns to her.

"Do you want me to go and speak to the station master? Shall I have a word with him?"

"Well . . . yeah." Through years on her own, a first marriage, many boyfriends, she carried her heavy packages herself, stood alone at bus stations waiting at one in the morning, figured out how to get through the weekend on twenty dollars. She watched other women's boyfriends pick them up from work, drive them away to weekends in the country. Then Max came.

Now he puts both his arms around her and smiles happily because Tess is looking up into his face. He likes Tess to look to him, to need him. He had lived alone for many years before they met. Tess's need of him made him the center of something. She came with a large, complicated world: sisters, nephews, cousins, and friends. He had been invited to a gathering. In turn Max's isolation gave Tess sanctuary, a place to retreat, a deal like any other made of longing.

"Let's go home, get in bed, and lie back into all of our pillows and pull up our thick comforter and read," Max says. This is one of Max's ways of making love to Tess. Max, like Mikhalkov, understands romance.

Tonight, implying a rescue from this miserable subway station.

"When I'm this cold I feel as if I live in a world without beds," Tess says.

"Are you kidding? Our bed not exist? When they write the history of love, one chapter is going to be about our bed."

"A bower of bliss," he had said when she had bought new bedding recently. She stood considering the effect before she raced back to their store. "What you do with a bed, Caravaggio did with color." He had sat on the bed that day and lain back against the dark red pillows to show his appreciation.

"Ya think? Not too much? All the dark reds?"

Picturing the piles of red pillows, Tess sees the telephone next to the bed.

"Max, did you give Paul a real curfew? I get so frantic until he's home safe."

Their son has only recently been given permission to stay out late with his friends.

"I told him absolutely no later than midnight. I don't want you going through what you went through last week. I know it drives you red with the crazies. I *know* he'll be okay, just *trumpenicking* around with his friends." He looks at her with his, "aren't I a good husband" look. "But a mother worries. Look, we'll go home. We'll drink a glass of that good port. We'll climb in bed, read, doze, and he'll be home."

Now, the Broadway local rams into the station, screeching, bellowing, murderous. Tess put her hands over her ears. The platform isn't crowded at this hour. The impulse of these tired New Yorkers to crush each other at the subway doors is only weakly in place. Everyone is too cold to do anything but squeeze into themselves against the weather.

When they get home Max goes right to the kitchen to get something to drink. Tess goes to see if there is a phone message from Paul. He'll be home in an hour, "I promise Mom, I'm coming uptown with Ed and James. We'll share a taxi. I promise." His message releases Tess to find her way back to the atmosphere that Max had created on the damp subway platform. Paul has remembered to call. For the next two hours she is released from imagining someone holding a knife to his chest. She hurries into her nightgown and climbs into bed.

Tess hears the icy rain against the panes. The dark colors of the walls, the patterns of the worn rugs, the long curtains all collect and reflect a glow from the incandescent lighting.

When Tess climbs into bed on these nights it's onto the island that is home to her marriage, the place where husband and wife come upon the heat of the other's limbs in the dark, feel the shudders of each other's dreams.

"Max, come to bed. It's so cozy in here." Her feet are stiff with cold.

"I'll be there in a minute," he calls from several rooms away.

"Where *arrrre* you? Hurry." As soon as he arrives, they'd read, be next to one another in the good housing of blanket and pillow.

Tess's eyes wander the room as she hears the creak of the medicine chest, the rattle of an aspirin. She hears the dangle and clang of his pee hitting porcelain, then the scrape of a page turning, lost in whatever book he's picked up. He's alone in the frame of his own movie, Tess knows. She wiggles down into the bed, rubbing her feet back and forth against the sheets, trying to hurry warmth into her cold toes. Why can't she feel the undiluted pleasure of her life more often?

Max comes in now, reading as he walks. As soon as he stops fiddling around and climbs into bed the glow will wash back over the room.

He stands by the bed now, lost in his book. After a little he puts the book down on his night table, looks around the room as if he is surprised to find himself there. He stares off into the bookcase near his bed. Then he turns to find Tess in bed. "What did you do with it?" He asks this question every night. He's looking for the sweatshirt he wears to bed.

"Where do you think it is Massimo?" Tess is not up for this particular running bit tonight. It had taken her fifteen years of nagging to get him not to leave his newspapers, coffee cups, or whatever has recently been in his hand on whatever surface is closest. She has only recently abandoned trying to explain to him there were certain times when an endless stream of jokes erodes pieces of her that she seems to have lost the ability to replace.

He comes and flops on top of Tess, "What did you do with my nighty?" He delights in using the diminutive names he gives to ordinary objects to keep the song in his head going. He pins back her arms as if she were his enemy or his boyhood friend whom he wants to wrestle with.

"Come on Max, just go get it." He walks to the closet and stands there, a gentle curve of relaxed belly, underwear sagging with ease and wear.

She can see his sweatshirt under her bathrobe from where she is. But lifting a bathrobe is apparently beyond him. She forces herself to turn away and look at the wrinkle in the rug next to her bed.

"Oh, so here's where you hid it." From behind her, Max continues playing his game by himself: "I've found it." He turns his head smiling, waiting for Tess to join in. "See where you hid it?"

Tess picks up a magazine lying next to her, concentrating on the mailing label in the lower left corner. Their name is still misspelled.

"Hey. Want to watch *Seinfeld*?"

"Nah, we've seen every one of them too many times."

"I'm just not ready to climb into bed." Max is already on his way to his chair in front of the television.

She could call the subscription people again. The last time she did, asking for a simple Max Luria, they changed it from Prof. Maxim Luria to Dr. Luria Prof. She flips through the pages of *The New Yorker*. The sounds of the laugh track arrive from the living room. Oh it's that one, about the stupid dog barking.

Tess forces her attention back to *Slave of Love*. A question about the way Mikhailkov uses the luxurious images first to conceal and then to reveal the ascending violence begins to flutter up in Tess's brain. The synaptic impulse rises, almost forms into an idea about the movie, then it darts off again.

The mood she had been trying to hold onto since she had left the movie theater, this amalgam of art and spirit, has slipped into a corner of the room, crouched there under a chair, waiting to see if Tess was capable of calling it back to her. She can't hold onto her suspicion about what Mikhalkov has been up to. The cold, the subway, Max not coming to bed have each had their effect. She'll have to wait until it floats back to her of its own accord. She'll have to make do with reading *The New Yorker*.

When Max climbs into bed thirty-five minutes later, he picks up a book and leans contentedly back into the pillows, declaiming, "*Questo si chiamo vivendo!*"

"That's not . . . the right way . . ." Tess stops herself, and looking around the room, her eyes come upon the telephone sitting blankly on Max's night table. "What should we do if Paul isn't home in an hour?" she asks.

"He'll be home."

"But what if he isn't, like last week?"

"You'll wake me up, and we'll discuss it then." She'll wait to hear the clicks of her son's key in the lock. Tess knows that in an hour or so she'll nudge Max. In an hour and a half, he'll stir, moan, and plead, "Please, I'm so tired. Leave me alone."

Anticipating this scene, Tess gets out of bed and yanks her bathrobe off its hook in the closet, ripping the loop by which it hung. The sleeve of Tess's bathrobe is turned inside out. She punches at it trying to use the force of her fist to open the sleeve. "Fuck you," she mutters.

Tess goes into the kitchen, puts a flame under the kettle, and slaps her body into a chair. Sometimes . . . she thinks as she curls over the stainless steel tabletop, dropping her head onto its cool metal surface. The cold from the kitchen floor is drawn up into her feet. Freeze goddamn it, she thinks furiously about her swollen, aging feet. Then she tries again, out loud this time. "Sometimes, I just . . . I just . . ." But as the final words begin to form, she stops them from emerging.

She will wait in the kitchen alone. She will call her son's phone over and over, which will go to message again and again. When he does arrived at four thirty, a sloppy smile on his face as he drapes his stoned love over his mother and says sweetly, "Hi Mama. How are you this lovely night?" his eyes are both glazed and alive to all the particles in the air around him, though he's not alive to his mother's terror and definitely too stoned for reasonable conversation. "We danced all night Mama, all night. I can really dance." Tess will feel her wet terror drain away, and at that moment know only the queasy joy that her son is home. He's only stoned. He hasn't been chewed up by the late night of the city. He looks especially filled with sweetness and light; he could be a Renaissance angel; he's that beautiful, so filled is he with the glow of his young outlaw maleness. What Tess will know at that moment is that Max and she have made this young man, and now he is starting to belong only to himself. After Paul goes to bed, she'll fling herself in next to Max, crawl up against his broad back, and whisper, "He's home," with incredulity and relief. Max will pull her flank closer to him.

But right now, in the misery of her expectation and in her home, still empty of Paul, before any of that takes place, the kettle's whistle ascends into a piercing screech.

———•———

Acknowledgements, with gratitude and love:

Bill, Lucia, and Myra who have read, reread, and reread this manuscript in all of its iterations. And who always had useful things to say to help me push my work in the direction I was attempting to go. Kathy Bernard for her invaluable editorial comments, kindness, and support. John Herman whose advice is always impeccable.

Lisa Wilde for the fabulous map she drew for this book and her wonderful friendship. Stacy Karzen for her gorgeous cover.

James Peltz, Amanda Lanne, Jenn Bennett, and Fran Keneston, all of whom make an amazing team at SUNY Press and who once again made this such an lovely publishing experience.

Toby Miroff, Theresa Ellerbrock, Edvige Giunta, Annie Lanzilotto, Nancy Carnevale, George Guida, Joseph Sciorra, Peter Covino, Pat Ranard, Louis Phillips, Jane Olian, Amy Burton, John Musto, Pam Katz, Beatrice Becce Avcolli, Donna Herman, Heather Barnard Herman, Anna Resnikoff, Ariella Resnikoff Diaz, Ronnie Herman, John Mudd, Anna Amelia Mudd, Benjamin Allen, William Mudd, Mallory Mead, Peter Mudd, Lisa Hickey, Leo Isaac Mudd, Ella Ferris Mudd, Rose Julia Mudd, and Jason Brynes, for family, friendship, and love.